SANCTUARY ISLAND

THE JAMES GANG

C. F. FRANCIS

PRAISE FOR C. F. FRANCIS

"Sometimes you read a book so good, a story you love so much, you want to shout its praises from the rooftops. **SANCTUARY ISLAND** is such a book. Launching a thrilling romantic suspense series, the story grabs you from the first line and captivates you so thoroughly you'll want the next book the instant you finish this one. It's that good. Everything a romantic suspense novel should be. "

—Sue-Ellen Welfonder, USA Today bestselling Author

LOVERS KEY *(Book two in The James Gang Series)* is "An Exciting and dynamic Romantic Suspense novel that is sure to have fans of the genre eager for their next fix."

—Toni Anderson, New York Times bestselling author

This book is dedicated to the men and women of our armed forces who can keep us safe. We can never repay you.

To: Sally
Enjoy the read
&
the stay
— C. F. Francis —
— 2022 —

ACKNOWLEDGMENTS

To my good friend, Cathy Schneider, who taught me to believe in myself and has never wavered in her support and friendship. To all my other writing friends, especially, Sarah, Anne, Joyce, and others too numerous to name, who have continually lifted me up. Thank you USA Today Best-selling author, Sue-Ellen Welfonder for your insights, support and generous promotions. And finally, thank you Elizabeth Stokes of estokescreative.com for the fantastic new cover for my 2016 debut novel. Your ability to bring the series together under one theme is amazing.

1

The Lincoln was back. Cat studied the vehicle currently framed in her rearview mirror. It had to be the same car. How many older model, gas guzzling, black Lincoln Town Cars habitually traveled this relatively quiet strip of road? Not many, she suspected, and this was the third time in as many days that she'd spotted the car behind her. Yesterday, when she noticed it for the second time, she'd thought it an interesting coincidence that she and the occupant of the other vehicle were on similar schedules. There'd been no reason to think otherwise – until now.

This morning, however, the owners of her rental cottage, Pat and Terry, had invited her to join them for breakfast. She'd spent a pleasant morning chatting with the two men but, as a result, she'd left for the beach considerably later than she had on previous days. What were the chances that the same car just happened to be behind her again? Taking another peek at the vehicle in her rearview mirror, Cat decided she didn't like those odds.

Stress, no doubt, was playing a big part in her uneasiness. She hadn't been sleeping well, which she'd written off to having too much on her mind. Still, that didn't explain the feeling that she was being watched. Even with her personal history, she'd never been paranoid. But stress did funny things to the mind and body. She knew that. But knowing it didn't change the way she felt.

Logic battled with instinct and instinct won out. At the first wide spot in the road she whipped her BMW Roadster around and headed for Lighthouse Point, the most popular and, therefore, most populated beach on Sanibel Island. August was the beginning of low season as far as tourists were concerned but with a few more weeks before school started there would likely be families gathered on the beach. In addition, there were security cameras in the parking areas unlike the private beach where she'd planned to spend the day. The Lincoln didn't follow. Thank God. She had enough to stress over without worrying about an imaginary stalker.

In a few weeks her friend, mentor and boss, Jason Waters, would announce his early retirement from the State Attorney General's office. His decision to step down earlier than planned left Cat with some decisions to make regarding her future. Jason had promised her a glowing letter of recommendation and had even made some preliminary calls on her behalf. She just couldn't garner much enthusiasm for the prospect of continuing on her current path. She knew what she wanted to do but having the guts to do it was another thing altogether. The plan had been to get out of town, clear her mind and hope the Southwest Florida sun would burn away a few layers of indecision. So far, the layers had remained stubbornly in place.

Over-thinking a problem had never produced answers for her. She needed to relax - to open her mind to all possibilities. Hopefully, by the end of this sabbatical she'd figure out where she was headed, both literally and figuratively. At the moment though, there was a little patch of sand with her name on it that she still had to find. Determined to make the best out of the remainder of her day, she took one last glance at her rearview mirror. No one appeared to be following her. So why couldn't she shake the feeling that she was being watched?

2

Colt wanted a few more shots of the Sanibel Lighthouse before the beach got any more crowded. Given a choice, he wouldn't be taking pictures of what he considered the less than aesthetic structure. But any calendar featuring the sights of Sanibel was expected to include at least one view of the historic tower. Yesterday he'd taken some photos as the sun was setting and then again at sunrise this morning. A couple more full daylight shots and he'd be done. The publisher could select the one that best suited the calendar's layout. There would be plenty of shots from which to choose and Colt would have managed to pull Gib's ass out of the fire - again.

His friend and business partner hadn't been able to complete the assignment. Yesterday afternoon Gib had called from the Keys, leaving Colt a voice mail begging him to help out. The reason behind his friend's sudden departure was, no doubt, a member of the opposite sex but regardless of the reason, he would always have Gib's back. He owed him for his sanity. When Colt had first arrived on Sanibel, he'd been trapped in a very dark place. If not for his friend, he might still be there – or worse. But that didn't stop Colt from wishing Gib had picked a better time for his disappearance.

The deadline for the photo spread was tomorrow. He still had to upload the pictures and then send them off to the publisher along with the ones Gib had already taken. Colt had originally planned to spend the morning at the "Ding" Darling Wildlife Refuge photographing some of the shorebirds that currently called the place home. A local magazine would be featuring some of his wildlife photos. The issue was scheduled to be on newsstands at the same time a small gallery on the island would be highlighting his art. He was hoping to get some additional shots to submit to the magazine and possibly include in his upcoming gallery show.

Colt shook his head, still finding it hard to believe that things were finally beginning to fall into place. His love of photography and plans for a career in the field had taken a back seat when the unimaginable had happened. His brother - his best friend – was killed while serving his country overseas. Colt had enlisted in the Army just days after the funeral. He'd wanted to finish what Taylor had started. Probably not the best reason to enlist but it had felt right at the time. With his keen eyesight and steady hands he'd been tapped for sniper school. He'd remained in the Army's Special Forces for twelve years, quickly moving up in the ranks to captain. But each tour had become more difficult for him and after the disaster of his last mission he just couldn't take any more.

He was beginning to put those days behind him. This place was helping him do that. Sanibel and Captiva were known as the *Sanctuary Islands* and they had become exactly that – his sanctuary. When he'd left the Army he had needed a place to mend. These islands had proved medicinal. Capturing their nuances through the lens of a camera became his therapy. He was finally sleeping better. Jolting awake less often from the nightmares that left him covered with a fine mist of perspiration. Photography, and this place, had centered him. With a gallery show on the horizon, he was more focused than he had been since his arrival here two summers ago.

Satisfied that he had all the shots he needed, and a few more besides, Colt packed up his equipment and headed for the parking lot.

3

C at swung her canary yellow Roadster into the paid parking area near the Lighthouse. The parking fees were another reason she didn't frequent the public beaches. She wondered if she'd made the right decision regarding her destination then gave herself a lecture for continually second-guessing herself. She was here now and she'd make the best of it.

After paying for all day parking, she placed the receipt on the dash of her car where the security patrol couldn't miss it, grabbed her stuff then made her way down the path leading to the water. It didn't take long before she was regretting her eagerness. Unlike the beach she'd been occupying the last few days, this one was a good distance from the parking area. In an attempt to avoid a second trip to the car, she'd grabbed everything from her trunk. Now she was struggling to remain upright on the soft sand while trying to balance her chair, cooler and the other items she needed for the day. To make matters worse, the sea breeze was blowing her unsecured hair across her face, almost completely blinding her. So far her morning had sucked.

All she'd wanted to do was plant her butt on a sandy beach but she was beginning to wonder if she was ever going to get there.

Instead of another self-directed lecture, she paused, closed her eyes and inhaled deeply, practicing the calming exercise she'd learned so many years ago. Taking slow, measured breaths she concentrated on the sound of the surf and the fragrance of the salt air. Slowly her tension receded - then returned tenfold as she was slammed to the ground.

Her cooler burst open, spewing ice and bottles of water over the sand. The contents of Cat's canvas tote spilled out across the path. Her beach chair, which had been firmly clamped under one arm, now trapped her to the sandy soil.

"Are you alright?" Colt asked the woman sprawled in front of him. Damn. He'd been focused on the sea oats, mentally framing a shot and wondering if he had time to take a few pictures of the reeds bowing to the ocean breeze. The lighting was perfect at the moment. He'd forgotten he was on a well-traveled path leading to the beach.

Setting his equipment aside, he dropped to one knee to untangle the woman from her chair.

"What the hell are you doing trying to carry all this stuff?" he snapped, noting the amount of gear the woman had been hauling. What was she thinking overloading herself like that? It was hard enough to navigate the soft, uneven pathways empty handed. Based on the items now strewn across the landscape it looked like she was preparing to set up camp.

Cat was considering the various ways she could do damage to the steamroller currently barking at her when she was suddenly - and effortlessly - hauled to her feet and came face to – ah, chest - with the man. And, Holy Mary, what a chest! Broad, tan and sculpted. She found herself fighting the sudden and unnatural urge to test its firmness. Instead, she craned her neck back to glare at the man. He was over six feet and as impressed as she was with the man's chest, it was the eyes boring in on her that made her breath catch. Cat wasn't prone to romanticize but at this moment she'd swear she was looking into a pair of Sorcerer's stones. Tiny flecks of silver danced in the discs of crystal blue – not unlike the waters she'd been heading toward. Against his deeply tanned face and coal black hair they sparkled like gems displayed on a jeweler's cloth.

Wrenching her eyes away from his she busied herself by brushing the sand from the seat of her shorts. "Are you hurt?" she asked, immediately realizing the absurdity of the question. Hurt? The man was built like a tank.

"I'm good," Colt answered, a smile slowly replacing his scowl. He studied the small, attractive package now fidgeting in front of him. He might have to thank Gib, after all, for being AWOL today. Her face had turned the same shade of red as the shorts she wore - shorts that showed off a pair of legs that couldn't possibly be as long as they appeared considering the top of her head didn't reach his shoulders. A white halter-top accentuated her small, pert breasts. Stirred by the breeze, her sable colored hair danced around her face. His masculine assessment of the woman surprised him. It had been some time since he'd felt this kind of sensual pull.

Ordering himself to stop gawking like a teenager, Colt turned his attention to the objects scattered across the beach. While she collected items that had escaped her tote, he tossed the bottled water back into the cooler and snapped it shut. "Where were you headed?" he asked, picking up the cooler in one hand while he slung his camera equipment over the other shoulder.

"Ah, thank you but I'm fine," Cat stammered, realizing his intent. Damn. She was feeling clumsy and awkward not to mention distracted. She'd come to Sanibel to chill out on the beach not warm up some guy's sheets. Whoa! Where had that thought come from? The man was only offering to carry her cooler not father her children.

"My mom would horsewhip me if I didn't see you safely to your destination."

His slight Southern drawl only added to his sensuality. It wasn't his words, though, but his unyielding stance that told her he wasn't going anywhere until she was settled in. Resigned, she glanced up and down the beach looking for a spot to claim for the day. Aesthetically, the shoreline wasn't much different from the private beach she'd been visiting. It had the same sparkling blue water, silky white sand with an occasional tree for shade. The major difference was the people. They were everywhere. Well, wasn't that the reason she'd come to this location?

"It's been awhile since I've been to this part of the island. I was hoping for a quiet spot - if there is such a place."

"The farther away from the lighthouse, the quieter it tends to be. Let's try this way." Colt slipped on the sunglasses that had been dangling around his neck then took the chair from her before heading up the beach.

"If you see a spot you like, just holler."

Cat considered "hollering" as she watched his retreating backside. The man looked as good going as he did coming. She shook her head as another bad pun popped into her mind. What the hell was wrong with her today? The guy probably had a harem. Besides, she didn't need that kind of distraction. At least the encounter had taken her mind off the reason for the detour. The sudden image of the menacing, dark Lincoln brought her to a grinding halt. She'd wanted to be near people, she reminded herself. Not follow a stranger to a secluded area. "This'll do," she announced sharply.

Surprised by her tone, Colt turned, studying the woman. She looked like she'd just spotted Ted Bundy's ghost.

"Are you sure you're okay?" Colt asked. Maybe she'd been injured when he'd knocked her down. It was certainly possible. She was small - even by most women's standards. Tiny compared to his large frame. He wouldn't call her pixie-like, though. There were some sharp edges reflected in those dark, round eyes. Bedroom eyes, he mused then smiled as that thought conjured up an image of her body tangled in some well-worn sheets. The image, though, quickly disappeared as he recognized something else that he'd seen far too often to ignore. Fear. He scanned the area behind her - his protective instincts kicking in.

"No. I mean, yes. I'm fine. It's just been a weird morning." Was she whining? She never whined. God, how much more could she embarrass herself? "Thanks for your help," she clipped, turning her back to him. Hopefully, he'd take the hint and leave.

"My pleasure," he drawled, intrigued by her blatant attempt to get rid of him. He wasn't quite ready to go. No woman had peaked his interest in years but this one did – and in a big way. There was also that flash of fear he'd seen in her eyes. No, he wasn't ready to leave just yet. "I'm Colton. My friends call me Colt."

The man was either slow or stubborn Cat decided as she turned around to acknowledge the introduction. She was surprised to find his hand extended. A Southern gentleman? She'd long suspected the species was extinct.

"I'm Cat," she said, taking his hand.

"Cat? As in 'here, kitty, kitty'?" His large hand swallowed hers yet her grip was surprisingly firm. The lady was full of interesting contrasts.

Cat ignored the pun. She'd heard them all. "Cat. Short for Catherine." She noted the professional camera equipment he'd carefully set on the ground. "Are you working?"

"Helping a friend out this morning. I'm not usually at this beach myself. What brought you here?" Not that he was complaining.

"My imagination," she muttered to herself. His single raised eyebrow told her she'd spoken the thought aloud. His arms, now folded across his chest, told her he wasn't moving until she elaborated.

"I thought someone might have been following me," she admitted, sheepishly.

Colt's head snapped back in the direction they'd just come from. "Followed? Are you sure?"

"No," she responded slowly, intrigued by his reaction. The man had gone from curious to alert in an instant. "As I said, it was more than likely my imagination." Yet the hairs on the back of her neck still tingled.

"Okay then, what made you *think* someone was following you?" Colt watched her fight for - then gain control of her nerves. Hell, he told himself, he could very well be the reason she was on edge. For her sake he hoped that was all there was to it.

Not slow, she decided, just stubborn. Sensing she was stuck with the man until he heard the details, Cat quickly related the tale, fully expecting him to dismiss it or laugh. He did neither.

"And the car was back again this morning?" Colt asked. Warning bells he hadn't heard in years began clanging inside his head.

She shrugged. "Yeah, but like I said, when I changed directions he didn't follow. Still, it gave me a creepy feeling so I decided I'd try my luck here today."

"I'm glad you did," Colt flashed a grin but then quickly sobered. "That was a smart move. If you see that car again, though, call the police. We don't have much crime on the island but you should play it safe."

She nodded but she had no intention of repeating the story to anyone else. Verbalizing it had made her realize just how ludicrous the account sounded and she wasn't anxious to come across as an idiotic tourist, particularly to the police.

Her gaze, which had been refreshingly direct, now shifted toward the water. Something had banked the fire in those eyes and Colt felt responsible for that loss. Too bad he was on a deadline because he had an unexpected desire to rekindle that spark. It had been a long while since he'd spent time in the company of a woman he found interesting. Gib had been riding him to get back into the dating scene. He'd had no desire - until now.

"Can I interest you in dinner tonight? It would give me the chance to properly apologize for running you over."

She wavered for a split second before reminding herself that she hadn't come here to get tangled up with a man - no matter how appealing a picture it made. "Thanks but I plan on spending a quiet evening with my friend here," she said indicating the book she'd tossed on to her oversized beach towel. She preferred old-fashioned, hard cover novels to electronic devices when she was spending the day at the beach.

In spite of her negative response, Colt had caught her moment of hesitation. "Come on. I'll be good," he cajoled, adding a wink. He couldn't remember the last time he'd hit on a woman. He was rusty has hell and wondered if he was doing more to scare her away than aid his cause.

She'd just bet he was good. Her skin warmed and it had little to do with the Florida sun climbing higher in the sky. What was it about this guy that had her thoughts running in that direction?

"You've got to eat," he coaxed but decided not to push. She still appeared a bit skittish and coming on too strong might backfire. "Give it some thought," Colt suggested as he pulled a business card from the side pocket of his camera bag. "Call me if you change your mind or you could just meet me at the Mucky Duck. Say around 7:00 tonight?"

Cat was familiar with the local pub. The popular Captiva bar located at the water's edge was famed for its picturesque views of the setting sun.

"We can grab a burger and a beer." Colt suggested.

"I'll think about it," was all that she'd promise.

Colt knew that the non-committal response was as good as he was going to get. "Good," he said as he picked up his equipment.

"Do you have a last name, Cat?"

"Storm."

"Storm," he grinned. "Suits you." Halfway back up the beach he shouted over his shoulder, "See you tonight."

AFTER SETTLING her chair in the limited shade of a palm tree, Cat tried to relax. She wasn't succeeding. The whole morning had done nothing but wind her up instead of down. Now she was looking at the prospect of a date with a very attractive man. His last remark was an obvious attempt to influence her decision. Even so, it seemed to be working. What harm would it do to meet him for a drink?

Having her own car would give her the means to escape if she felt uncomfortable.

She hadn't been on a date since the disaster with Michael last year. That guy had had some serious issues. Issues that she'd been surprisingly slow to pick up on. Considering her history, she should have immediately recognized his violent tendencies. As soon as she did, though, she'd given him his walking papers. To say Michael took the news badly would be putting it mildly. Thinking about him and the business that followed still gave her chills.

Since then she'd become "a project." There was something about approaching thirty and being single that brought out the matchmaker in people. People she hardly knew had a "friend." Cat had never considered marriage a goal. She wasn't even sure she was cut out for the institution. Having been on her own since her teens, she was independent as hell and liked it. She'd proved she could manage just fine without a partner. That didn't mean she was adverse to the idea or didn't enjoy a man's company.

Realizing she had just read the same paragraph for the third time and still had no idea what the author had written, Cat put down her book and picked up the business card Colt had given her. The card was by no means ordinary. The business name, *Island Images*, along with his name and profession were superimposed on a captivating shot of the beach at sunset - obviously one of his photos. Stunning was the word that came to Cat's mind as she studied the miniature print. It was as compelling as the man.

Well, Mr. James, maybe we will see you later.

4

C olt sat at one of the outdoor tables enjoying the show put on by the setting sun as it shimmered across the waters of the Gulf of Mexico. He didn't think he'd ever get tired of these islands. What artist would? They changed with the movement of the sun yet remained constant. The islanders knew that the beaches and the wildlife made the place unique and most were committed to preserve its natural habitat. Hurricane Charley had cut a wide path of destruction when it roared through in 2004 but in the years that had followed, the residents had done their best to restore it. Nature was doing the rest.

Leaning back against the table, his long legs stretched out before him, Colt smiled at the sentiment of the Jimmy Buffett tune drifting down from speakers mounted high on palm trees surrounding the patio. The bar catered to both tourists and locals although depending on the time of year, you'd find more of one than the other. Colt occasionally came here during the off-season, when it was considerably less crowded, to enjoy a brew and the view.

Tonight, though, he was looking forward to enjoying Cat's company. That thought had kept a smile on his face for the remainder of the day. She'd peaked his interest - not to mention his libido.

She also concerned him. He hadn't imagined her fear this morning so after he'd left Lighthouse Beach he'd cruised the nearby parking areas looking for a black Lincoln. He hadn't found one. For good measure he'd stopped by the Sanibel Police Department to have a word with his friend, Rick Wilcowski.

He and Rick had been Army buddies, having served on the same Special Forces team until Rick had opted out to return home to Chicago to help his ailing dad. He'd joined the Chicago PD and had been able to share a few good years with his father before he'd lost his battle with heart disease. Shortly after Colt had settled in on Sanibel, Rick had come down to check the place out and, like Colt, decided to stay. The Sanibel PD was glad to have him and Colt was glad to have his friend near.

No suspicious vehicles had been reported – Lincoln or otherwise. But the more Colt thought about it, the less easy he'd become. He'd gotten the impression the lady didn't rattle easily but she'd been afraid of something this morning. He'd learned to listen to his instincts and they'd been shouting at him ever since Cat had related her story about the car. Colt was anxious to know if the vehicle had made a reappearance.

He'd made a point to arrive at the bar early. Not pushing her for a date had been a gamble. She hadn't called and there was always the chance she wouldn't show. He'd find out shortly if he'd bet wisely.

It wasn't long before he sensed her arrival. Turning toward the bar he caught sight of her as she rounded the corner of the building from its parking lot in the rear. Wearing sandals and a sundress splashed with bright colors, she looked like a tropical flower - fragile and exotic. He didn't think she'd like the fragile part of his appraisal, though. Tonight there was a definite spunk in her step. Whatever had been bothering her this morning had vanished. The change made him certain of one thing - he hadn't been the cause of her apprehension earlier today. That knowledge lifted his spirits another notch.

Cat scanned the tables and quickly spotted Colt. Her heart actually fluttered at the sight of him. "Get a grip," she muttered. As she approached the table, Colt rose to his feet. He looked as imposing and sexy as he had earlier in the day. Khaki shorts hugged his hips while a white polo shirt stretched across his broad chest. It was a shame to hide something that magnificent. The patio was crowded in spite of the summer's heat. Mostly women she noted and suspected her date was the reason so many females had chosen the hot, humid outdoors to the air-conditioned interior of the bar.

"Is poaching illegal on the island?" she asked, as she approached him.

"Poaching?" It wasn't exactly the greeting he'd expected.

She tipped her head to indicate the ladies who were now moving to take refuge inside. One particular blond had yet to take her hungry eyes off of Colt. "I think a few of them would like to have me charged with the crime."

Colt followed her gaze and saw the women filing into the bar. Confused, he asked, "Would you be more comfortable inside?"

Obviously, the man didn't realize he'd been in the sights of a hunting party. "I think we're both safer out here."

The Florida heat had never been a problem for Cat. The bar's misting fans were helping to cool things off. Together with the setting sun and a soft sea breeze, it was comfortable by her standards. "Besides, I like the view," she added, eyeing the water.

Gazing at the woman now seated across from him, Colt couldn't argue. The view was pretty damn exceptional in his opinion. Cat's shoulder length hair still hung loose. The dark strands, treaded with a gold that didn't come from any salon, framed her small face. Everything about the woman was petite except for those eyes. A man could get lost in those large, coffee-colored, eyes.

"What would you like to drink?" Colt asked.

A bottle of beer from a local microbrewery sat on the table in front of Colt. "I'll have the same," she said, indicating the bottle.

While Colt went to the outdoor bar to place their order for burgers and beers, Cat turned toward the water and relaxed. Inhaling the air deeply, she cherished each salty breath. The ocean settled her. It always had. She felt as if some part of her was missing when she was away from its shores.

"How'd the rest of your day go?" Colt asked as he set the drinks on the table. The wait staff would bring out the food when it was ready.

"Things improved after you left." At his raised eyebrow she laughed then quickly clarified, "Let me rephrase that," she said, smiling. "Nothing out of the ordinary happened after you departed."

"No more Lincolns?"

"Nope. Not a one." She had pretty much dismissed the car to her overactive imagination. "I know I sounded like an idiot this morning."

"What you sounded like was someone who was smart

enough not to take chances." He reached across the table and laid a hand over hers. "I stopped by the police station this afternoon. I have a friend on the force. He did some checking." Her reaction told him he caught her by surprise. Those big, brown eyes actually grew rounder.

"And?"

"Nothing unusual has been reported - which doesn't mean that you imagined it. He wants you to contact them if you see that car again."

"I certainly didn't mean for you to go to any trouble. Thank you, though."

"You're welcome and it wasn't any trouble." But he noticed the fire in those beautiful eyes had banked again. He also noted that she hadn't agreed to call the police.

"Where are you staying?" Colt asked, sensing the need to change the subject. Her choice of hotels was another concern that had been on his mind.

"The Sunset Cottages. Do you know them?"

Colt was familiar with the quaint string of cottages. Painted in the Florida's signature colors of pastel pink, green, yellow and blue, they sat on the Gulf side of Sanibel not far from Bowman's Beach. Colt had taken the photos used in their current brochure. He also knew the owners. Terry and Pat were characters but well respected in the community. Still, free standing units like the cottages didn't offer much in the way of security.

"I know them. They're right on the water. So why did you have to hunt up another beach today?" Although he was grateful that she had.

"There's a young family staying in one of the cottages through the weekend. The kids are cute but are over-flowing with energy. I came here to think and couldn't do that while ducking Frisbees." She thought of the six-year-old twin boys who had almost decapitated her that first afternoon on the beach. Their mother had been genuinely embarrassed and had done her best to keep her sons under control the rest of that day but Cat decided it would be better if she found another place to lounge, at least temporarily. The kids would feel free to enjoy themselves and she would find the solitude she needed. Pat had recommended the secluded spot that she'd been visiting before her imagination had gotten the better of her this morning.

"What needs so much thought?" Was there a man that required her attention? The idea set his teeth on edge.

"Work. Or a lack thereof," she sighed. "My boss is retiring. It's time I decided what I want to do about my future."

Colt let out the breath he'd been holding. "Why is that giving you trouble?" He'd have to clarify the boyfriend issue but things were looking better.

"Because I'm not sure if I want to stay in Tallahassee or even continue working in an office, for that matter. The easy thing to do would be to stay put. Avoid the hassle of having to find another place to live, pack, move, etcetera. I'm not even sure where I'd go if I decide to leave. But Tallahassee has never felt like home to me and I'd prefer living in a place where the word "freeze" refers to a frozen concoction rather than the weather forecast."

Things were, without a doubt, looking up, Colt thought. "What would you do if you didn't work in an office?"

"Something to do with plants or landscaping. Maybe even start a small nursery business. I've been designing and planting gardens for some time." Working in the soil had actually become her passion. Plants didn't judge or complain. She liked the solitude she found digging in the soil and she preferred baking in the sun to freezing in air conditioning.

"Are you any good at it?"

Her broad smile answered his question.

"So what's stopping you, then?"

"Fear," Cat found herself admitting. "All the 'what-if' scenarios you can imagine. What if I don't succeed? What if I don't like it? Yada, yada, yada. Anyway, I was hoping to tackle some of those fears during my time off." Cat looked toward the water wishing it held the answers then decided she wasn't going to worry about it anymore tonight.

"I like your business card. A sample of your work?"

Colt smiled at her not so subtle change in topic.

"Yeah. Birds are my favorite subject but with the sand, surf and setting sun, Gib thought it would be good for business."

"Gib?"

"Gibson McKay, my partner. He's the reason I was at the lighthouse this morning. I was filling in for him. We have a small studio on Periwinkle Way. We specialize in photography for brochures, calendars, that sort of thing. When those jobs are light we supplement our income photographing social events and weddings. Not our favorite type of work but the money is good."

Cat pushed her plate toward the center of the table. Colt wasn't surprised half of her burger remained. Where would she have put it?

"Do you sell your pictures? As works of art?" If his business card was any example of his skill she could imagine his photographs gracing any home, including her tiny apartment.

"Occasionally. Gib and I display some of our photos at

the studio but we don't get a lot of foot traffic. That wasn't our intent when we opened the business but that might change shortly. I have a show coming up in a couple of months."

Cat couldn't help but smile at the enthusiasm she saw on his face. "Really? Where?"

"Right here, or I should say, on Sanibel since we're technically on Captiva. A small gallery there."

Cat raised her beer in a toast. "To the success of your show."

Colt touched his bottle to hers. At the moment, though, he was hoping for success of another kind.

The sun had set as they lingered over their drinks. Colt stood, stretched - and then held out his hand. "Care to join me for a walk on the beach?"

Cat studied the hand he'd offered. Did she really want to do this? She was having enough difficulty staying focused during this trip. Still, she wasted no time slipping her hand into his. The invitation, like the man, was hard to resist.

The sound of the surf calmed Cat and the sugary white sand felt like silk between her toes. The breeze had grown stronger, helping to keep the insects that would normally plague them this time of year at bay. With the setting sun, the temperature had dropped to a comfortable level.

"So, what brought you to Southwest Florida?" Cat asked then immediately regretted the inquiry when she felt the slight hitch in his stride. "Sorry. It's none of my business," she quickly added. God knew there were things in her past she didn't talk about. As a result, she made it a point not to pry into other people's history.

Colt was surprised that she'd picked up on his hesitation. "Are you always so perceptive?"

"No, but I am serious. I didn't mean to pry."

Colt stared out toward the darkened water. Few people knew why he'd come to these shores. It was a connection to another time and place he'd been trying to forget. For some reason he couldn't explain, he didn't just want to tell Cat – he felt the need to tell her. Was this the next step in the healing process? Maybe, or maybe it was something about the woman whose hand he held. Either way, impulse had him pulling his shirt over his head and laying it on the sand.

"Have a seat," he suggested, indicating the makeshift blanket.

Cat didn't know what to make of the gesture. She wasn't concerned that it was a prelude to something sexual. His mood was too somber - almost sad. So she took the seat he offered and silently waited.

Lowering himself onto the sand next to her, he draped his arms across his knees. He continued his study of the breaking surf for some time before speaking.

"I came here for basically the same reason you did – hoping the trip would clear my mind." He dropped his head between his arms as he continued. "I'd recently resigned my commission in the Army. I'd left the battlefield but the battlefield wouldn't leave me. When I'd returned to Savannah I couldn't pull myself together. I isolated myself. Work was impossible. There were flashbacks. I couldn't sleep. When I did doze, nightmares were common. Drinking was fast becoming my favorite pastime."

"Post-Traumatic Stress Disorder?"

"That was one diagnosis. When some friends headed down this way on a fishing trip, they all but strapped me to the bed of their truck hoping the trip would accomplish what the doctors couldn't. They were worried about me. I can't say I blamed them."

"Then, a few days before we were scheduled to head back to Georgia, I wandered into one of the small shops that line Periwinkle Way to pick up a gift for my mom. It sold mostly souvenirs but they also processed photos. The walls of the place displayed some stunning shots of the wildlife on the island. As I studied the photographs, it hit me. I'd been on the island for nearly two weeks but I'd been totally blind to its beauty."

"The guy running the processing equipment turned out to be the photographer. We struck up a conversation. He invited me to join him the following day on, what he called, one of his photo safaris." Colt thought back to that day and how it had saved his sanity. Maybe his life.

"That evening, for the first time in years, I was looking forward to something. After a day viewing the island through the lens of a camera, I was seeing things other than the pictures that had been trapped in my head. When my friends left, I stayed. I had my mom ship my things down and the rest, as they say, is history."

"The guy in the photo shop? That was Gib?"

"Yep." He smiled thinking about his unusual friend. "Our personalities are pretty much opposites in every respect except for our love of photography but for some reason we clicked. About a year ago we pooled our resources and purchased a building that was in need of some work. We fixed it up and opened our business downstairs. We live in the two units above." Colt paused, "I still have a lot of baggage but, for some reason, it seems easier to carry here."

Cat looked at the man whose attention was now fixed on the darkened horizon. No one had to tell her that mending a shattered soul took guts and determination. Apparently, Colt had both.

Sensing her gaze upon him, he turned his attention

back toward the woman at his side. Her petite frame made her look delicate. He was almost afraid to touch her for fear she'd break but he suspected that her frame was made of steel. His fingers brushed the soft skin on the back of her neck while his thumb stroked her cheek. What would she do if he kissed her? Pull away? Return the kiss? He was going to find out.

The air crackled around them as Colt lowered his head to hers. My God, she thought, we're going to be struck by lightning. She felt heat as his lips touched hers then a gentleness that surprised her. The kiss was soft and warm. He nipped her lower lip then traced it with the tip of his tongue. Just when she thought he would deepen the kiss, he slowly - reluctantly - lifted his head, gathering her into his arms.

"I promised myself I wouldn't touch you tonight." He'd planned on being a gentleman. Give her some time to get comfortable with him. She'd been frightened once today. He had no intention of scaring her by coming on too strong but it had taken every ounce of his control to pull back from the taste of her - fighting the desire to lay her down and take her right there on the beach. He wouldn't have let it get that far – at least that's what he told himself - but she'd surrendered to him so completely, he'd been blindly tempted to continue.

She rested her head against his chest and listened to the sound of his racing heart. It would have to speed up, though, if it wanted to catch hers. Had a kiss ever had her responding so strongly? Time to slow things down.

"I should get going," she mumbled against his chest.

"I scared you," he stated flatly.

Despite his obvious reluctance to let her go she leaned back and scowled at him. "I don't scare that easy," then added with a smile, "What you are is tempting."

He studied her face in the moonlight. No, she wasn't afraid. "Tempting?" he chuckled as he rose to his feet in one fluid motion. Reaching for her hand, he helped her off the sand. "I'll work on irresistible. Come on. I'll follow you back to your cottage."

5

_____

Cat glanced at her rearview mirror, confirming Colt was still behind her. He drove one of those big, four-door Jeep Wranglers. The ability to go off-road probably came in handy in his profession. His vehicle was certainly a more comforting sight than the ominous Lincoln had been. She almost laughed out loud. Comfort was not what she thought about when she pictured Colt. Hot, steamy, sex was more like it – which surprised the hell out of her. She needed to exercise a little more self-control she told herself as she pulled into a parking space near her unit.

Colt was at her side almost immediately after she exited her vehicle. "Any chance you're going to invite me in?" he whispered in her ear then began to nuzzle the skin beneath it. "What about it?" he added softly when she didn't respond. He brushed her hair aside then began sampling the skin on her neck and shoulders.

"What about what?" she mumbled, her head rolling to one side. Why couldn't the man just shut up and concentrate on what he was doing?

"Are you going to invite me in?"

The question finally permeated the thick fog of passion that filled her brain. When she looked into those hungry eyes she almost forgot the question for a second time. She'd never reacted to a man like this. Common sense battled with desire. Fortunately - or unfortunately - common sense won.

"Not tonight," she managed - although she knew she hadn't sounded all that convincing.

In spite of her response, Colt was still smiling. He couldn't remember any woman ever melting in his arms the way Cat did. It was a heady experience.

"In that case, can I interest you in doing something with me tomorrow?"

"Like?"

"Breakfast. Bicycling. Boating…"

"Ahh, the B list of vacation activities. Okay, but I draw the line at bailing out of airplanes."

"Damn. No skydiving."

Still smiling, she rattled off her cell number. As she watched him punch the number into his phone she admitted to herself that she'd lied to them both earlier. He wasn't just tempting. He was, in fact, irresistible. Still, she surprised herself when she reached up and tugged on the collar of his shirt to pull him closer.

The moment his lips touched hers, the gentleness of his earlier kisses was gone. He was consumed by a savage hunger. Colt quickly forgot his promise of restraint. He wanted her. No, he realized, he needed her. How could that be? This soon? This fast? His tongue stroked her lips, seeking entry. When she opened for him, he stopped trying to reason and took everything she offered.

Cat anchored her arms around his neck, bringing the two of them even closer. A moan escaped when she felt his erection press against her abdomen. Climbing his tall frame until his ridge rubbed against her core struck her as a good idea but when his hand found her breast she was too shaky to attempt the feat. Cat had no idea how they'd managed the steps to her unit but was thankful for the support of something solid. She leaned back against the door - then gasped as it gave way behind her.

UNTITLED

"What the hell?" Colt tightened his hold on Cat, preventing her from tumbling through the doorway.

"I locked it. I know I did." Cat was almost obsessive about security. No way she'd left the door unlocked. She stepped into the cottage but firm hands gripped her shoulders and pulled her back.

"Don't even think about it," Colt warned. He deftly lifted her off her feet and deposited her safely out of the way. "Call 911 - and stay put," he ordered as he hit the light switch just inside the door. "Shit!"

"What?" Cat tried to push past him to look inside but Colt blocked her attempt.

"I said, *stay put*. Now make that call."

Glaring at his wide back she pulled out her phone. She bristled at taking orders – even when they were warranted.

Colt took stock of the destruction. It was immediately obvious to him that this wasn't an ordinary break-in. The place looked like a hurricane had passed through it. He recognized the book she'd had with her at the beach earlier that day, although just barely. The pages had been ripped from the binding and torn into pieces. They now littered the room like confetti. The floor of the small kitchenette was covered with what looked like the contents of the unit's compact refrigerator. A badly damaged iPad could be seen beneath the mess.

Although he hadn't thought it possible, the bedroom was in worse shape than the living area. Broken glass covered the floor near the window, most likely the intruder's point of entry. The door to the small closet had been left open. Its contents, along with apparently every piece of clothing from the small dresser, had been sliced into ribbons and were scattered across the room like colorful streamers.

Not surprisingly, the tiny bathroom was the final casualty. Every container, whether it be cosmetic, lotion, or toothpaste, had been emptied. The tub, sink and toilet played the canvas for their contents. Anger changed to a bone-deep fear when Colt spotted the message slashed savagely across the bathroom mirror in lipstick. *YOU'RE MINE.* This wasn't a random act. It was personal and Cat had been the target.

"Oh. My. God."

Colt spun around to find Cat standing in the center of the bedroom, her eyes wide as she took in the destruction.

"I told you to wait outside!"

"Why?" she snapped, recovering quickly. "You didn't."

Swearing under his breath, Colt headed to intercept her. She'd have to be told about the message. He just couldn't bring himself to do so now.

"The police are on the way," she said, absently. She was no longer paying him any attention. Instead, she stared at the scraps of fabric that littered the room wondering why someone would do this to her. The thought was a selfish one, she realized. What made her think she was the only victim? And in that instant she thought of Pat and Terry. Spinning on her heels, she raced through unit and out the door. If the same lunatic had broken into their place, they could be injured or worse.

Colt caught up with her halfway across the courtyard, pulling her to a halt. "Where the hell do you think you're going?"

Instantly she began struggling, violently trying to break free of his grasp. "Let go of me," she demanded.

Her frenzied - almost panicked - reaction took Colt by surprise. "Calm down," he told her. He was forced to repeat the command several times - each time with more emphasis yet she continued her frantic attempts to escape. He considered releasing her but feared she might bolt and he couldn't take that chance. The bastard could be hiding in the thick vegetation that surrounded the complex of buildings. Instead he pulled her to his chest, wrapping his arms around her shoulders to hold her firmly, but gently, in place.

"I'm sorry, Cat," he said calmly. "I didn't mean to frighten you." He knew that's exactly what he had done. Contrary to his training he'd allowed his anger to take hold. When she had disregarded her own safety, that anger had boiled over.

"But you shouldn't have run off like that. Whoever ransacked your place could still be nearby." He scanned the area surrounding the cabins while he continued to gently stroke her back.

Sanity slowly returned - allowing his words to sink in. He was right. She needed to calm down. Hysterics wouldn't accomplish anything. Closing her eyes she took several deep, cleansing breaths. Intuitively she knew that Colt would not harm her but when he'd grabbed her, the action had been frighteningly familiar.

"I was going to check on Pat and Terry," she explained. And if, as she hoped, the men were safe then she wanted to be the one to tell them what had happened before the police arrived.

"Alright then," he said tucking Cat firmly against his side. "We'll do it together."

Colt banged on the door to the bungalow belonging to the owners, shoving Cat behind him as he did. It was apparent she wasn't happy about his protective posture because she immediately tried to step away. The corners of his mouth twitched as he shoved her behind him again. While it was highly unlikely that the person who'd broke into Cat's place would answer the door, he wasn't taking any chances where her safety was concerned.

Terry opened the door, obviously confused when he recognized Colt. His confusion quickly turned to alarm when he spotted Cat peeking out from behind Colt's large frame. "What's wrong?"

"Somebody broke in and tore up Cat's cottage," Colt told him.

Cat scowled up at her white knight. Was the man always this blunt?

A series of rapid-fire questions and answers ensued between the two men. Since she didn't appear to be needed, Cat decided to head back to her unit for a more thorough look at the damage and wait for the police. Colt apparently read minds because his arm tightened around her waist, effectively pinning her to his side. She was considering a well-placed kick to his shin when the flashing lights of the police cruisers filled the lot.

Cat sat with two of the responding officers at one of the picnic tables that circled the cottages' courtyard. She was doing her best to answer the questions they were throwing at her. *Yes*, she was sure she'd left the cottage a little after six-thirty. *Yes*, she was sure she'd locked the door. *No*, nothing but her digital camera appeared to be missing although she'd only done a quick check of the living room and bedroom before Colt ushered her back out. When they asked about the writing on the bathroom mirror her eyes snapped to Colt. So that's why he'd rushed her from the unit. What? He thought she couldn't handle it? She turned her attention back to the officer. She needed to finish with them before she told Colt what she thought of his inter-ference.

Colt sat with Rick at a nearby table. He had called his friend as soon as the police had arrived. The two of them had completed their examination of the cottage's rooms and surrounding area and were now waiting for the officers to finish their questioning. Colt was convinced this wasn't a random burglary. Only Cat's personal possessions had been targeted. Property belonging to the cottage had been left untouched unless it happened to get in the way. With the exception of the broken window, Pat and Terry would likely be out only the cost of a good cleaning. Cat's prop-erty, on the other hand, was completely destroyed. Then there was the ominous message scrawled on the mirror – which, based on the scathing look he'd just received, she was now aware of.

"What do you think?" he asked, turning his attention back to Rick.

"That someone isn't very happy with your Ms. Storm. Any ideas?"

"No, but I intend to find out."

Rick noted that Colt's eyes rarely left the petite woman. His friend hadn't shown any interest in dating since his return from Afghanistan, claiming he had too many issues to deal with without adding a woman to the mix. Well, he'd either dealt with a few of those issues or this particular female was too appealing to pass up.

"Any reason to think she might be involved in something that would warrant this kind of attention?"

"What are you implying, Rick? She works for the State Attorney General's office, for God's sake. There's sure to be a background check in her file. If you ask real nice, they might even share it with you."

Rick ignored his friend's sarcasm. It was his fierce defense of the woman that captured his attention. Very interesting indeed.

A screened door slammed shut snapping their attention back toward the cottages. Colt immediately relaxed as he spotted the two proprietors exit their living quarters and make a beeline for Cat. The smile on Cat's face telegraphed her relief. She welcomed the interruption.

As the two men approached, Cat couldn't help but grin. They were such an odd couple. Pat was tall, handsome and muscular while Terry had always reminded Cat of an absent-minded professor. The pair was the main reason she stayed at the cottages when she visited the island. They were funny, considerate and always made her feel like she was at home.

"You doing okay?" Pat asked, concern evident on his face.

Before she could respond, Terry handed her a small canvas tote bag along with a room key. "We put some toiletries together along with one of our souvenir t-shirts for you to sleep in. You're in Unit 2 now - next to us. Don't you worry about a thing. As soon as they allow us into your old unit, we'll get it cleaned up and salvage anything we can."

She started to argue. It was her problem and she'd deal with it but she was suddenly so very tired. Instead, she nodded her thanks and turned toward the officers. "Are we done?" she asked, hoping she didn't sound as impatient as she felt.

One of the men handed her a card containing his contact information. "If you think of anything else, contact me."

"Come on," Colt said, as he joined them at the table. "Let's get you settled."

"We put an extra toothbrush in the bag," Pat said quietly to Colt as he turned to leave.

"You are *not* spending the night!"

Although she had managed to keep her voice low there was no mistaking Cat's anger. Colt had been expecting this volcano to blow. He'd seen the steam building with each question put to her by the police. The problem was he hadn't seen any way around it.

"I'm staying or you're coming home with me," he told her firmly as he snatched the key from her hand and headed toward the building. "You've been followed. Your personal possessions have been destroyed. It looks like somebody wants to harm you. At the very least, he wants to terrorize you. So, lady, if you think I'm leaving you alone tonight, you're crazy." His voice had risen with each statement but, damn it, what did she think he'd do? Just walk away?

Cat had to almost run to keep up with Colt. His long, angry strides telegraphed his mood. Well, she wasn't real happy herself. "I let my imagination get the better of me this morning," she countered. "The damage was most likely the result of some kids looking for drug money. More importantly, *I don't need - or want - a keeper*."

"If you can't see that you have a problem then maybe you do need a 'keeper.' That must be one hell of an imagination you've got. You were pretty damn shaken up this morning. As for your room - nothing in it was damaged *except* items that belonged to you! Explain that!"

"Don't forget the message on the bathroom mirror!" His eyes narrowed at that statement. "What? You didn't expect me to hear about it? Did you plan to tell me?" She didn't like being controlled. No one would ever do that to her again. "Even if your theory is correct, what are you planning to do about it? Hire on as my personal bodyguard?"

He'd wanted to tell her that protecting her was exactly what he planned to do but this didn't appear to be a good time to mention that fact so he held the comment in check. He watched as she took several deep, slow breaths. He was quickly recognizing the action as a coping mechanism. She made her way to the small kitchenette. Leaning back against the counter, she closed her eyes and continued to inhale deeply, slowly letting out each breath. Her clenched fists gradually unfurled. Colt stood silently, watching the transformation. Finally, she opened those big eyes and looked directly into his.

"If, and I repeat, *if* there is someone after me, I will deal with it. It's my problem. Besides, do you think I'd put you between me and some nutcase?" Her heart had stopped when he'd disappeared into the cottage.

Colt saw the fear return to those wide eyes. He realized she was afraid - for him. He stepped forward and gently pulled her into his arms.

"I learned a few things in the Army." He brushed her hair with a kiss. "Think of this as doing me a favor. I wouldn't sleep a wink worrying about you. Let me camp out on the sofa tonight. We'll sort through this in the morning when we're fresh." He paused. "Deal?"

The adrenaline rush was fading as exhaustion seeped in. Silently she admitted that she didn't have it in her to argue any more tonight. Cat left the security of Colt's embrace and returned a minute later with sheets, a blanket and pillow from the small linen closet.

"The couch opens up," she told him although she doubted it would fit his large frame. Tossing the bedding onto the sofa she turned back to her unwanted guest. "I really do appreciate all you've done. Most guys would have run in the other direction as soon as the police were finished with them." With a crooked smile, she added, "I bet this ranks up there as one of your strangest dates."

"It does that," he said as he ran his finger down the bridge of her nose then used it to tilt her chin up so that her eyes met his. "But I like the way it ended. After all, I'm spending the night with a very beautiful woman."

6

As the bright Florida sun squeezed its way through the slits of the plantation blinds, Colt sat at the kitchenette's small table with a cup of coffee he'd just finished brewing. The caffeine was needed. He'd gotten very little sleep. The cause of the sleepless night, however, was something other than the nightmares that had often kept him awake.

For the first couple of hours he'd lain awake on the stunted sofa bed trying – and failing miserably - not to picture Cat asleep in the next room with her t-shirt bunched up over her hips. He'd sent her off to bed with only a pat on that tight, little ass of hers. If he'd done anything more, he wasn't sure he would have been able to stop. The urge to hold her - to kiss away her fears - had been strong. But he wanted to give her time to get her feet back under her. When he made love to her - and he had every intention of doing so - he wanted all her wits about her. He didn't expect he would have to wait very long. It was obvious the steel in her backbone ran deep.

After wrestling his sex drive under control, he sorted

through what he knew about Cat – which wasn't much. Twenty-four hours ago he hadn't known she existed so that tended to limit the information available. He needed all the pieces to the puzzle before they could start putting the picture together. This morning he was going to sit her down and dissect the past few days. He also needed to delve into her background. He had no doubt that she would balk at his help. It hadn't taken him long to figure out a couple of things about her - she possessed an independent streak a mile wide and she wasn't the least bit keen on taking orders.

He'd briefly wondered if she might decide to head home to Tallahassee but dismissed that idea almost immediately. Partly due to the fact that he didn't want to consider that possibility – which was a sobering thought - but mostly because he didn't believe she'd let someone run her off. If anything, he'd bet she'd dig in.

CAT FOLLOWED the aroma of coffee into the small kitchen where she was greeted with a steaming cup and a dazzling smile. Butterflies took up residence in her stomach again. Colt had stayed. The fact that he was still here didn't surprise her. What startled her was that she was comfortable with the idea. Bossy, protective men normally irritated her. Last night, Colt demonstrated that he was both. But for the first time, Cat realized, those weren't necessarily bad traits if they were mixed with a healthy dose of respect.

"A man after my heart," she said, taking the cup he offered. She inhaled its fragrance deeply. "Beats flowers and jewelry any day."

"I wish someone had told me that secret years ago. It would have saved me a lot of money."

"Generally speaking, that rule only applies to caffeine addicts such as myself. I'm sure your gifts were greatly appreciated." She stared into the contents of her cup - thankful the man couldn't read minds. The thought of him giving gifts to other women annoyed her - which was just plain stupid. She'd known him for less than a day and she'd be leaving shortly. No sense getting worked up over his sexual history. She remembered her initial reaction to him, reminding herself he might still have that harem she'd imagined. No, she thought, nothing would be gained by worrying about his gift-giving habits.

"I'm going to take a rain check on whatever you had planned for today. I need to do some shopping." She plucked at the skirt of the sundress she'd been forced to put back on this morning. "I can't wear this thing for the rest of my stay."

Colt mentally ticked off a point for himself. She wasn't running anywhere.

"Why don't we grab some breakfast? We can talk about what we're going to do to keep you safe over a plate of hotcakes - then we can hit the mall."

Cat watched Colt through the steam still rising from her mug. What was going on here? Did he actually think she wanted his services as a bodyguard?

"Colt, while I'd enjoy having breakfast with you, I'm far from convinced my safety is an issue. I can also assure you that I'm quite capable of shopping without your aid. Don't you have some things you need to do?"

Colt pushed away from the counter and added another point to his mental scorecard. When her scowl deepened he was tempted to give himself extra points.

"Don't get your back up. I have no doubt that your shopping skills far exceed mine. However, I have nothing pressing for the next couple of days and I would very much like to spend that time with you."

Her frown changed to a reluctant grin. The guy was good. If she refused his offer she'd be rejecting his company along with his protection. The man had missed his calling as a salesman.

After last night she could understand why Colt might think she had a stalker. She hadn't helped matters by relating the ridiculous story about the Lincoln. Taking into consideration a stubborn streak that seemed to match hers, she relented – for the time being. "Alright. Let's see if you can convince me I'm in mortal danger," and, she added silently, keep up with her at the mall. The day just might prove to be entertaining.

As HE DROVE, Colt contemplated the fact that he'd just won a potentially difficult battle with relative ease. He was sure he'd detected a hint of mischief when she'd finally agreed to his suggestions. Perhaps he was the one who needed to watch his back today.

Turning into the parking lot of the Sanibel Cafe, Colt checked his rearview mirror again. No one followed. That would have been entirely too easy, he admitted. But the absence of a tail didn't comfort him. Something wasn't right and his internal radar rarely failed him.

He ushered Cat into the small eating establishment. As soon as they settled into a booth they were immediately greeted by a perky young blond carrying a pot of coffee and two mugs. Colt ordered the special, which Cat good-naturedly labeled "a heart attack on a plate," while she opted for yogurt, fruit and a freshly baked muffin with homemade jam.

While waiting for their order, Cat glanced at her

surroundings. Each table in the café was actually a shadowbox filled with seashells that were laid out in geometric patterns beneath a thick slab of glass. Booths and chairs showed signs of age but were clean and well-kept. Shells filled glass containers on half-walls separating the booths. Light spilled into the room from the plate glass windows lining the front. It was cozy and relaxing.

Her eyes wandered back to Colt. His long index finger traced the rim of his cup as he stared out at the parking lot. She couldn't tell if he was on guard or just deep in thought. "All right, Magnum. Ask away." Deep in thought, she decided when his head jerked back in her direction.

"Magnum?"

"As in Magnum, P.I.?" Cat smiled, thinking the comparison to the 1980's television character wasn't that far off. "You did want to ask me some questions, didn't you?"

Colt jumped at the opening she gave him. "You don't really believe the break-in was random, do you?"

"I'm not sure what to believe. I'm not blind or stupid. I saw the destruction. Throw in my story about being followed and I can see where you'd get the idea something was going on."

"Are you saying you weren't followed?"

"No. I'm saying what I've been saying all along I'm not sure, although I think it's unlikely."

"What about last night? Everything, with the exception of what you were wearing was destroyed. And don't forget the message on the bathroom mirror."

"Were you going to tell me about that or did you hope to keep it to yourself?"

"I was going to tell you. Eventually."

She shook her head. His instincts were to shield others. He'd probably always been that way but his time in the

Army had most likely reinforced his need to protect. "Why would anyone follow me, trash my things or threaten me? It doesn't make any sense."

"Cat, I'm not a detective but I am pretty good at putting puzzles together. The police will look into this but there's not much they can do. They'll send out a description of your camera to local pawnshops and check a few websites to see if anyone tries to sell it but I don't think it's likely that it will lead anywhere. This doesn't have the feel of an ordinary break-in. I'm asking you to give me a chance to get to the bottom of it."

She reached across the table and placed her hand on top of his. "Why is this so important to you? I'd think you'd have better things to do than spend your time attempting to solve a mystery – one that most likely doesn't exist. I don't want to sound ungrateful - but I am curious."

And cautious, he thought. She probably considered the depth of his interest a little disconcerting given the fact that they'd just met. He understood that. His interest surprised him as well. Turning his hand over, he anchored her fingers in his.

"My gut tells me something's not right here. I haven't had this feeling since I left the Army and it was right more often than not. If I'm wrong - and I hope that I am - then the worse that comes from this is that I get to spend some time with a very compelling woman – a woman I'm very much attracted to."

Cat wanted to trust him. Whether she should, remained to be seen. But she had instincts as well and, for the time being, she'd go with them. "Alright, Magnum, what do you want to know?"

Colt visibly relaxed. "Why don't we start with the obvious? Is there a boyfriend, significant other, somebody that might be angry with you for one reason or another?"

The look she gave him could have fused sand. She snatched her hand back.

"I wouldn't be here - with you - if I was involved with someone else," she stated emphatically. "Were you fishing or just trying to piss me off?"

Colt made no attempt to hide his amusement.

"Can't blame a guy for wanting to know if he's got competition." His grin widened when he added, "And I like the way your eyes spit fire when you get riled." He laughed when her glare deepened.

"Okay. What about ex-boyfriends, disgruntled coworkers, any weirdoes you may have come in contact with—job related or otherwise?"

Cat didn't need any time to think about the answer to that one. "Michael Montgomery would fit into two of those categories: ex and weirdo. He's ancient history, though. As for anyone else? I'm sure Jason and I have made a lot of people unhappy over the years but no one I can think of that would carry a grudge or, at least, direct it at me."

Her quick response about Montgomery set off alarms.

"Tell me about the ex-boyfriend."

"Technically, I wouldn't call Michael a boyfriend, ex or otherwise. We only went out a couple of times before I realized that he had a nasty temper. Although nasty is too mild a word. Anyway, I called a halt to things after a couple dates. It wasn't very pretty. I'm afraid he didn't take the rejection well."

"Did he hurt you?"

"Not then. I had enough sense to break the news to him in a public place but it was still a frightening experience. He went ballistic over dinner. Accused me of being a tease. Made a lot of threats. It was quite a scene. Fortunately, the restaurant manager stepped in and asked him to leave before the police were called. I kicked myself for days for not breaking the news to him over the phone instead of face to face but later it became evident that it wouldn't have mattered how I'd told him."

"That wasn't the end of it, was it?" Colt pressed. He knew with certainty that she'd been hurt and the damage hadn't been just physical. Her intense reaction when he'd caught up with her in the courtyard was proof of that.

"Several nights later he grabbed me as I was leaving my apartment." She shrugged as she raised her eyes to meet his. "He roughed me up a bit but he'd made it clear that his ultimate goal was rape. Fortunately, it didn't get that far. I was able to land a solid hit to his family jewels. It gave me enough time to get away."

If there was a God, Colt thought, the bastard's balls would still be stuck in his throat. "You pressed charges?"

"For all the good it did. Michael claimed that I was mentally unstable. Even threatened to file charges against me for assault. My injuries, he argued, were the result of him trying to defend himself. Nobody actually believed him but it boiled down to his word against mine. He had no record. No history of violence – domestic or otherwise. He put on one hell of a show. I'll give him that." To this day Cat was still surprised at Michael's ability to spin the truth. "He was contrite to the police. During the hearing, he apologized profusely to the judge for not handling the situation like a gentleman. Swore he'd stay away from me if I agreed to keep my distance. He was ordered to take an anger management class and was free to go."

The son of a bitch walked! Colt sat silently while he wrestled with his temper. How the hell could anyone believe that a woman the size of Cat would attack a grown man? It wasn't until he saw Cat grimace that he realized he still clutched her hand and was squeezing it tightly. He relaxed his grip.

"Do you know where he is now?"

"I haven't seen or heard from him in over a year." Thank God, she added silently. "Why would he wait until now to get back at me? And why here when it would be easier to come after me at home?"

"You're probably right but it wouldn't hurt to have Rick check on his whereabouts." Besides, Colt really wanted to find this guy. "Other than Montgomery, anyone else come to mind?"

"I can't imagine anyone being so pissed off that they'd go to these lengths."

"Nothing else unusual happen since you got here – other than the Lincoln?"

"Does being knocked on my butt by a macho photographer count?" she asked with a grin.

"Hopefully it counts for something."

7

Before they headed off island, Colt wanted to grab a shower, change clothes and pick up a sidearm. He had a permit to carry a concealed weapon in Florida and would feel better with one close at hand. He didn't like it but he'd left Cat in the studio below. Whether she'd just needed space or possessed a natural inclination to rebel, she had refused to wait for Colt upstairs in his unit. Instead, she'd insisted on viewing the photos he'd referenced the previous evening. Figuring he'd pushed his luck as far as he dare in gaining her cooperation, he'd directed Cat to stay put before activating the security alarm and heading upstairs.

Cat was tempted to leave just to spite Colt but admitted the notion was a stupid one. Safety aside, her car was several miles away and she had no desire to walk back to it. Instead, cursing chauvinistic throwbacks, she headed to the front of the business where Colt said she'd find the photography display.

When Cat reached the small lobby her mood transitioned from irritation to awe. The walls were covered with the most extraordinary, magnificent photographs she had ever seen. Seashells, sea oats, beaches, and birds - so many stunning birds – covered the walls. She imagined every species of fowl that called South Florida home had been captured in remarkable detail. She had to wrench her eyes away from each photograph to view the next. What a rare and amazing talent to be able to capture nature in such vivid detail. This man deserved the recognition of his own show. She found herself wondering if she could arrange time to come back for it. Whoa! Stop right there. She'd just met the man. Why would she be thinking of him in terms of months from now? Her emotions were on a fast track where he was concerned. It was time to take a few steps back.

She was mentally listing the reasons why she shouldn't get involved with this sexy, talented man when he entered the lobby looking good enough to eat. His coal black hair, still damp from his shower, curled behind his ears. The granite jaw she'd admired at breakfast was now clean-shaven. But it was those turquoise eyes that, once again, drew her in. One look into them and she could feel those wings fluttering in her stomach. With his snug fitting jeans and a tropical print shirt that hung open - framing both his solid chest and abs - the man personified sex.

"You ready?" he asked.

Ready? Was he kidding? She was more than ready. Shaking her head to clear her thoughts she looked back toward the images on the wall. "Are these for sale? I'd like to buy one, if I could, to take home with me."

Her reference to going home did more to cool the fire burning inside Colt than the cold shower he'd just endured. When he'd stepped under the pelting spray, he'd fantasized about heading back downstairs and convincing Cat to join him. He imagined shampooing that silky hair and watching the bubbles trail over her tanned skin until they reached the dark curls at the junction of her thighs. He'd wanted to take one of the small, firm breasts that he'd caressed the night before into his mouth. The images of her naked and wet had been so powerful that he could not remember ever being so painfully aroused. He'd been forced to finish his shower sans hot water.

Tonight, though, he had plans and they didn't include a cold shower. Now she was talking about leaving. Well, he wasn't convinced that's how things were going to play out. Not yet, anyway. There was something going on between the two of them and he intended to find out what it was before she packed up and headed north.

"Pick one," he snapped as he turned toward the door. "It's yours."

8

While Sanibel was home to a variety of great specialty shops and boutiques, there were no malls on the island - which was just the way the residents liked it. Ordinances were in place guaranteeing that they would never sprout up. It kept the natural feel of the island intact but, as a result, serious shopping was done on the mainland.

Keeping one eye on his rearview mirror, Colt drove across San Carlos Bay and into Fort Myers. If they were being tailed, he hadn't been able to spot anyone. He glanced at the glove compartment where he'd stashed his Glock before retrieving Cat from the studio. He would have felt better if he carried it on his person but he wasn't sure how Cat would react to that. Besides, they were going to an area that would be busy with pedestrians. It was unlikely anyone would try something there.

Eventually they pulled into the parking lot of an open-air mall. The place was huge and housed a large variety of middle to upscale retailers. Outparcels accommodated many well-known "big box" stores. Cat wouldn't have any problem replenishing her losses here. Exiting the vehicle, she surprised herself by grabbing Colt's hand and tugging him along. The foul mood that had come over him at his studio had faded during the ride across the causeway. She intended to keep things upbeat.

On the few occasions Colt had been suckered into a trip to a mall, he recalled that women made their way through the shops with excruciating slowness. Cat, obviously, hadn't attended the same class on shopping. The woman moved like a small tornado. Hitting one store, grabbing what she needed and then blowing on to the next. If she slowed down a fraction it was when she shopped for clothing. Then she'd take the time to try on her selections. Occasionally, when the whim struck her, he'd be treated to a brief fashion show. They'd developed what Colt considered a rhythm despite the whirlwind pace but as they approached a shop dedicated to lingerie he hesitated instead of blindly trailing behind her.

"Problem?" Cat asked, smiling. Colt had been a good sport - following her into every store and hauling her purchases with only one comment about his status as a pack mule. She'd intentionally left the purchase of intimate apparel until the end – trying to gauge what his reaction would be when it came time to make this stop. In her limited opinion, men usually fell into one of two categories when it came to lingerie – those who wouldn't go anywhere near a store of this type and others who felt their opinions should be the deciding factor.

As he eyed the window display, a devilish grin slowly crossed his face. "Do I get a say in your selections?"

"Only if *you* plan on wearing them."

"Not in this life time," Colt chuckled. "What about modeling them for me?"

"Here? I don't think so," she laughed.

Colt's eyes darkened. "Later," he said. "At my place." His voice had turned husky and the heat in his eyes was so intense Cat thought she just might melt into a puddle at his feet.

"Ah, maybe it's best you wait out here," she stammered before retreating into the store. She hadn't known how to respond to Colt's remark. There was no doubting her body's response, though. The desire he telegraphed had her body reacting in unfamiliar ways. It was a unique and scary feeling that she tried, unsuccessfully, to push aside as she went about the task at hand.

Normally, Cat didn't give much thought to shopping for bras and panties but she was certainly giving it some serious consideration now. Should she buy the practical but boring styles she usually wore or some sexy pieces meant to raise a man's blood pressure? She'd never bought something for the sole purpose of arousing a man. She'd never considered herself sensuous or sexy yet whenever Colt looked at her with those hooded eyes she felt that way. She didn't do flings or affairs. Casual sex just wasn't for her. Yet here she was thinking about purchasing items with the intention of making the man drool. The idea made her smile. Well, wherever this chemistry was leading them, she wouldn't get there hiding in the panty section.

Colt kept an eye on Cat through the large display windows at the front of the store. The wheels were turning in that pretty little head of hers. He imagined he could hear them grinding from his position on the sidewalk. Then she started to gnaw on her bottom lip. Something was causing her stress and, he realized, he didn't like that one bit. Before he could move from his spot on the pavement though, her expression suddenly brightened and a wide grin spread across her face. She had gathered herself once again. Colt found himself hoping he'd factored into that smile.

When Cat emerged from the dressing room with an armful of delicate looking undergarments Colt decided this would have to be their last stop. It wasn't going to be possible for him to maneuver through any more stores. Imagining her in the skimpy scraps of fabric she'd handed over to the cashier was giving him a hard-on that would make walking extremely uncomfortable not to mention embarrassing. Fortunately, he'd held on to Cat's purchases. He shifted the shopping bags in an attempt to hide the obvious state of his arousal.

The wail of a child snapped Colt's attention back to the world around him. A little carrot-top boy lay sprawled on the ground just a few feet away. The toddler, who had apparently stumbled, was screaming over the mishap. In addition to a good set of lungs, the kid had some water-works going for him. Tears raced down his freckled cheeks as his mother knelt beside him trying to sooth him. Colt took a step back, giving them more space. A large, unfamiliar man would do little to calm the child. He kept an eye on the pair, though, in the event they needed assistance.

CAT WASN'T aware of the mini-drama unfolding outside. Her mind was on the sexy bras and panties now stuffed into the little pink shopping bag - and how Colt would react when he saw them. She was so involved in her private fantasy that she didn't notice the man who had quietly materialized behind her. The sweaty palm covering her mouth was her first indication of trouble. As he muffled her cry with one hand, he clamped his arm around her waist, trapping both arms against her body. With very little effort, he lifted her off her feet and sprinted out the side entrance.

It only took seconds for Cat's anger to leapfrog over her shock and fear. She had no intention of becoming anyone's victim – not again. With all the force she could muster she kicked back at her assailant but her sandaled feet had little effect. She didn't give up, though. Couldn't. Kicking and squirming, she managed to free one arm. Reaching blindly behind her, she clawed at his face with her free hand. As soon as she made contact, she dug in – her nails scoring down his cheek. While the idea had been to gain her freedom, she hadn't anticipated being thrown to the ground. She landed hard. Ignoring the pain, she scrambled across the sidewalk on her hands and knees, scanning the area for help as she made her escape. Where the hell was everybody? It was a mall, for God's sake. She'd only managed to put a few feet between them before the man grabbed a fist full of her hair, lifting her off the ground. Then, for the second time in minutes, she found herself careening toward the sidewalk.

COLT WATCHED the mother and her whimpering child until they'd disappear into a nearby ice cream shop then turned his attention back to the store. He was immediately alarmed when he didn't spot Cat. She should have finished checking out by now but she was nowhere in sight. Holding his breath, he raced inside. When he noticed the side entrance his stomach dropped. Why the hell hadn't he checked the place out before she'd gone in? He told himself not to panic. She might have returned to the dressing room. However, if she'd gone out the side door, then something was terribly wrong.

The instant he'd cleared the exit he spotted them. A

large, burly man had a fist full of Cat's hair, yanking her up off the sidewalk. His free hand was raised - poised to strike. For the first time since leaving the Army, Colt thought about killing a man.

As soon as he reached them, he locked his arm around the man's throat and hammered his fist into the attacker's kidney. The action had its intended effect. Cat was free but dropping like a stone. With nothing to counter their weight, the two men stumbled backward. As they slammed against the pavement, Colt just managed to avoid cracking his skull. The impact, however, broke his hold. The would-be kidnapper didn't hesitate at the opportunity and bolted toward the parking lot. Damn it! Colt wanted the guy. He needed this piece to the puzzle. His eyes flashed from the retreating assailant to Cat and he instantly forgot all thoughts of pursuit.

When Colt reached her side Cat was cussing up a storm. No words had ever sounded sweeter. As he eased her into a sitting position, he assessed her injuries. His concern mixed with fury when he saw her bloody knees. Slipping one arm beneath them Colt started to lift her off the pavement – all thoughts directed to getting her some-place safe. Cat stopped him with a smack on the shoulder.

"I can walk," she stated firmly. If she could move under her own steam, she would damn well do just that. Colt returned her scowl but didn't push. Instead, he supported her as she pushed to her feet. Blood trickled down her legs - the sensation making her shutter. Her knees had taken the brunt of both falls but she was certain nothing was broken. The palms of her hands were scraped and embedded with bits of dirt. The discomfort she felt in her extremities, though, came in a distant second to the cauldron of pain that sat on her shoulders. Hell, it felt like she had been scalped. Tentatively, she ran a hand through her hair to assure herself that it remained attached and paid the price for her curiosity. Closing her eyes, she held her breath until the wave of pain subsided. Fortunately, Colt held her close while she gathered herself.

A young, dark skinned woman pushed her way through the crowd of on-lookers, her arms loaded with shopping bags. "I think these are yours," she said, holding out the packages Colt had dropped as he'd dashed out of the store. Thanking the woman, he took the bags with his free hand. His other arm remained firmly locked around Cat's waist.

Mall security officers arrived and began breaking up the crowd that had gathered while asking any witnesses to stay and talk with the police. A manager hurried out of a nearby clothing store and offered them the use of his office while they waited for the authorities to arrive. Colt had to fight the urge to disregard Cat's wishes and sweep her into his arms. Her legs wobbled with each step. He suspected the only thing that kept her on her feet was her stubbornness.

The paramedics entered the small office minutes after Colt had settled Cat into the manager's chair. One EMT checked her vital signs while the other assessed the damage and began tending to her injuries. She soon forgot about her discomfort, though. Instead her pity turned toward the paramedics. Colt bombarded the men with questions about each scratch, cut or bump. When Cat refused transport to the hospital she thought Colt would blow a blood vessel. This wasn't the first time she'd been on the receiving end of a fist. She'd recover. Colt wasn't convinced. He wanted her in the ER. She had no intention of going.

Over Colt's rather loud objections, Cat requested and was given a release to sign. As the paramedics made their escape, two deputies with the Lee County Sheriff's office took their place. Apparently, they'd been waiting their turn just outside the door of the small office. After cursory introductions and some basic information, Cat related the incident to them. They remained quiet, taking notes, until she finished.

"Did you recognize the guy?" the younger of the two asked.

"He grabbed me from behind. I never got a good look at his face. He was taller than me but, then again, who isn't…"

"Six feet," Colt started. "About two hundred and thirty pounds. Late twenties or early thirties. Short, dark brown hair. Caucasian." His words were clipped. He was angry. Angry at Cat for not going to the hospital. Angry at the bastard who tried to grab her. But mostly, he admitted, he was angry with himself for allowing this to happen.

"Did he say anything? Give you any indication what he wanted? Why he targeted you?" the older deputy asked.

"I don't think he said anything. If he did, I didn't hear it."

"And you have no idea why he grabbed you?" the first deputy asked, his skepticism obvious.

"Look, officer," Cat said sharply, her frustration rising to the surface. "I don't know what's going on but I will admit I'm getting pretty damned tired of it."

"Her cottage was broken into last night," Colt explained, anticipating their next question. "Check with the Sanibel PD if you need the details," he added. He wanted the interview over so he could get Cat out of here. Neither officer moved.

"Your place is burglarized then someone tries to grab you off a public street and you're asking us to believe that you don't have a clue about what's going on?" the young officer asked in obvious disbelief.

Colt stepped between Cat and the deputies. "Are you

accusing her of something? Do you plan on charging her with a crime? If not, then finish your damned questions so I can take her home."

Cat had been about to tell the officer where he could stick his insinuation when Colt had jumped to her defense. She wasn't sure which irritated her more – the officer's tone or Colt thinking she needed rescuing. She clasped a hand around Colt's forearm in an attempt to gain his attention. His muscles were coiled so tight beneath her fingers she wondered if they might snap. Kicking him was an option but she had no desire to inflict further injury on herself.

"Colt!" she said, tugging on his arm. "It's okay. I'll handle this," she added firmly when she finally got his attention.

"No, it is not okay," he said, choosing to ignore the rest of her statement. He hadn't been able to prevent the attack but he sure as hell could keep her from being badgered. "You didn't cause any of this and they don't need to be insinuating that you did. They're forgetting who the victim is here."

"And just who, exactly, are you?" the young officer asked.

"A friend," Colt snarled.

"Well, *friend*, I need to get some information from you."

Colt took a business card from his wallet. "You can call me with any questions."

The deputy ignored the outstretched hand. "Let's step outside."

It had been a long shot so Colt wasn't surprised when the officer didn't play along. Before following the deputy, he hesitated long enough to rub his palm reassuringly over Cat's shoulder. "Don't go anywhere until I come for you."

She watched them leave, praying Colt would hold on

to the temper she saw simmering underneath the outward calm. She turned back to address the remaining deputy. "I honestly do not understand what's going on. I'm at a loss to explain any of it. I don't know if this assault is connected to the break-in - although I'd be crazy to dismiss the idea altogether. However, I can't add anything to what I've already told you. Perhaps if you and the Sanibel PD talk to one another you could make some sense of it. Right now my head hurts so bad I'm having difficulty putting two coherent thoughts together. I promise to call if something else does come to mind."

Fortunately, the officer didn't press her further. He informed her she'd be hearing from one of their detectives, handed her his contact information and left. It didn't take long for the quiet to get to Cat. Maybe she shouldn't have chased the officer away. Talking to him would have kept her mind from wandering and worrying about Colt. He'd been so angry when he'd left. The affectionate pat on her shoulder was in steep contrast to the tension etched in his jaw. What if they had taken him in for questioning? Did they actually think he had something to do with the attack? She'd been aware that he'd been struggling with his anger since he'd reached her side. Did he finally loose that grip on his temper? Could that be cause for arrest? Anger, mixed with a hefty dose of fear, began to work its way to the surface. She didn't know why she'd been targeted but she knew damn well Colt wasn't the one behind it. And if he did lose his temper it was only because he was trying to protect her.

Deciding she'd waited long enough, Cat ignored her body's protests and pushed to her feet but before she could order one foot in front of the other the door opened and Colt walked into the room. Relief overwhelmed her as she dropped back into the chair.

In an instant, Colt was crouched in front of her gently tilting her chin so he could study her face. "What's wrong?"

"I thought you'd gotten yourself arrested," she told him as she swiped angrily at her tears with the back of her hand. She wasn't sure why she was crying. Relief. Frustration. Pain. It didn't really matter. She hated tears. "You looked like you wanted to pound that deputy into the ground."

"I managed to restrain myself," he said, attempting to smile. "If you're sure you're okay, Security has a cart waiting outside to take us to the car. Can you walk that far or are you going to let me carry you?"

"I can walk," Cat stated emphatically but she couldn't stop the groan from escaping as she got to her feet.

"You are, without a doubt," he announced as he lifted the protesting woman into his arms, "the most stubborn female I've ever met."

9

"This isn't my cottage," Cat stated flatly as they'd turned into the parking area of Colt's studio. Stupid observation, she admitted. But stupid fit the way she was feeling at the moment. Stupid, hurting and confused. None of what was happening made any sense. On the trip back to Sanibel she'd mentally gone over the events of the last few days trying to unravel the mystery that surrounded her. The exercise helped to keep her mind off the pain in her head and her aching muscles. But now that they were back on the island, all she could think about was getting some relief.

She hadn't given any thought to their final destination but she realized she shouldn't have been surprised when Colt pulled up to his place. An alpha male, she reminded herself - and not a very happy one at the moment. He hadn't responded to her remark and the determined look on his face told her that the subject wasn't open to discussion. Yeah, right.

"Colt, I'd appreciate it if you would just take me back to the cottages. I really want a long soak in a hot bath."

"You should have been checked out at the hospital," he started in again, slamming his vehicle into park. "But no. You're too damned mule-headed. I'm not taking the chance of something else happening to you – not on my watch. You'll stay here where I can keep an eye on you and you'll get your damn bath even if I have to give it to you!"

Cat swung her head around so fast she felt her brain ricochet inside her skull. Ouch! "The hell you will! I can take care of myself."

Colt was around the vehicle and yanking the passenger door open before Cat could unlatch her seatbelt. Ignoring the scathing look she shot him, he lifted her out of the car. It was obvious she didn't like being carried - or cared for - for that matter. Tough. She'd have to get used to it. Other things, however, weren't quite so clear.

"Why is it so difficult for you to accept my help?" he asked as he started up the rear steps. "Damn it, woman," he spewed, frustrated at her lack of understanding, "it's my fault you were hurt!"

Stunned, the words she'd been about to throw back at him froze on her lips. "Why would any of this be your fault?"

"That bastard shouldn't have gotten anywhere near you today. A hell of a lot of good I did being there."

She adjusted herself in his arms until she could see his face clearly. The man was serious.

"Are you arrogant or just plain stupid?"

Her caustic tone had him hesitating. She had every right to be angry. He should have been protecting her today. Instead, he'd been fantasizing about getting her naked.

Cat took a deep, calming breath before resting her head against his chest. In deference to the pounding in her head she lowered her voice before continuing. "Granted, you're one of the finest specimens of the male species I've run across but that alone doesn't qualify you as a super-hero. For Christ's sake, Colt, you stopped that guy from taking me out of the mall. If you hadn't, God knows where I'd be at this moment or in what condition. I'm safe, and relatively sound, because of you. *So get over yourself!*"

In spite of his anger – in spite of his guilt - Colt looked down at the slip of a woman he held in his arms and started to laugh. How the hell did all that sass fit into such a tiny package? "Alright," he finally agreed, "I'll do my best but on one condition. You stop fighting me about this."

She pressed her head deeper into his chest. "I think you're going to win this argument by default. Get me some aspirin and I'll agree to anything."

When they reached the deck at the top of the stairs, Colt easily balanced Cat in his arms as he unlocked the door to his unit. His home took up the northern half of the second floor. His friend and partner occupied the other half. At one time he and Gib had considered sharing a single unit and renting the second. Economically, it would have been a smart move. Rentals went for a bundle on the island. Fortunately, they'd decided against it. Gib was a player and since Colt's departure from the Army, he preferred quiet and solitude. The current arrangement suited them both.

He carried Cat through the kitchen and down the long hall to the master bedroom. Both upstairs units were laid out "shotgun" style - with the hallways running down the inside of the building and the living areas positioned against the outer walls. The design maximized the use of the natural lighting and tropical breezes, when the temperature allowed, and the hallways acted as an additional buffer against sound between the units. "Rest here a minute," he told her, gently depositing her on his king size bed. "I'll be right back."

Sprinting back down the steps, he retrieved the drugstore purchases. On the return trip to the island Colt had stopped at a pharmacy, parking in the handicap spot in front of the door. He wanted Cat in plain sight and hadn't given a damn if he was breaking any laws. He'd have felt better having her by his side but she looked so miserable curled up against the passenger door he couldn't bring himself to roust her. Instead, he'd unlocked the glove box, making her aware of the gun he'd stashed there earlier. She raised an eyebrow at the sight of the weapon then suggested he hurry or she might have to use it on him.

Returning to the bedroom, Colt dropped two tablets into her outstretched hand then gently held her head while he tipped the glass of water for her to sip. The sideway look she gave him told him that she wasn't the least bit happy about his ministrations but he suspected she was hurting too much to argue.

Settling her back against the pillows, he left to run water for her bath. The master bath housed a separate shower in addition to the large garden tub. After Colt and Gib got their business up and running they'd gutted the upstairs. Initially, he hadn't planned anything close to this spa-like space but Gib had been incessant about the upgrades. *"Women will love it,"* his friend had sworn. Colt hadn't had any intention of inviting a woman to share his bath but he'd given in just so Gib would shut up. Now he wondered what Cat would think of the finished room. He added some of the scented bath gel that he'd grabbed from an end cap on his sprint through the drugstore to the running water. While the tub filled he set out some clean towels then lowered the toilet lid to give her a place to sit while she undressed.

Cat studied the room she'd been deposited in. It was orderly – probably a result of his days in the service – yet it had a comforting feel to it. The two large windows on either side of the bed made the place sunny and bright. The bedspread and side chair both sported tiny palm trees. The walls were painted a soft tangerine color. Odd choice but it worked, making the perfect backdrop for the pictures that adorned the walls. She immediately recognized the stunning photos as Colt's work. Everything about the space suggested a tropical paradise. She wondered if he'd had some help with the decor or if the finished space was the result of his artist's eye. She wanted to believe it was the artist in him. Any outside help he might have received would probably have been from a woman - and that didn't sit well.

What was wrong with her? She had no claim on him and no right to be jealous of anyone - let alone someone who might only exist in her imagination. She settled back into the pillows and she closed her eyes. What she needed was an attitude adjustment but at the moment she was too tired, confused and miserable to make the effort.

When Colt returned to the bedroom he was surprised to find that Cat had not only remained where he'd laid her but that she appeared to be resting. He didn't think she did much of that. That thought alone concerned him. The dark circles that had formed under those big brown eyes added to his worry. Bruises were now evident on her exposed skin. Blood dotted the gauze pads the paramedics had applied to her knees. Why wouldn't the damn woman listen and go to the hospital? It wouldn't have hurt to be checked out.

Cat sensed she was no longer alone. When looked up she found Colt studying her - concern written all over his face. She didn't like that look. It made her feel frail and vulnerable. She was neither, damn it. To prove the point she swung her legs over the side of the bed then immediately regretted the sudden action. Burying her face in her hands she waited for the throbbing in her head to ease.

"Take it easy. Are you alright?"

"I'm fine unless stupidity counts as an ailment."

"No, but stubbornness might," he said, lifting her into his arms.

"You are not giving me a bath," she warned him, remembering his earlier threat. Taking a deep breath, she added, "Please, Colt? Put me down. *I* need to do this."

Of course she did. He understood that yet he continued to carry her toward the bathroom. "I'll leave you be in just a minute but right now *I* need to do this."

She gnawed on her bottom lip as he settled her onto the commode. She managed to remain silent while he carefully removed the bandages from her knees. When his attention turned to the straps of the sundress she reached for his hand.

"Relax," he said. "This is as far as I'm going – *tonight*." He untied the remaining strap then left without saying another word.

Cat finished undressing then slowly lowered herself into the tub. The heated water felt like heaven to her aching muscles. Resting her head against a rolled-up towel she allowed herself to get lost in the moist heat.

While Cat soaked Colt made another trip down the stairs to retrieve the remaining packages. He sorted through the bags until he found the one from their last stop. Only a thin blanket of bubbles remained on the surface of the bath water when Colt poked his head in the bathroom a few minutes later. The bubbles did little to hide the curves of her petite body. Colt stared like a kid getting his first glimpse of a woman's flesh. He couldn't help but

68

marvel that even battered this one was beautiful. Her small, round breasts were perfectly suited for her compact frame - and his palm. Her tiny waist flared nicely at the hips drawing attention to the triangular thatch of dark curly hair at the junction of her thighs. His rising lust was quickly dampened, though, as his eyes were drawn to the raw skin on her exposed knees. He cleared his throat and his thoughts.

Cat's eyes flew open.

"I didn't see where you bought anything to sleep in," he said quickly, "so I dug out one of my t-shirts. It's old but clean." He laid the tattered shirt that was a remnant from his Army days on the granite countertop along with a pair of lace panties she'd purchased earlier.

"Do you need any help getting out of there?"

A scowl answered his question. It was probably just as well. He wasn't sure what he'd do if he put his hands on her in her current state of undress. No, he thought, that wasn't true. He knew exactly what he'd like to do but he should be shot for thinking about it in her present condition. "Wait here when you're done. I want to re-bandage those knees," he said before pulling the door shut behind him.

When he returned, Cat was impatiently sitting on the lowered lid of the commode. The faded, green t-shirt engulfed her, falling off one shoulder, exposing her tanned skin. He forced himself to concentrate on her wounds. He cleaned her cuts and scrapes with antiseptic before applying ointment and bandages. When he was finished to his satisfaction, he scooped her up and returned her to his bed. Pulling the covers over her, he kissed her lightly on the forehead and silently left the room.

10

When Cat opened her eyes, the room was in shadows. Night had fallen. She suspected there must have been a sleep aid in the pain meds Colt had given her. She'd slept soundly in spite of her aches. Her eyes caught the small sliver of artificial light that stretched across the hardwood floor from the door that had been left ajar. Deep voices rumbled from down the hall. Colt had company.

She sat up slowly not wanting to repeat her earlier performance. Every muscle in her body protested. Too bad, she thought, touching her feet to the floor, they'd have to get used to it. Besides, nature called.

As she flicked on the bathroom light she immediately noticed the cosmetic and hygiene items she'd purchased that morning. Colt had taken the time to remove each item from its packaging and had set them out on the massive vanity for easy access. Why did that simple, thoughtful act have her on the verge of tears? Duh. She was hurt and, admittedly, a bit scared. She hadn't felt this vulnerable since she was fifteen. She didn't like the feeling. Suck it up and move on. Going back to that time was not an option nor would it help.

She gingerly washed her bruised face then returned to the bedroom in search of clothes. None of her belongings were in the room. Not her sundress or the clothes she'd purchased on her shopping trip. The shirt Colt had given her to sleep in wasn't fit for friends or strangers. She had no intention of going through Colt's drawers or closet so she could either wrap herself up in a sheet or borrow the robe that hung on the bathroom door. She opted for the robe. It was a little less material than the sheet - though not by much.

Colt didn't know whether to be aggravated or pleased as he watched Cat through the crack in the bedroom door. Muttering as she made her way around the room, she was too stubborn to let her discomfort get the upper hand. He'd come close to putting a stop to her struggles but he'd seen the determination etched across her forehead. She was proving something, if only to herself.

When Cat stepped out of the bedroom, the same massive chest she'd run into on the beach greeted her again. She waited for Colt to move. He didn't budge. She didn't have to look at his expression to know what he was thinking. Well, she was done being toted around and made it clear with one stern look.

Grinning at the unspoken admonishment, he finally stepped aside.

Rick stood in the middle of the living room eyeing the two of them as they approached. Although she hadn't paid much attention to him the evening before, Cat recognized Colt's friend. The man was attractive - in a rugged sort of way. His size, age and build were similar to Colt's. The stunning difference between the two, though, was the hair. While Colt's hair was dark and long enough to curl where it touched his collar, Rick wore his military short. The color was so blond it could easily be mistaken for silver.

"Hi," she said.

"Hi, yourself," Rick responded, smiling at the sight in front of him. The surplus of terrycloth puddled at her feet made the woman look like a child playing dress up.

Cat was aware that Colt was hovering, watching her like a hawk, waiting to see if he needed to catch her should she collapse. Well, she'd had all the coddling she could take for one day. She ignored his stare, lifted a handful of robe off the floor then headed toward the kitchen. "Would you mind if I got something to drink?"

Colt gently took her by the shoulders and steered her toward the couch. "I'll get it. You sit."

Cat scowled at Colt's retreating back. "I don't like macho men," she stated firmly. She caught his shrug as he disappeared into the kitchen.

Rick grinned. "Then why are you hanging around with that guy?"

Cat was about to respond to Rick's remark when she noticed a pair of scissors and price tags scattered across the dining room table. Her new purchases were carefully draped over the chairs that circled the table. Mystery solved.

Colt returned with a bottle of water and a can of soda. Indicating the two partially consumed beers that shared the table with the discarded tags, Cat asked, "You guys drink all the beer?"

Colt's head snapped up - a lecture ready on his lips. Then she smiled. "Very funny."

"Lighten up, Colt. I'll live."

"Damn right you will." He didn't try to disguise the order.

Rick could feel the electricity crackling between the

two and grinned. Very interesting, indeed. "I ran a check on your old friend, Montgomery," Rick said, breaking the tension. "That guy is a real piece of work. It appears you were the first in a string of woman he's assaulted."

"Shit!" She'd figured out pretty quickly that the guy was trouble. She should have done more to get him off the streets but she'd let the matter drop. Glad to be rid of him. "How many? How bad?"

Colt instantly knew the direction her thoughts were heading. She was laying those attacks at her feet. "What happened to those women wasn't your fault, Cat. You did everything right. The system failed them - not you."

Cat wanted answers not sympathy. She repeated the question to Rick, more firmly the second time. "I asked how many? How badly were they hurt?"

"They were all beaten - and raped," he added reluctantly, "but the investigating officer told me they've all recovered."

"Wanna bet?" she asked sarcastically. How did you recover from something like that? "How many?"

Colt pulled her firmly against his side before he answered. "Four that we know of."

"Four?" She would have launched herself off the couch if Colt hadn't had such a firm hold on her. "Four? How the hell could that happen?"

"Charges were either dropped or were never pressed."

"I don't understand."

"Two of the women never filed charges against him. The two that did eventually dropped the charges. The police suspect Montgomery threatened them but can't prove it. There was nothing the authorities could do." Rick had spent quite a bit of time on the phone this afternoon with the Tallahassee detective who had been assigned to the cases. Detective Corello's frustration had been evident.

"Son of a bitch."

"There's another problem," Colt told her. "Montgomery's gone."

Cat eye's shifted from Rick's to Colt's and back again. "What do you mean 'gone'?"

"Corello did some checking after Rick's call. Montgomery was fired from his job a few weeks ago. Shortly after that he dropped out of sight. He could be anywhere."

"Including here," she said, thoughtfully. "I don't buy it. He had his shot at me."

"And look how that turned out. You fought back. You pressed charges," Colt reminded her. "He can't be very happy about that fact. You stood up to him, Cat. You're the only one who has."

"But he, more or less, won that battle. Besides, that was more than a year ago and it still doesn't explain the guy at the mall today. Those two might be cut from the same ugly cloth but that wasn't Michael who grabbed me."

Cat raked her hands through her hair. None of this made any sense. One thing was certain, though; her problems started after she'd arrived on this island. It was one thing to be stubborn. Another to be stupid.

"Well, guys, I can't say this hasn't been interesting but I think it's time I headed home."

Colt wasn't surprised she wanted to leave – to go where she felt secure - but it was a mistake for her to think she'd be safe at home.

"I don't think that's such a good idea."

Cat shot him a questioning look. "Colt, if this is about us…"

"Jeezus, Cat," Colt said, jumping to his feet. "Do you think I'd put you in danger just for the chance to crawl between the sheets with you?"

"No! No," she repeated the second time more softly.

She may not have known this man long but she knew that angle would not have entered his mind. She massaged her temples. "Sorry. My brain's still a little fuzzy."

Colt sat back down, pulling Cat close so he could tuck her head under his chin.

"Rick and I were knocking around a few theories while you were getting your beauty sleep." He smiled briefly when he felt her huff at his remark but she managed to keep any comment to herself. He suspected that required a monumental effort on her part. "Whatever that guy wanted today must be pretty damned important to attempt a kidnapping in broad daylight. We both agree that it's likely you're still a target. Going back to Tallahassee won't change that."

"You really know how to cheer a girl up."

"Colt's right," Rick added. "That stunt today was desperate and stupid. You'll be safer here than you would be on your own at home."

"Colt can't be with me 24/7. He has work to do. A show to get ready for. What happens when it's time for me to leave?" Frustrated, she was on her feet now, facing Colt. "Do you plan on following me home?"

"Why do you keep throwing the fact that you'll be leaving back in my face? Is that some sort of defense mechanism you use to keep your distance?" he asked, rising to tower over her.

"Whatever you want to call it, Colt. But the fact remains - I don't live here!"

"Well, maybe you should!"

The picture the pair made was comical. Colt, twice Cat's size, was leaning over her like a drill sergeant dressing down a new recruit. Cat, petite and battered, was glaring up at him, not the least bit intimidated by Colt's size or temper. Rick hadn't seen his friend this animated or emotional in a very long time. If the situation hadn't been so serious, he'd have cheered.

"Children," Rick said, raising his voice to draw their attention, "we're getting away from the issue here." He turned to Cat. "At this moment, you're safer on Sanibel than you would be if you went home. The best the Tallahassee PD might be able to do is have a police unit drive by every so often. Given what little we have to go on, that's not likely to happen. In addition, the Sanibel PD and the Lee County Sheriff's office are working on both these incidents. It would be easier on everyone if you were to stay in the area for the time being." The second part of his argument was flimsy and Rick suspected, with her background, she knew it. Investigations were completed on the phone all the time but Rick figured he owed it to his friend to try. Besides, the fire she'd lit under Colt was one he didn't wish to see extinguished.

Cat understood they meant well. They just didn't understand how hard this was for her. "Look, I don't mean to be uncooperative but the last time I had a keeper I was fifteen years old. I didn't like it then and I don't like the idea any better now."

11

Rick leaned against his Silverado as he glanced back up the stairs. "Montgomery makes a good suspect, Colt, but logically I just can't see him connected to the shit that happened today. His type doesn't send someone else to do his dirty work. He'd want to experience her fear first hand." He held up his hand, anticipating his friend's argument. "I'm not discounting the chance that it's him but I think it's unlikely. I'll call FDLE in the morning. Hopefully, they can get a lead on him. They should to be notified about the events here anyway since she works for the AG's Office." Among their other responsibilities, the Florida Department of Law Enforcement oversaw security at the state capitol, which included the State Attorney General's Office. "Until we get something more concrete, though, I'm not sure there's much we can do other than try to keep her safe. I suggest you don't let her out of your sight." He looked up toward Colt's unit a second time. "Does the Pentagon know about her?" he asked, grinning.

"She's a pistol, isn't she?"

"With a hair trigger." Rick looked at Colt thoughtfully. "What's your plan?"

Colt knew Rick wasn't talking about his plans for Cat's safety. "The first thing I have to do is to get her to stop backing away from me."

DESPITE HIS SILENT promise to let her rest, Colt found himself opening his bedroom door. He'd just poke his head in and check on her. See if she needed anything. While he knew what she needed was sleep he was still glad to find her awake and sitting up in bed. The energy she'd exhibited during their heated exchange was gone - her fatigue and discomfort now obvious. Against the crisp, white sheets her bruises appeared darker than they had earlier in the day. If Colt knew where to find that bastard, the man wouldn't see the sun rise tomorrow. He tempered his anger and forced a smile.

"You doin' okay?"

"Gettin' there. I'll be fine in the morning."

She'd be sore as hell in the morning but he knew she'd never admit it. She'd see it as a sign of weakness. Colt lifted a protesting Cat into his arms then lowered himself to the mattress's edge. Settling her onto his lap, he began to rock, holding her to his chest. If asked to explain his actions, he'd be at a loss to do so. He wasn't sure who needed the comforting more, him or the woman in his arms. After a few minutes he felt Cat relax and he was able to do the same.

"What did Rick want to talk to you about?" she asked, breaking the spell.

He kissed the top of her head and smiled. He'd known she wasn't going to stay quiet for very long. "He told me to keep an eye on you." He chuckled when she spit out her feelings on that subject.

"He doesn't want anything to happen to you, Cat. Neither do I."

"He doesn't think it's over, does he?" It was a rhetorical question. "Makes sense. If the person who's targeting me is still out there, it stands to reason there will be more trouble. "

"Can you cut me a little slack here?" Colt asked. "It's obvious that it goes against your grain to have someone watch your back but for us 'macho men' what you're asking is damn near impossible. Why is it so hard for you to accept a little help?"

She'd been expecting Colt to push on this subject. Not that she blamed him. He'd been bending over backwards for her since they'd met and she'd been resisting every step of the way. Leaning on others, particularly men, was not something she did easily.

A psychologist would have a field day with her but she didn't need one to tell her where the root of her problems lay. What she didn't know was whether she was capable of sharing that information. She never talked about her past. Not even with Jason - although she was sure he suspected much of the truth. She accepted her history because she could do nothing to change it. Her early years had shaped her. They'd made her strong but they had also made her cautious and slow to trust. She preferred to keep that part of her life firmly locked away. Now this man was asking her to open the door to her past. She hated going back - remembering the betrayal. But Colt hadn't hesitated today. He could have been hurt or, God forbid, killed. Didn't that earn him the right to an answer? In her book of fairness, it did. With a heavy sigh she reached for the key that unlocked the door.

"My dad preferred beating my back to watching it," she stated bluntly. She felt Colt flinch as his arms tightened around her but, thankfully, he remained silent.

"Anything, and I do mean anything, I did without his express permission resulted in some form of retribution."

"One night I was suffering from a nasty case of stomach flu. I was throwing my guts up when he came in from the garage and found me in the bathroom. He went wild. You see, I'd been told to stay in my bedroom. He took his belt, his weapon of choice at the time, and lashed into me. That was the night of my epiphany - the night it finally became clear that things would never change. Up until then I'd held on to the hope that the man who had loved and cared for me when I was a child would miraculously reappear. That whatever had caused him to turn into this frightening monster would change and I'd have my old dad back. But with each sting of his belt that hope slipped away until it was completely gone."

She remembered that evening with such clarity – and heartache. She realized that the father she'd loved and idolized as a child had ceased to exist. He didn't see her as his loving daughter any longer. What she'd become to him wasn't clear – had never become clear after all these years - but she'd known then with certainty that the essence of the man who had been her father was gone.

"The next morning I stuffed what I could safely hide into my backpack, left for school and never returned. I was just a few weeks shy of my sixteenth birthday. I've been handling things for myself since."

"And your mother?"

"She died in a car accident when I was ten. It was the evening of her funeral that the beatings began. Up until then, we had an average, loving family or at least I remember it that way. But something in him snapped that day. I suppose mom's death was some sort of trigger. At the time, I didn't much care why he started hitting me. I just wanted him to stop - to be my dad again."

"Why didn't anyone step in? Aren't teachers and doctors supposed to report that sort of thing?"

"They'd have to know about it first. He never hurt me where it was obvious or couldn't be explained and I was very good at keeping the secret." She answered the question she knew was on his lips. "Looking back, I know I should have gotten help but things weren't as obvious to me then. Fear, pride or shame. I'm not sure which motivated my silence more but I didn't want anyone to know what was happening."

"Go on," he said, tightening his hold. The thought of what could have happened to a fifteen year old alone on the streets terrified him.

"I found an abandoned property and spent some nights there. I didn't drop out of school, though. Initially I was terrified that he'd come looking for me there. He didn't. Once that fear subsided I was able to concentrate on ways to survive and stay under the authorities' radar. It turned out it wasn't all that difficult to fool the system." She'd learned some things from other kids on the street. The rest she'd figured out on her own. Still, she considered herself lucky to have avoided the whole social services thing. "Eventually, I earned a small scholarship to a local community college. I graduated with a degree in business."

"Your dad never tried to find you?"

"Not that I know of. I haven't seen him since that night."

"I'm sorry, Cat." He pulled her closer.

"Why?" She didn't want or need his pity. "I'm a firm believer that things happen for a reason. I am who I am because of my past and for the most part I'm not unhappy with the results. There are a few things I'd like to change. I'm working on lowering my bitch factor. I'd also like to bust a few more holes in the protective wall I've built around myself. I'm making progress in both those areas." She tilted her head and gave him a timid smile. "After all, I'm sitting on your lap telling you my life's ugly story."

He knew both were major concessions. "Has it occurred to you that fate may have brought us together?" He wasn't above using her comments to boost his cause. "I'm not asking you to commit to anything, Cat. God knows it's too soon for either of us. All I'm asking is that you keep an open mind." And an open heart he added silently. "You've admitted you don't know what your plans are for the future," he continued. "I don't know where this is going but I'd like the chance to find out. I'll work on my 'macho' tendencies but when it comes to your safety I can't promise I won't revert to my Neanderthal ways."

The image of Colt in a loincloth made her smile. Relaxing a bit, she became conscious of how much energy she'd put into fighting him. The more he pushed, the more she dug in. No man had ever tried this hard to break through her shields. They were normally long gone before they made a dent. But Colt wasn't only sticking around - he wanted more. Earlier today she accepted the fact that she would share his bed. Perhaps it was time to knock another hole in that wall.

"I don't know that I have it in me to give you what you're asking for, Colt."

"Right now, all I'm asking for is some time."

Colt tipped her head back and saw the vulnerability in her eyes. She didn't back away though, and he already knew it wasn't in her nature to run. Instead, with a curt nod she reached up and brought his head down to meet her lips. Immediately, he began to struggle against the need to possess her. He pulled away sharply before he reached the point where stopping would be impossible. He stroked her forehead then brushed it with a kiss. "Get some rest," his voice was rough as he pulled the covers over her.

She rolled to her side, closed her eyes and took a few measured breaths to slow her racing heart. She'd been fully aware of the battle Colt had just fought and won. But it was the tenderness of his last kiss that drifted with her into a deep sleep.

12

C olt jolted awake, instinctively reaching for the Glock that he'd placed on the nightstand before crawling into bed with Cat. Thunder rattled the windows and he relaxed his grip on the gun. It was just a storm. A nasty one from the sound of the rain beating against the glass. The power had gone out, making the room black as pitch. He checked the display on his cell phone - 4:10 a.m. Surprisingly, he'd slept for several hours.

Lightning flashed, illuminating the small body curled up next to him. Without air conditioning the room had rapidly warmed. In an unconscious effort to keep cool, Cat had kicked the sheet away. As he'd imagined the night before, her t-shirt had worked its way above her hips. This time the vision revealed a pair of sexy black lace panties. With each flash of lightning he imagined sliding the delicate fabric lower until she was free of the dainty lace, then staring into those dark eyes as he filled her.

Instead of giving in to the carnal urge he slipped from the bed and went to the window, forcing his thoughts to the storm raging outside. This room, as with all the rooms on his side of building, overlooked the drive that led to the private parking area in the rear. Just past the drive was his neighbor's extensive garden. As lightning danced across the sky it cast an eerie glow over their tropical wonderland. The rain was coming down in sheets. The fronds of the palm trees were being blown horizontally by the strong wind. The locals would call this a "palmetto pounder." Colt had yet to decide whether the term referred to the plant or the large, flying cockroach - both abundant in the area.

His eyes had adjusted quickly to the darkness and, as he glanced back at the bed, he could see Cat trembling in her sleep. He wasn't surprised she was having a nightmare – not after the past two days.

Leaving his post he settled on the bed next to her and began to gently stroke her hair – shushing her softly as he did. If he had to wake her he would but she seemed to instantly calm at his touch, giving him an unusual sense of satisfaction. When, at last, her breathing steadied he reluctantly removed his hand and left the bed. Stepping into a pair of jeans, he returned to his position by the window. There would be no more sleep for him tonight and if he stayed in bed with Cat, her hair wouldn't be the only thing he'd be stroking.

He wanted to explore every inch of that sensuous, petite body. His desire for her bordered on primal but he also acknowledged that there was more to it than a sexual pull. She intrigued him. She was strong, smart and independent as hell. She had worked her way into his heart at a speed that was both frightening and exhilarating – not unlike a roller coaster ride. Well, if he wanted to ride this car to the end he would need to keep Cat safe. Then, as if on cue, the heavens lit up and Colt caught a glimpse of a man sliding around the corner to the back of building.

．　．　．

COLT GRABBED his sidearm and silently exited the room, closing Cat inside. After giving the front door a quick glance, he made his way down the hall toward the kitchen. It was the only point of entry from the rear. He stopped just outside the kitchen, straining to hear sounds other than those of nature's fury. When the rumbling thunder began to fade he was able to distinguish the unmistakable creak of wood over the pelting rain. Concentrating, he briefly divided his attention between the front and back of the unit. With the squall still raging outside he couldn't be sure but he didn't hear anything unusual emanating from the front. Attempting to break in from the street side would not have been the smartest move. The police routinely patrolled Periwinkle Way keeping an eye on the numerous businesses that occupied the strip. Even in this weather there was a fair chance someone would be spotted attempting to break in. Bringing his full attention back to the door nearest him, Colt could hear their visitor working the lock. Good luck with that. A safe cracker would have difficulty getting past the dead blots he and Gib had installed.

Colt waited. It was the only thing he could do. The trespasser was mostly likely armed so charging the door would be idiocy. The second option of slipping out the front - assuming that path was clear - and coming up behind the bastard would take too long. The guy could be gone or, even worse, make his way to Cat before Colt made it around the building. If his objective was to kill, it would only take seconds to accomplish that goal. So Colt stayed put and continued his silent vigil.

The scratching at the lock ceased. It was followed by the faint creaking of wood as the target crossed the deck toward the bank of windows at the corner of the kitchen. Prior to turning in last night, Colt had made the rounds, checking every point of entry. He knew these windows were secured so the next sound he expected to hear was breaking glass. Instead he heard – what? It took a moment for the sound to register and when it did, it told him that the man outside was a professional. He was using a glasscutter.

Once a section of glass large enough for his hand had been removed, it was a simple matter for the man to unlatch the window. Humid air, driven by the storm's wind, filled the room as the window was raised. The sudden influx of air forced a door deep inside the unit to shut solidly. The intruder halted, listening for any sign that the unit's occupants had been alerted to his presence.

Colt remained motionless in the dark – his sniper skills kicking in. He hadn't lost any of those skills since leaving the Army. He used them routinely in his photography work. The ability to remain stock-still was an asset when trying to capture birds and other wildlife through his viewfinder. But instead of a camera, his hands once again held the means to kill. Memories of his last deployment bubbled to the surface. He quickly shoved those thoughts aside, refusing to go there now. They would only serve to distract him. A distraction that could cost Cat her life.

Apparently satisfied that no one had been disturbed, the intruder slipped through the opening, lowering himself to the bench seat beneath the window. His stealth-like movements confirmed that this was no amateur. Everything about this guy telegraphed his expertise.

At the sound of sirens in the distance, the intruder froze, no doubt trying to decide whether the emergency vehicles should concern him. Colt and Gib had installed an alarm system on the ground floor to protect their expensive photography equipment but had decided against doing so on the second floor. Alarm codes were a necessary nuisance to protect their investment but neither man had wanted to be bothered dealing with them in their living quarters. This guy wouldn't know that. He was probably wondering if he'd missed a silent alarm. When the sirens and flashing lights came to a halt in front of the building the intruder quickly made his decision and bolted back toward the window. Colt wasn't about to let this one get away.

"Hold it right there!" he shouted. Unfortunately, the man didn't heed the order. Instead, he rounded on Colt. Instinct had Colt rolling across the floor. As he did, Colt heard the repeated spit of a silenced weapon. He fired back. A grunt told him he'd hit his mark. The thud of a body collapsing to the floor told Colt he'd done more damage than he'd intended. As silence settled over the room he grabbed the flashlight from the top of the refrigerator.

More police units were arriving - pulling up behind the building now. Colt's attention, however, was focused on the body before him. The hum of the refrigerator signaled the return of electricity. He flicked on the closest light source. Blood was already pooling beneath the black clad figure, channeling the grout lines on the tile floor. Kicking the gun away from the limp hand he checked for a pulse. Damn.

"Colt? Are you okay?" Cat called out from down the hall.

"Stay where you are," he shouted back.

"Answer me! Are you hurt?" she persisted. Her voice was shaky but demanding.

"I'm fine, Cat; but I need you to stay put until I let the police know what's going on." For once he hoped that she'd listen to him. No matter how well trained, the sound of gunfire sent the senses into overdrive. The police were no exceptions. He wanted her safely tucked away until the cops confirmed that the threat was over.

When Colt heard the police make their way on to the back deck, he identified himself through the closed door, placed his weapon on the counter and slowly opened the door. With his hands raised, he stepped outside into, what was now, a light rain. One officer ordered Colt to the side while the others prepared to enter the building. He recognized several of them but familiarity wouldn't stop them from following procedures and assessing the situation.

"There's a woman in the master bedroom," he told them as they crossed the threshold. "She's with me. Keep her in there if you can. She doesn't need to see what's in the kitchen."

"Your night life has certainly picked up."

Colt's head whipped around in the direction of the familiar voice.

"What the hell are you doing here?" he asked Rick, surprised to see his friend.

"Who do you think called in the troops?"

"You?" Colt asked, puzzled. "How'd you know there was trouble?"

"Cat."

"Cat?" Colt glanced into the unit. He was definitely having trouble connecting the dots.

"She called me." As a precaution, the two of them had exchanged cell numbers before Rick had left earlier that evening. As soon as he'd seen her name displayed, he knew something serious was going down.

Colt's mouth went as dry as the Sahara. "Thank God she didn't decide to investigate." He didn't believe the woman sat still for much.

"She threatened to do just that if I didn't - and I quote - *'get somebody's ass over here pronto'.*"

The sound of a pair of stampeding feet had them both turning to see the subject of their discussion racing down the hall. She was zeroed in on Colt and he prayed her attention stayed focused on him because there was no time to stop her before she reached the kitchen. Fortunately, she made a beeline into his arms.

"Are you okay? Are you hurt?" She fired the questions at him as she wrapped her arms around his waist and pressed her head to his chest.

He held her tight and touched his lips to her hair - a habit he was getting into, he realized. "I'm fine. Not even a flesh wound," he answered lightly, hoping to reassure her. Instead, she stilled, took a step back and glared at him. If those dark eyes had been weapons he'd be as dead as the man on his kitchen floor.

"What the hell did you think you were doing?" she yelled at him. "Who do you think you are marching out here with no backup, no help. You could have been killed!" She punctuated the tirade by turning her back to him.

Colt eyed the urchin now clutching the deck's wooden railing. His t-shirt had dropped off her shoulder again, exposing a fair amount of flesh. The cotton material was so thin he had no trouble seeing the pattern of lace on her panties beneath it. The gods must have been looking out for him tonight because the rain had stopped. If it hadn't, the shirt would have been plastered against her skin, leaving nothing to the imagination of those who were gathered on the deck.

"Ah, Cat?"

"What?" she snapped, keeping her back to him. She wasn't finished being mad.

"Do you think you could change your clothes? As much as I'm enjoying the view, I'd rather not share it."

Crap. She hadn't given any thought to her clothing - or lack thereof. The shirt she was wearing had holes in it the size of grapefruit while being about as dense as a window sheer. There was no way out of this gracefully. She whirled around and stormed back toward the door only to have Colt pull her to his side. No one stopped them as he escorted her through the kitchen - shielding her from the grisly scene.

Rick joined Colt in the living room a few minutes later. "He's not the guy from the mall, is he?" he asked, indicating the kitchen.

"Not even close."

"You know I've got to ask her to take a look at him."

Colt nodded. "I'd rather she not see him like that. When they get him bagged, we'll see if she's able to identify him." What would she think of him when it sunk in that Colt had killed the man? It wasn't the first time he'd taken a life. He'd done it with regularity while in the Army. It was his job and he'd been good at it. But those deaths hadn't touched her. This one did and, once again, the blood was on his hands.

"Any identification?" Colt asked, although he already knew the answer. A pro wouldn't be that stupid and this guy had been a pro.

"Not on him. We're looking for his vehicle now. It's unlikely he was on foot in that storm. Of course, he could have had an accomplice who took off when he heard us coming."

Rick stood as a uniformed officer led the medical examiner through the living room. "I'll need to talk to both of you," he told Colt. "Think she'll be up to it?"

"You're asking the wrong person," Cat stated as she walked into the room.

"Should've known the answer to that one," Rick said as he left to join the ME in the kitchen.

CAT HAD USED the time it took to dress to calm her rattled nerves. She'd known something was wrong the moment a noise had awakened her. Her first indication of trouble was that Colt was not in the room. When she'd awakened hours earlier she'd been surprised to find herself nestled up against his large frame but at the same time she'd felt an unfamiliar sense of rightness. Too tired to question it, she'd drifted back to sleep with her backside planted firmly against his hip. It had felt good.

But when she'd awakened the second time, she was alone in the room. She knew something was wrong. She immediately looked for the gun she'd seen earlier on the nightstand and noted it was missing as well. Its absence confirmed that something was happening and it probably wasn't good. No one had to tell her that leaving the room would have been a bad idea. If Colt was out there armed, he was hunting. She didn't understand how she knew that but she'd known it with certainty. She'd also known better than to get in his way. But she had needed to do something so she'd called Rick and - bless the man - he hadn't hesitated.

Now there'd be more questions. If only she had answers. She could think of no explanation for the things that were plaguing her. And if this last attack, like the others, had been directed at her, then she'd put Colt in danger – again.

"You both believe this is related to the other incidents, don't you?" Colt's nod confirmed what she already knew.

"Does he need me in there?" She spent enough time around law enforcement to know what would be asked of her.

"Not yet." He reached for her hand, tugging her down next to him on the couch.

Cat closed her eyes and she rested her cheek against his chest. It was becoming so easy to lean on this man. The thought scared her, though not as much as it would have a few days ago. Her biggest fear now was that in leaning on him she was putting him in danger.

"When they're through with me, I need to get out of here."

"We can do that. As long as Rick knows how to reach us…"

"I'm not talking about us, Colt. I'm talking about me. I'll be leaving here alone." She had expected outrage but was met with stony silence instead. "I've put you in danger. You could've been shot or even killed tonight because of me," she choked out. "I'll get my stuff together while they're finishing up."

A chill settled over Colt that had nothing to do with the damp clothes that still clung to him. He continued to hold her close.

"What are you saying? That you're worried about me? That's the reason you want to leave?"

She looked up at him, puzzled. Isn't that what she'd just said?

"I'm asking if you're leaving because you're afraid for me - or afraid *of me*."

Cat's eyes widened in surprise. "Why on earth would I be afraid of you?"

"I just killed a man," Colt snapped.

Comprehension quickly struck. "Oh, Colt. I'm sorry you were forced to do that but I don't think you could ever frighten me. What does scare me is that it could have been you bleeding out on that floor and I refuse to be responsible for that possibility."

Why did he continue to underestimate her? Probably for the same reason she thought she could just walk away. In spite of their bonding under fire these last few days they were still relative strangers. Well, that was going to change – and change quickly.

Clasping her by the shoulders, he gave her a gentle shake.

"Let's get something straight. None of this is your fault. I chose to get involved and I don't give a damn what your presence brings through that door. I want you here - with me. That hasn't changed. Won't change." He couldn't explain the need to keep her close but it was so strong there was no hiding from it.

"Let me finish," he said when he saw her on the verge of protesting. "This works both ways. Do you think I could step aside and let you walk out that door knowing what might be waiting for you? I was trained for situations like tonight. I can take care of myself - and you - if you'll just let me. Trust me, Cat. " He hadn't asked anyone to trust him in years. He'd sworn he'd never take on the responsibility for another human being again but he needed to protect her. He needed her to believe that he could. "Please?"

Rick entered the room and immediately came to a halt. It was obvious he'd interrupted something. The tension there was palpable. He debated giving them a few more minutes but with an almost imperceptible tilt of the head, Colt gave him the signal to come forward.

"I'd like you to take a look at the guy and tell us whether you recognize him," Rick said, squatting in front of Cat. "You okay with that?"

"Anything that'll help," she agreed but Rick didn't move. Instead he remained where he was, studying her. "Don't worry, I'm not going to fall apart," she assured him.

He squeezed her hand. "Wait here a minute."

The gurney squeaked slightly as it was maneuvered out of the kitchen and into the living area. Rick lowered the zipper on the black body bag a few inches. He carefully spread the thick plastic so that only the face was visible. The man had light skin which was even paler in death. His blond hair was matted and still damp from the rain. A thin, inch-long scar sliced diagonally through his right brow. Cat guessed he was somewhere in his mid-thirties or early forties. He looked vaguely familiar. The question was did he just remind her of someone or had she seen him before? He wasn't the guy from the mall. That man had been dark and stocky.

Colt stood at Cat's side, his arm around her shoulder. He hadn't been sure how she'd react to seeing the dead man so he'd stood ready to pull her away if it proved to be too much. Instead, her study of the body was intense.

"Do you recognize him?" Colt asked.

"Maybe." She moved toward the end of the gurney, changing her angle of sight. She had seen this man - and not too long ago. But it could have been anywhere. At the mall, in a restaurant, on the beach...

"On the beach! I saw him on the beach!"

"What beach? When?" Rick zipped the bag closed.

"Off Smuggler's Lane this past... Tuesday," she added after she mentally calculated the days. "When I arrived that morning, there were two guys having what looked like a serious discussion. I remember them because at first I was disappointed that I didn't have the beach to myself but as soon as it dawned on me that they wouldn't be staying long I forgot about them and got myself settled in for the day."

"How did you know they weren't staying?" Colt asked.

"Their clothes. That guy," she said, indicating the gurney that was now being rolled toward the front door "was dressed casually but not 'beach' casual. He was wearing a white button down shirt but the collar was open and his sleeves were rolled up. He had on khaki colored chinos, I think. The other guy was dressed in a suit."

"Can you describe the other man?" Rick asked.

"Not really. His back was to me so I didn't get a look at his face. Like I said, once I figured they'd be leaving shortly, I went about my business."

"Tell him what you can remember," Colt encouraged her.

She closed her eyes and tried to picture the scene from the beach. "The guy in the suit was a little shorter and heavier than this guy. He looked solid, though, not fat." Cat sighed frustrated, "I'm not very good at guessing weights or heights."

"Relax. You're doing fine," Rick assured her.

Cat took a deep breath and continued. "He was Caucasian. His hair was light brown, cut short and neat. The suit was dark – navy, I think. I do remember thinking 'nice suit.' Pretty sure it wasn't an off-the-rack piece of clothing. Looking back, my guess is that it was tailored to fit." She considered the image in her mind for a second more, "Sorry, that's about it."

"Age?" Colt asked.

"I'd be guessing. I don't remember seeing any gray hair, though."

"Did you overhear anything?"

"I could hear their voices but couldn't make out what

they were saying. They were too far away. I did get the impression that neither one of them was happy.

"Did they see you?"

"Not while I was looking at them but considering their positioning, I'd say the chances are pretty good that the guy who was here tonight saw me. I can't say it for certain, though." Cat nodded toward the hallway. "Do you know who he is?" she asked Rick.

"No, but we'll find out."

13

Colt and Rick were alone in his unit. Cat had been desperate for coffee but Colt had refused to let her make use of his kitchen until all traces of the shooting were erased. So at sunrise, Colt had let her into Gib's place and left her there to make a pot. Rick had sent an officer with them on the pretense of helping but Colt new better. He suspected Cat did as well but she'd held her tongue. More than likely she wanted the caffeine more than she wanted to argue and was smart enough to have figured out that neither man intended to let her go anywhere alone - not until they had some answers.

"This doesn't make any sense," Colt stated.

"What specifically are you talking about? Because not much about this case does."

"The escalation of events. First, the sporadic tail. Then the ransacking of her cottage followed by an attempt to kidnap her. Now this – which, based on the fire power that guy was carrying, wasn't just another attempt to snatch her." Knowing she'd been the target of an assassin chilled Colt to the bone.

"If someone wants her dead, why screw around with the other shit? They could have simply waited until I'd left her at the cottage that first night. Breaking in only served to raise our guard. And what was so damned important about that meeting on the beach that it necessitates the killing of a witness?"

"The body might lead us somewhere," Rick said. "After I leave here, I'll check out that beach. It's doubtful, but maybe I'll get lucky and turn up something. Want to tag along?"

Colt thought about it for a second but Cat was his first priority. If there were something to find, Rick would find it. "Actually, if you're okay with it, I'd like to get Cat away from here for a couple of days." It would give Rick some time to get a handle on things and, while she would never admit it, he suspected Cat could use some down time.

"I don't see any problem with that." The shooting was a clear-cut case of self-defense. Forensics had already dug two bullets out of the kitchen wall that obviously hadn't come from Colt's gun. "As long as I can reach you. When and where?"

"When we're done here. I'm thinking the Keys."

"Go. This might have taken care of the problem but I'm not laying odds on it so watch your back. I'll call you as soon as I know something."

"I'd like to borrow your truck. That thing she drives is a neon sign – assuming I can even fit in it. And if our visitor had friends, my vehicle has been made by now."

"Go ahead. I'll take your Jeep when I leave," Rick said, tossing his keys to Colt. "Do you need a weapon? It will be a while before we can release yours."

"Gib and I have another one in the safe downstairs." Which reminded him, he needed to contact his friend and bring him up to speed.

"I'll arrange for someone to clean up the kitchen while you're gone," Rick added, lowering his voice when he heard Cat enter the front door.

Colt nodded his thanks. He'd been planning on asking Gib to see to the task but Rick had contacts that would be accustomed to cleaning up messes like this one.

Cat set the makeshift tray with the coffee, cups, creamer and sugar on the coffee table in front of the two men. "What?" she asked, when she realized they were studying her. Did they expect her to collapse? Admittedly, she looked pretty bad. The vision that had greeted her in the bathroom mirror earlier hadn't been an attractive one but she assumed these two had seen worse.

"You feel up to a trip?" Colt asked, still scrutinizing her.

"A trip?"

"Yeah. Ever been to Key West?" The more he thought about it, the more he liked the destination. It would be easy to spot a tail on the two-lane road to the small island and he suspected Cat would enjoy the quirky little town.

"We're free to leave?" Cat asked, surprised. She'd worked for Jason long enough to know that people involved in a shooting would often have their movements restricted initially, regardless of whether the shooting was justified.

"I think it's a good idea," Rick told her as he got to his feet.

Cat wasn't ready to let him escape. She snagged him by the arm, raised herself up on her toes and pressed a kiss to his cheek. "Thanks for trusting me when I called last night," she said softly.

"I figured it was that or get my ass kicked. Take care of her, Captain," he said to Colt then headed out through the kitchen.

Cat cocked her head, "Captain?"

"A previous life," he sighed. One he really didn't want to revisit at the moment.

A shadow seemed to pass over his face. A history with painful memories was one thing she could relate to so she didn't push. "Do we have time for a shower?" she asked instead, changing the subject. When the sparkle returned to his eyes, she clarified, "Do *I* have time for a shower?"

He'd been thinking about getting her into the shower since the day of their first meeting. But now wasn't the time. "Go ahead. I'll start throwing some stuff together." He counted his blessings that the subject of her leaving had not been resurrected.

Colt exited the bathroom after his shower to find Cat standing in the exact spot he'd occupied the night before when he'd first caught a glimpse of the gunman. Her eyes were wide and fixed. Her attention riveted. His senses went into high gear as he quickly closed the distance between them.

"How could I have missed that yesterday?" she wondered aloud. After gathering what she needed for the trip, Cat had become restless. She'd been tempted to wander outdoors to get some fresh air but thought better of it. No point in making the boys in blue Rick had left stationed outside nervous. She settled for opening the blinds hoping a little sunshine would elevate her sinking mood. When she peaked through the slats the gardens below had stunned her. The variety and array of bright, tropical colors exploded against a lush, green backdrop.

Colt followed her line of sight then smiled. "That's the Copeland's place. Beautiful, isn't it? I spend a lot of time over there with my camera."

"Do you think they'd let me looked around?" she

asked, full of anticipation. She had yet to remove her eyes from the view, Colt noted.

"I'm sure they'd enjoy showing it off once we know it's safe for you." As soon as the words were out of his mouth he regretted them. Her childlike enthusiasm swiftly melted away. Surprisingly, it was sadness, not fear, he saw reflected in those dark, round eyes. Still, he couldn't promise her the freedom to roam. Not yet. Something ugly was going down and she was in the center of it.

COLT LED Cat into the studio's office. She wasn't happy. Her brief sadness had been replaced by familiar stubbornness. She'd wanted to look at the photos in the lobby again while he was collecting items from the office for the trip. He had firmly nixed the idea. He wasn't comfortable letting her out of his sight. Hell, he'd found himself rushing through his shower, nervous because she wasn't within arm's reach. He was concerned, not possessive, he'd argued silently as he checked his spare weapon and tucked it into the back of his jeans. He had to keep her safe. He could only do that if she stayed by his side. Satisfied with his logic, he tossed some extra ammo into the large duffel bag.

Colt glanced up to see Cat staring at him. Her expression was disarming and difficult to interrupt.

"Something wrong?"

"No," she answered quickly. "It's just the way you move..." As she'd watched him gather his supplies her irritation had faded. She found herself fascinated by his movements. The silent, lithe and deliberate motion reminded her of one of the endangered Florida Panthers. It was no wonder she hadn't heard him last night in spite of her intense listening. Was he always that smooth? That agile?

Cat suddenly pictured his body wrapped around hers and flushed. Her color deepened further when she realized that Colt had not only followed her train of thought but her eyes as they focused on the "gun" tucked low in his jeans.

Cat's obvious appraisal of his body had him hard and hurting. If there hadn't been several officers outside awaiting their departure, he'd be tempted to take her back upstairs. Instead, he rose. Pulled her against him so she could feel his desire and whispered against her lips, "You haven't seen any moves yet."

14

They were on the road before noon, which Colt considered a feat considering the night they'd had. He'd taken numerous false turns on the way out of town with one eye glued to the rearview mirror. Once he was certain that they hadn't been followed, he placed an overdue call to Gib.

His friend started in with lighthearted protests about having his tryst interrupted but as soon as Colt mentioned trouble, Gib immediately quieted - only interrupting to clarify a point or to question Colt about his resurrected love life. Before the conversation had ended, Gib's car was packed and he was on his way back to Sanibel to take care of any business that might come up while Colt was away.

From her end of the conversation, it was evident to Cat that the partners shared a mutual respect for one another. More than that, they cared about each other. The tone of their exchange varied from concern to good-natured ribbing. A little stab of jealousy settled in her gut. What would it be like to have a friend like that? With the exception of Jason and Ellie, she'd made it a point to keep people at a distance. It was safer that way. Still, she couldn't stop her wistful feelings.

Her ringing cell phone pulled Cat back to reality. She recognized Jason's ring tone but was still surprised by the call. Normally, he didn't contact her on her time off.

"Hi, Jason. Is Ellie okay?"

"She's fine. Cat. What in the blazes is going on down there? FDLE just left here. Are you all right? Why didn't you call?"

Why hadn't she thought to call him? She should have realized the authorities would be in touch with him.

"Damn, Jason, I'm sorry. Everything's okay. We're fine."

Like the good lawyer he was, Jason didn't miss a beat.

"Who is 'we'?"

The question was asked with a mixture of worry and interrogation. Cat smiled. "I seem to have acquired a white knight. Never thought I'd say this but they can come in pretty handy. He's saved my butt a couple of times these last few days."

"Okay, Cat, start at the beginning. The State boys weren't very forthcoming."

Cat attempted to give Jason the abridged version of events but, not surprisingly, his questions were detailed and thorough. His shock at hearing about last night's break-in along with the death of the intruder confirmed that state cops hadn't shared very much of what had transpired.

"You mean to tell me they let you take off with a man who'd just killed someone? What kind of police department do they have down there?"

"Whoa, Jason. Slow down. First of all, you of all people know that no one 'lets me' do anything. Leaving Sanibel with Colt was my choice. My decision. He was free to go because the shooting was justified. His actions most likely saved my life." She looked deep into those crystal blue eyes that had flashed on her, "I trust him, Jason."

Jason let out a breath, apparently appeased. He knew she didn't place her trust in anyone lightly. "As long as you're okay. What's the name of that detective, again? I want to talk to him. I'll see if there's anything I can do to help."

She gave him Rick's contact information. Hopefully, he wouldn't mind Jason butting in because he was going to do exactly that whether Rick liked it or not.

"You're sure Ellie is okay?"

"I told you she was fine. Now will you stop trying to change the subject? What's your next move?"

"For the moment we're staying out of the way and letting the police investigate. With any luck they'll know the name of the gunman shortly and things will fall into place." One could only hope.

"What about protection? Is Wilcowski arranging it?"

"On what grounds? The black cloud I have hanging over my head?" A series of coincidences is how the authorities viewed the events of the last few days according to Rick, even though he disagreed. She simply was not a candidate for police protection but she suspected that wouldn't stop Jason from trying.

"Let me see what I can do," he responded, confirming her thoughts.

"Thanks, Jason."

"You be careful and tell your white knight he'll have to deal with me if anything happens to you." He paused, "Cat, you do know I'm going to have him checked out, don't you?"

"Would it make any difference if I objected?"

"No."

"Didn't think so."

She dropped her head back against the headrest as she disconnected the call.

Colt glanced over at her. "Your boss?"

"Yeah. Apparently, FDLE showed up there this morning and scared the crap out of him." Damn. Jason shouldn't have heard about her difficulty second hand. "I hadn't even thought about calling him."

"You had other things on your mind."

"He's got enough to worry about without adding me to the mix." She explained about Ellie's recurrence of breast cancer and Jason's plans to retire early so he could be with his wife while she went through treatment.

"He sounds like a good man."

"You might not think so when I tell you he's going to run a background check on you."

He digested that for a minute. "I'd probably do the same thing under the circumstances." He just wasn't so sure the man was going to like what he discovered.

"I suspect you two are alike in that way..." Cat said absently, staring out the passenger window, "...very protective of the people you love."

He managed to keep his eyes on the road and his hands firmly wrapped around the steering wheel even though her slip of the tongue shook him to his core. She knew. Not consciously, he'd swear, but on some level she knew that he'd fallen in love with her. He'd come to that stunning realization this morning. He wouldn't have believed it possible to tumble so quickly. If anyone had told him it could happen he'd have laughed in their face. He wasn't a schoolboy with his first serious crush. He'd enjoyed his share of women. Some had been more special than others but those relationships paled in comparison to his feelings for Cat. Nothing else could explain the emptiness he felt whenever she left the room, the panic that rose in him when she talked about leaving or the way his soul settled by simply having her close.

The big question was what was he going to do about it? She'd run if he told her - which would probably be the smart thing for her to do. He wasn't exactly a good bet since Afghanistan. He'd yet to pick up all the shattered pieces of his life. Didn't think he ever would. Could she accept damaged goods? Did he have the right to ask?

15

When crossing the southern tip of Florida, most motorists elected to take Interstate 75 or - as it was locally known - Alligator Alley. Colt opted for U.S. 41. It was the older, less traveled of the two available routes. If someone were following, he'd have no trouble spotting them on the two-lane highway. Even if he hadn't been watching for a tail, Colt preferred this more leisurely route. The Tamiami Trail would take them through the Big Cypress National Preserve before skimming the northern edge of Everglades National Park. Once they were headed south on U.S. 1, a series of bridges along the Overseas Highway would take them across pristine blue waters as they made their way through the chain of islands known as the Florida Keys. It was, in Colt's mind, one of America's most beautiful routes.

Colt loved the Everglades. The only place of its kind on earth, there had once been a danger of losing this environmental wonder to agriculture and development. Initially, it was thought of as a giant swamp that needed to be converted into usable land. But fifty years ago a woman with foresight, Marjory Stoneman Douglas, wrote a book about this unique environment and virtually saved it single-handedly. "The River of Grass" extolled the beauty and necessity of this ecosystem. Colt was personally grateful for her efforts. The Park and its inhabitants were an endless source of subject matter for his art.

Even though she'd grown up in South Florida, Cat had never taken the time to visit this part of the state so she was captivated by the stories Colt told about his trips deep into the wilderness and the creatures he was fond of photographing. When they reached Key Largo and began their trek south, Cat was so taken in by the quaint communities and sparkling waters that connected them, the reason for their flight south slipped pleasantly to the back of her mind.

It was early evening when they pulled into the small parking area of The Gardens Hotel. Colt knew the place well. He'd done a photo spread for them the previous year. With Cat's love of anything green he suspected this unique bed and breakfast would be a treat. Colt considered himself fortunate that he was able to snag the room he'd wanted when he'd called.

Cat couldn't take the place in fast enough. It wasn't a hotel as much as a group of quaint, two story houses surrounding a courtyard, pool and gardens. The buildings were painted white with black shutters that set off the colors in the landscaping. Each building had a veranda or balcony complete with wicker furniture and ceiling fans. Cat sipped her complimentary Mimosa as she followed Colt to a secluded area of the property appropriately named the Garden Rooms.

Once inside, she crossed the hardwood floor and opened the door to the veranda. Palm branches hugged the second story porch. They were virtually hidden as a result of the lush vegetation and the angle of the building. Their own private tree house.

Colt wrapped his arms around her waist, gently pulling her back against his chest as she gazed out at the gardens. "Is this going to work for you?" he asked. It struck him how important it was that she was comfortable - in this place - with him.

She turned in his arms, tilting her head so she could look into those dazzling eyes. "It's beautiful."

"And the sleeping arrangements?"

She pretended to study the king size bed through the open doors. "That bed could probably sleep four. I won't even know you're there."

"You're going to know I'm there, alright," he whispered before smothering her smug grin with a kiss.

THE EVENING AIR was thick - hot, humid and smelled of rain - but after being in the car for six hours they'd both agreed they'd prefer to walk to dinner. With his arm comfortably anchored around Cat's shoulder, they headed toward the Marina. Colt steered clear of Duval Street and its bustling nightlife. It would be near to impossible to spot a tail in the hordes of people that had already begun filling the well-known street. Instead, he took side streets, detouring several times to ensure there was no one following.

Cat didn't mind the convoluted route. She was enjoying the mystique of the Key West night. The small gingerbread style houses that lined the narrow streets of Old Town captivated her. And, my God, the flowers! Bougainvillea grew everywhere - producing an amazing kaleidoscope of color. Most of the homes were built on postage stamp size lots, tucked behind white picket fences that set off the fluorescent shades of the cascading flowers.

When they reached their destination - a quaint waterfront café - Colt won the seating argument, requesting a table in the air-conditioned interior rather than one on the covered, open deck. The woman never seemed to get enough of the outdoors. He was beginning to think if he'd given her a choice she'd have preferred to camp on the beach. Small wonder she was considering leaving the restrictions of the white-collar world behind.

The meal passed as the trip south had - with casual conversation. Neither of them touched on the reason behind their visit to Key West. Colt had been tempted to call Rick before heading out to dinner. He was anxious to find out if they'd identified the intruder but then decided against it. He'd hear from Rick when there was something to report. Besides, he wanted this evening to be untouched, if possible, from the troubles that had chased them here.

The journey back to their room was a far cry from the walk to dinner. Cat's unease was telegraphed with each step. Colt's attempts to engage her in conversation were met with monosyllable remarks tossed absently his way. You didn't have to be Dr. Phil to know what was on her mind. In spite of that steel in her spine it was obvious she was apprehensive about what the rest of the evening held.

As soon as they returned to the room, Colt suggested Cat relax in a warm tub. She was relieved when Colt hadn't suggested he join her as she'd half expected. Instead, he'd kissed her soundly, patted her on her ass and told her to hurry.

She didn't hurry. She stalled. What the hell was wrong with her? She'd slept with men before. Granted, not many and those memories had long ago faded. But hadn't she wanted this? Yes, she answered her own unspoken question

- then amended that to *hell, yes*. And that, she realized, was the problem. She'd never wanted a man like she did Colt - and the depth of that desire frightened her.

What if she disappointed him? What if he found her lacking in some way? Those damn "what-ifs" again. Cat stared at the woman in the mirror and shook her head in disgust at her timidity. One thing was certain, if she didn't leave the bathroom shortly she'd not only disappoint Colt but herself. So, wearing only the inn's fluffy, one-size-fits-all robe - and a bad case of nerves - she opened the door.

Her heart rate kicked up another notch when she took in her surroundings. The reasons Colt had opted out of joining her were now evident. Candles flickered on the small tables. Two flutes of champagne sparkled on one of the nightstands, shimmering as the flames from the candles reflected in the bubbling liquid. Several foil packets lay beside the stemmed glasses. When had he arranged all this? She pressed a hand to her stomach trying to calm the mass of fluttering butterflies.

"You alright?"

She turned toward the husky voice. Colt leaned casually against the frame of the French door, arms crossed over his bare chest. Jeans hung low, clinging snugly to his long legs. His feet were bare. Lord, he was exquisite. The butterflies fled – chased away by a herd of stampeding buffalo.

"I'm fine," she lied.

She looked ready to bolt and short of a fire, he had no intention of letting her out of this room. He quickly closed the distance between them. Cupping her chin, he tilted her face, studying it. "I thought you'd gone down the drain."

Cat forced herself to hold his gaze. Who was this insecure woman who'd taken over her body? She couldn't remember ever being this unsure of herself.

Colt could almost see the nerves dancing across her skin like heat lightning on a Florida summer night. "Second thoughts?" he asked then wished he hadn't voiced his concern. What would he do if she had changed her mind?

She shook her head, sensing his immediate relief. "But I'm not what you'd call experienced," she admitted softly, shrugging her shoulders, hoping she sounded casual - which no small feat under the circumstances.

Colt froze. No way. She couldn't be. Until this minute it had never occurred to him… "You're not telling me you're a… That you've never…?"

In spite of her nerves, or maybe because of them, she laughed. The panicked look on his face was priceless. "No," she assured him. "I'm just giving you fair warning that this may not turn out to be the evening you're anticipating."

He let out the breath he'd been holding then touched her forehead with a tender kiss. He followed it with one to her temple, then another near her ear… and then another. He left a trail of soft, tantalizing kisses along her jaw until they led him back to her parted lips.

With her arms trapped between their bodies she spread her fingers over his chest. She needed to touch him - to feel the warmth of his skin beneath her fingertips. When he groaned as her thumbs brushed over his nipples, Cat's insecurities began to fade.

Pulling away from the slow, lingering kiss, he attempted to catch his breath - then decided breathing wasn't a priority. Finding the sensitive patch of flesh behind her ear, he pressed another kiss to her skin. With one hand he slowly traced the curve of her throat then followed that path with the touch of his lips, claiming every inch of her skin for his own. When the robe halted his trek he gently pushed it off her shoulders. She smelled of jasmine. He remembered the lotion she'd purchased on that fateful trip to the mall. He'd be buying it by the gallon after tonight. The robe fell away but stopped short of revealing her breasts - taunting him.

She extended her neck, giving Colt access to the newly exposed skin. Her nipples ached. Liquid heat pooled between her thighs. When he slipped his hand inside her robe and cupped her breast, her knees gave up the fight.

Colt caught her, lifting her into his arms, half expecting her to protest. Instead, she nuzzled his chest then tentatively flicked her tongue against his skin. It was his turn to stumble. The bed seemed miles away. Willpower won over lust and he managed the remaining steps. Lowering her onto the cool sheets, he grasped the robe's belt and slowly unwrapped the gift before him.

Cat watched as Colt took in every inch of her with those Sorcerer's eyes. He was hungry and she was the feast. It was both unsettling and emboldening. She reached for the zipper of his jeans.

He took a step back - out of her reach. He knew he wouldn't last a minute if she laid a hand on that rock hard portion of his anatomy and his plan was to take his time. Still, he quickly shed his remaining clothes.

God, he was gorgeous and... big. Cat stared at his jutting erection. She couldn't help it. Doubts began to filter back in.

"What is it?" he asked, seeing her anticipation change to unease. He slipped in bed beside her, resting his substantial weight on one elbow as he brushed the hair from her face. Not surprisingly, his fingers weren't entirely steady.

"Unlike the robe, I'm not sure that's a one-size-fits-all," she stated, awkwardly.

He didn't know whether to laugh or console her. "Trust me, Kitten." It was a request as much as a promise. He kissed the tip of her nose before capturing her mouth again. His hands traveled over her breasts, caressing them, rolling the nipples between his fingertips, delighted as they hardened under his touch. Following the path forged by his fingers, his tongue circled the taunt peak. She arched, inviting him to take more. He did - capturing her small mound in his mouth. After savoring the small, firm raspberries he continued his journey, touching, stroking, and lapping every warm, sensual inch. Butterfly kisses dotted the skin over her womb as he parted her legs and brought her knees up to give him access. He knew the instant she'd realized his destination. Cat stiffened.

"Relax, Kitten. Let me get you ready." Inserting one finger into the valley beneath the dark curls, he watched her eyes begin to lose focus. "You're tight," he blew a soft breath across to her tender flesh then he dipped his head to taste her sweetness. Suckling her sensitive folds, he inserted another finger, stretching her - making it easier for her to accept him.

An unfamiliar but overwhelming sensation traveled through her. Good God, it consumed her. Muscles tighten around his fingers. Her vision darkened as spasms racked her body. Her heart slammed against her breastbone as she called out to him - not sure if she wanted him to continue or end the exquisite agony. Before her head cleared enough to reason out that puzzle, Colt slipped between her legs.

"Look at me, Cat."

Her brown eyes flew open as he sank into her moist, warm sheath. Immediately he felt her tighten around him. This was not going to be the slow, tender lovemaking he had envisioned. Not this time. When her muscles constricted again, he lost all control.

· · ·

CAT LAY LIMP - TOTALLY DRAINED. Only her heart and lungs seemed to be functioning and they were working double time. "I lied," she whispered when she managed to take in enough air to speak, "that *was* my first time. And my second..." The admission made her smile.

Colt raised himself so he could admire the look of satisfaction on her face. She was even more beautiful lying sated beneath him. Her skin was pink where his stubble had chaffed her. He'd have to shave more often, he noted. Perspiration beaded between her small breasts. Knowing that she had not experienced the "little death" at the hands of another man made him possessive - *and hard* - as hell. He wanted her again. This time he'd take her without setting a land speed record.

"I'm sorry, Cat," he said, tracing the line of her jaw. He'd gone off like a teenager in the backseat of a Chevy. Not even in his youth had he been that quick on the trigger. "I'd planned to take my time, to do it right," he said.

"Are you serious?" she asked, reaching for the sheet. "Anything better would probably kill me."

Sporting a cat-that-just-ate-the-canary grin, he said, "You'll live - and enjoy it." He picked up the flutes of untouched champagne and held one out to her. His intent had been to give her a little romance. Some tenderness. Not a quick roll in the hay. Obviously, his body had had other ideas. But she'd been so responsive there'd been no controlling his reaction to her.

As she took a sip of champagne he laced his fingers through her free hand. "Are you okay? I wasn't exactly gentle." He leaned his head back against the headboard as an exasperated breath escaped. "I've never lost control like that."

His confession both surprised and touched her. He hadn't been the only one who'd lost control. Nothing she'd ever experienced came close to making love with this man. It had left her feeling down right giddy. The night was full of unexpected emotions. For once, she allowed them to rule her actions. Putting on a solemn face, she tried her hand at a little acting. Grimacing, she wiggled her bottom against the mattress, "Well, I am a little sore."

Both glasses disappeared as the sheet was snatched away. "Do we need a doctor? Should I take you to a clinic?" Colt asked frantically while he scanned the length of her. What he was looking for, he had no idea.

Her career in Hollywood was over before it started. A giggle turned into full-blown laughter, earning her a lecherous look. Grabbing her ankles, he yanked her flat on to the mattress.

"Just for that," he threatened as he straddled her, "I'm going to torture you for the rest of the night."

16

The heavenly aroma of coffee pulled Cat from her slumber. She pried her eyelids open and sought out the source. Across the room a freshly showered Colt lounged in a guest chair sipping from a steaming cup. Even half-awake it was hard to miss the satisfied gleam in his eye. She knew immediately that she was responsible. Who'd a thought?

"I was wondering when you were going to get up. They won't be serving breakfast downstairs much longer and I worked up an appetite last night. Come on, Kitten, let's get a move on," he cajoled.

"Kitten." He'd used the term of endearment throughout the evening. From any other man, she'd have considered it degrading. From Colt, it felt like a caress.

"Speaking of getting up…" she tucked the sheet under her arms as she surveyed the room. "That might explain why I'm so tuckered out. I seem to remember you getting *it* up several times last night."

That he had. A victory grin spread across his face. It was a wonder either one of them could stand this morning.

She continued to scan the room. He knew exactly what she was looking for. He'd returned the robe to the hook behind the bathroom door and that's where it was going to stay until she got that naked little ass of hers out of bed to retrieve it. "Looking for something?" he asked.

The smug look telegraphed his thoughts. Well, if he wanted a show she'd give him one. Amazing how she'd gone from insecure to brazen in the short space of one night. "Too bad you've already showered," she said coyly as she began to close the bathroom door. "You could have joined me." She barely got out of the way when the door flew open.

THEY MANAGED to make it to breakfast before the morning buffet had been cleared away. Temporarily satisfied and fortified, Colt grabbed his cameras and they headed out to explore the island's Old Town on foot. He was reasonably comfortable that they hadn't been followed on the trek to the Keys but for insurance he led them through a series of streets and alleyways. By the time they reached The Audubon House & Museum, Colt felt secure that they had no tails.

The historic home was noted for its collection of naturalist prints but it was its tropical gardens that seized Cat's interest. Orchids, bromeliads and other plants filled the courtyard. Bright colors and lush fragrances assaulted her senses.

Colt snapped shots while she investigated every corner of the landscaping. As he followed her around the premises, he was amazed that she'd managed to stay confined to an office for as long as she had. She was animated and vibrant as she explored the plants in the courtyard, going from one to another like a hummingbird seeking nectar. This was her element. Her hesitation at leaving the office world puzzled him. It was obvious she had the backbone, intelligence and stubbornness to succeed at anything she set her mind to. When you added her love of gardening, Colt could not imagine her failing at the endeavor. Perhaps she just needed a little shove - some encouragement to bury the doubts that kept popping up. He could do that. And if she wanted his help - hell, even if she didn't – he'd be there for her.

After enjoying the mandatory "cheeseburger in paradise," they continued playing tourist, ending their day at Ernest Hemingway's Key West Home. They opted for a leisurely self-guided tour of the house and gardens of the legendary author then settled down to watch some of the descendants of the original six-toed feline that Hemingway had received as a gift from a ship's captain. Cat was sitting on the steps of the back porch, laughing at a kitten playfully chasing its tail, when the call Colt had been waiting for finally came through.

Colt stepped away for some privacy. "What's going on?"

"You're not going to like this," Rick started.

"I figured as much. Just spit it out."

"We've identified your shooter as Marcus Bookman. He is, or rather was, a contract killer. A professional - and a good one from what we've been able to uncover."

"Why would anyone want Cat dead?" Colt's heart was in his throat.

"My best guess? That meeting on the beach she witnessed was between a contractor and his killer for hire."

"Why the hell would they let her walk away from something like that?" If that was true, Cat should be dead. The thought made Colt's stomach tighten.

"I don't know but one thing I'm sure of is that if this

was about a murder for hire then the guy in the suit was most likely the one calling the shots or we'd be investigating two bodies turning up on that beach."

Rick didn't have to elaborate. Cat had told them that the beach had been empty that morning with the exception of the two men. If the other man were the target then the killer would not have hesitated to eliminate the witness along with his target at the time.

"Could the guy Cat saw be connected to what's been happening?"

"But you don't believe that," Colt stated flatly.

"No. Bookman wasn't on that beach to socialize. I'd bet this week's paycheck that he was with the contractor."

"Then the question still stands. Why leave Cat alive?"

"Maybe the guy in the suit is squeamish. After all he's hiring someone to handle his dirty work. Or he wanted to be sure he was somewhere else when the deed was done. We've got more questions than answers right now."

"Colt, there's something else," Rick continued. "I played a hunch and had your vehicles checked out. We found tracking devices on both."

"Son of a bitch. That explains how the bastard found us at the mall and tracked us back to my place." Still, things just weren't adding up. "But why tag our cars? The only time he could have gotten to both vehicles was at the cottages so he already knew where she was staying."

"Insurance maybe? Right now I'm focusing on finding the guy that was with Bookman on that beach."

"And how do you propose to do that? Cat can't identify him. She never got a good look at him."

"We're backtracking Bookman's whereabouts. That might lead us somewhere." It wouldn't be easy. The guy was a pro and Rick knew that even if they did get lucky, that angle might not lead them where they wanted to go.

"What about his car?"

"We've got it. So far, it's clean."

"And the make?"

"Typical run-of-the-mill mid-size rental. Not a Lincoln Town Car. It was leased the morning he broke into your place. He might have changed cars, though. We're looking into that possibility."

"This whole thing is screwy. Why would someone that savvy drive a vehicle as distinctive as a Town Car in the first place?"

Rick silently agreed that the question needed to be answered but at the moment he had another problem. "Colt, the FBI is involved now. Bookman's name has been linked to a number of hits including the one on that federal judge up in Delaware last year. They're sending two agents down from Tampa. They want to talk to Cat. We need her back here."

Colt glanced over at the woman he'd held in his arms last night. He didn't want to leave. Not yet. But this kind of trouble would eventually find them. When it did he wanted the advantage of home turf.

"Have the chances of arranging for some protection improved now that you've identified our visitor?"

"We're still having a problem in that area. The general assumption is that with Bookman dead, Cat is no longer in danger."

"That's bullshit and you know it. If there is a contract on her it didn't fall apart with Bookman's death. She needs protection, damn it."

"I'm working on it."

17

A fter Colt relayed the news to Cat, they made plans to return to Sanibel the next morning. Remaining in Key West had never been an option but the brief escape had allowed her time to regroup. She felt stronger both physically and mentally but it was time to face the devil. Colt had called Rick with a tentative timetable. Once back on the island they would go directly to the station. Rick would notify the FBI to meet them there.

They had this one last night in the Keys. Cat had been determined not to waste it but her plans changed when she received a call from Jason. He was not a happy man.

"Goddamn fools!" he snapped, venting about his lack of success in arranging for protection. Her eyebrows shot up several notches at Jason's remark. The man rarely swore. For years he'd been on a campaign to break Cat of the habit.

"Calm down, Jason." She could almost hear his blood pressure rising. "You knew it was a long shot before you made the first call. No agency these days has the staff or money to spend on protection duties especially since there's nothing to substantiate the risk. Just theories."

"We're talking about your life, Cat. Don't be so damn flippant about it."

"Trust me, Jason, I'm anything but flippant."

"I'm not done lighting fires. In the meantime, you swallow that stubborn streak and do what Wilcowski and James tell you to do. If you had to find this kind of trouble at least you stumbled on to the right people to help you out of it."

"I assume by that comment they meet your criteria?"

"Looks like your instincts were right about him. Darn shame what happened to James on his last tour."

"And what was that?" she asked, hoping for a little more insight into the man.

"His story to tell," he answered. "I will say this, Cat, I trust him enough to put your life in his hands and you know how important you are to me and Ellie."

Cat wasn't sure why Jason and Ellie had taken her under their wings but they had made her part of their family - the only family she had.

"Let me talk to James," Jason requested. When she didn't respond, he added firmly, "Put him on the phone, Cat, or I'll just get his number from Wilcowski and call him direct."

She marched out to the veranda where Colt had been waiting for her to finish her call. When she shoved the phone into his bewildered face, the unspoken question was evident. "Don't ask me," she snapped. "He insists on talking to you."

"Yes, sir?" Colt asked, taking the phone.

Cat could hear Jason's deep, resonating voice but she couldn't make out what he was saying.

"Yes, sir," Colt responded several more times before grinning slightly. "Yes, sir, I've discovered that."

A few more words passed between them before Colt said, "Yes, sir. You have it."

Colt ended the call and handed the phone back to Cat.

"Well?" She certainly didn't get much from Colt's end of the conversation.

If Colt hadn't already decided he liked Jason based on what he'd learned from Cat, he would have certainly held that opinion by the end of the lopsided exchange. It was obvious that Jason cared deeply about the woman standing in front of him. He wanted Cat safe regardless of what it took to keep her that way. He'd offered his leverage, and his finances, if they would help. He'd also warned Colt about her stubbornness and short fuse. That information had been a little late in coming.

Speaking of temper, the tips of Cat's ears were turning red while she waited for his response. Definitely not a patient woman.

He stroked her cheek with the pad of his thumb. "He wanted my word that I'd keep you safe. He needn't have asked. I'm not going let anything happen to you, Kitten."

Colt didn't know what to make of Cat's reaction. Her stare unnerved him but before he could question her, she turned away. As clearly as a tortoise pulling back into its shell, she'd withdrawn into herself.

"Cat?" Coaxing her to turn around until she faced him, he nudged her chin up to look into her tear filled eyes. They ripped at his heart. She had every right to be upset. Hell, she should be terrified. Still, this wasn't like the woman he was coming to know. The sudden change from bravado to tears worried him. "What's this all about, Kitten?" She shook her head, refusing to answer but he held her chin firmly in his grasp. "Come on, baby. What brought this on?"

"You!" she snapped accusingly, slashing at the tears that she couldn't seem to stop.

"Me?" He mentally did a quick accounting of the events of the day and couldn't come up with anything he might have done to upset her.

"What did I do?" he asked, perplexed.

"Your plan is to put yourself between me and a bullet. That's what! Who's going to protect you?" She stabbed him in the chest with her finger as the leaky dam that had been holding back the flood finally breached. Colt took her into his arms and carried her to the chaise lounge, cradling her while she sobbed. Her release was long overdue in his opinion. Most women – hell, some men – wouldn't have held up as well as she had under the stress of these past few days. Yet it was fear for his safety that had tipped the scales. How could he not love this woman?

Eventually, the tears ceased. Exhausted from the emotional release, she fell asleep in his arms. He carried her to the bed then settled in next to her, holding her close while she slept off the effects of the crying jag. When she stirred during the night, Colt slipped deep into her warmth – showing her with his actions what she wasn't ready to hear.

18

In spite of some early morning bedroom calisthenics they were on the road before dawn. Their eagerness to get started was rewarded with a breathtaking sunrise. Orange and pink pastels swirled with angel hair clouds as the sun began its rise over the Atlantic. And tonight, Cat smiled to herself, they would have an encore performance as the sun settled into the Gulf of Mexico.

It was just after noon when they turned into the Sanibel Police Station's parking lot. Cat studied the unique group of structures. Colt had advised Rick of their imminent arrival as they crossed the Sanibel Causeway. He was waiting, along with several uniformed officers, on the upper landing of the building. All the men were scanning the landscape surrounding the station. The picture they made was surreal. How could all this intrigue have developed from a simple trip to the beach? Cat took a breath to steady her nerves then opened the passenger door of the truck. Before her foot touched the ground Colt was at her side, scowling down at her like a pit bull with an attitude.

Yanking her up against his side, he rushed toward the stairs.

Cat almost tripped trying to keep pace with Colt's long legs. "Slow down," she snapped. "I can't keep up." In response, he tightened his hold on her waist and lifted her off the ground. With her tucked snuggly under his arm he hustled her up the steps. Only after they were inside and the door shut solidly behind them did Colt set her back on her feet.

Rick watched the pair as they squared off, amused in spite of the situation. Cat was fuming. Her skin was flushed and she had a death grip on the large handbag she carried. Rick wouldn't have been surprised to see her launch it at Colt.

Although he did his best to conceal it, Colt was enjoying Cat's anger as well. He was glad to see that her temper had returned. With what lay ahead, she'd need that fire in her belly. For good measure he decided to fan the embers. Taking a step closer he glared down at her, daring her to comment. He wasn't disappointed.

"Who the hell do you think you are carrying me up the stairs like a football? I'm capable of moving under my own power."

"What you're capable of is getting yourself killed. You had no business exiting that vehicle before one of us was there to protect you. From now on you wait for instructions."

Cat jabbed her finger into his chest. The fact that it was like poking a concrete wall didn't stop her. "Listen up, big guy. That is not the way this is going to work. I will not use you - or anyone else - as a shield. Nor will I 'wait for instructions.' If you need me to do something - ask." She stabbed at his chest again. "And remember this, *Captain,* I am not in your Army and I do not take orders!"

Rick didn't hide his grin as he stepped between the two, silently giving this round to Cat. "As entertaining as this is, I'm afraid we need to move on. The Feds have been cooling their heels for over an hour and I'd like to get them out of here."

"Sorry, Rick," Cat apologized but kept her focus on Colt. "General Patton here has me confused with one of his enlisted men."

Cat turned in the direction of a sign that indicated the restrooms. "I need to make a stop before we get started." She shot Colt a look that could have turned coal into diamonds. "Would you like to check the stalls first?" she asked sarcastically.

"Is the building secure?" Colt asked Rick.

Cat threw up her hands and stormed away, mumbling as she went.

"'Is the building secure?' What the hell sort of question is that?" Rick asked, turning to confront his friend. When Colt's expression changed from somber to amused, Rick smiled. How long had it been since he'd seen that mischievous look on his friend's face?

"It must have been a hell of a couple of days. Have you been riding her like that since you left?"

Colt's mouth ticked up at the corners as he remembered how that ball of energy had straddled him this morning. "I wasn't the one doing the riding."

19

Rick was deep in conversation with two men when Cat and Colt caught up with him a few minutes later. Colt had planted himself outside the ladies' room then escorted her down the hall to what looked more like a conference room than the interrogation room she had expected. When she spotted the agents, Cat had to cover her mouth to hide her smile. The "Men in Black" had arrived - complete with sunglasses sprouting from the pockets of their dark jackets. Rick introduced them as Special Agents Hernandez and Morgan. Hernandez, the smaller and older of the two men, spoke first.

"If you'll excuse us," he said, looking past Cat to address both Rick and Colt, "we have some questions for Miss Storm."

Colt immediately inserted himself in front of Cat but she quickly sidestepped his attempt to run interference.

"Am I under arrest?" she demanded. Judging by their expressions they hadn't expected her to go on the offensive. She wasn't surprised. Her size was in such contrast to her demeanor that she tended to take people off guard.

"We're only here to ask you some questions," Agent Hernandez replied, recovering quickly.

"And I'll be happy to answers your questions, if I'm able. However, right now I'm requesting that both Detective Wilcowski and Mr. James be allowed to remain in the room. If that's not acceptable, then your questions will have to wait until I can arrange to have an attorney present." She was pretty sure she'd just broken her own personal speed record for pissing people off but she'd be damned if she was going to let them dictate the tone of this meeting. Working with Jason had taught her a few things and one of those things was letting the other guy know who was in control.

"Is there a reason that you're hesitant to speak to us?" Morgan stepped closer in a blatant attempt to intimidate her. Clearly he'd missed Colt's attempt to do the same a few minutes earlier. It took a monumental effort but she managed to keep her tone civil.

"I did not say that I was hesitant to speak with you. And if you're going to continue to put words in my mouth then, obviously, my presence will not be necessary for this interview. What I *did* say was that I would like these gentlemen to remain while we talked. That should not be a problem under the circumstances. So, unless you plan to whip out the Patriot Act and - by some enormous stretch of your imaginations - designate me an enemy combatant, there is no reason why they cannot stay."

Colt didn't wait for an invitation. He pulled out a chair and lowered his tall frame into it while he struggled to keep a straight face. Rick fought a similar battle, covering an escaping laugh with a throat-clearing cough.

.   .   .

HERNANDEZ TOOK the lead in the questioning, establishing the timeline of her visit to Sanibel. They touched on her suspicion of being followed and the break-in at her cottage but their focus always returned to the meeting she'd witnessed on the beach. Hours passed as they picked apart that small span of time. When they were finally satisfied she couldn't add anything else, the agents rose.

"Will you be arranging a security detail for Miss Storm?" Rick asked before they could escape the room.

"Why would you think that?" Morgan asked.

Colt slammed his fist down on the conference room table. For the better part of four hours he'd sat quietly, watching with admiration as Cat fielded the tedious questions thrown at her. Her answers had been sharp and concise. The agents had tried every trick he'd learned for interrogation to trip her up. Her story never wavered nor did she let them rattle her. Colt had not interfered nor had he attempted to come to her rescue but with their obvious lack of concern for her safety, he was done sitting on the sidelines.

"For the same damn reason you're here! Something major is going down and she's in the middle of it."

"If she's in danger…" Morgan started.

"If?" Colt interrupted. "She's been the target of three attacks in less than a week. What would you call that?"

"Unfortunate but not grounds for a protection detail."

Unfortunate? Colt seriously thought it might be worth having his ass thrown in jail for the pure satisfaction of planting his fist in the asshole's face but while it might satisfy him it would do nothing to help Cat. He tamped down his temper and tried another tact. "If we can't count on you for assistance in that area would you be willing to share information?"

"What sort of information?" Hernandez asked, hesitantly.

"Anything we can get. We need to know what we're up against if her protection is going to fall solely on us."

The agents looked at each other for a minute then Hernandez nodded at Morgan.

Morgan sank back into the chair he'd been occupying. "As you now know, Bookman was a contract killer. Recently he began getting his contracts through an organization called Gravestone - a placement firm for assassins, you might say. While we've been anxious to find Bookman, bringing down Gravestone is the Bureau's goal. They've been a tough nut to crack. We need a lot more info or someone on the inside if we're going to succeed."

"Are we talking *Murder, Incorporated*?" Colt asked. He remembered hearing stories about the historical enforcement arm of the Mafia.

"In a sense − yes. Although they fit the legal definition of organized crime, we haven't tied them to any of the known *'Families.'* They appear to be independent - entering into contracts with anyone they can determine to be legitimate clients and who are willing to pay their exorbitant fees."

"Gravestone has developed a reputation for completing jobs and doing them neatly. Professional hits with no traceable evidence to them or to the person who contracted the killing." Hernandez added. "We can assume that, in this case, the target is high profile. That appears to be Bookman's specialty − or rather was his specialty. Rumor has him earning an average of $2 million for each hit."

"I guess I should be flattered," Cat commented.

"You're more than likely considered collateral damage," Morgan responded offhandedly.

Cat felt like she'd been slapped. Next to her she felt

Colt's body tighten, restraining his anger. She could sympathize but their current focus was on getting information.

"You haven't had *any* success against these guys?" Cat asked.

"They're ghosts. Most of what we know is based on rumor and hearsay. Very little of it can be substantiated but what we can confirm tells us they are more than just a rumor and are very good at what they do. We haven't been able to get anyone inside the organization. We've attempted to place contracts with them but they've yet to take the bait. These guys are sharp and buried so deep the CIA could take lessons from them."

"How did you manage to link Bookman to them?" Rick asked.

"Can't tell you specifics. We were able to put him in the area of some hits - not at the scene but in the neighborhood. We were hoping this was our break."

Cat understood. They wanted the client along with Bookman. With either, they might have a link back to the group. Without them, they were dead in the water – and so was she.

"Believe me, if I knew who the other guy was, I'd tell you. Hopefully, Gravestone will eventually realize that and leave me alone."

Hernandez pushed back from the table. "If - and I repeat - *if* they're concerned about you and what you may have seen then I think it is highly unlikely that they would change course." He picked up his laptop signaling they were done. "Give us a call if anything else develops," Hernandez added as Rick escorted them from the room.

"Like a gator coughing up my remains?" Cat muttered to the agent's back.

Colt whipped her chair around and hauled her to her feet.

"*Nothing* is going to happen to you," he told her through clenched jaws. "Do you hear me?"

When she looked into his eyes she realized he wasn't just making a promise - he was looking for one. She nodded as he took her into his arms.

Rick returned to the conference room a short time later but he didn't enter. Instead, he waited in the doorway, silently watching the two inside. Cat was wrapped firmly in Colt's arms, his cheek resting against the top of her head. Since Colt's arrival on the island, he'd been steadily beating back his demons. Rick admired him for the strides he had made but they were small in comparison to the advances he'd witnessed since his friend had tripped over this fire-eating pixie. There was no option but to keep Cat safe because if they lost her, Rick was afraid they just might lose Colt as well.

20

The sun was setting when the trio finally extricated themselves from the police station and headed out to get something to eat. Colt followed Rick into the parking area behind a small Italian eatery.

"I called Mama," Rick said as he led them through the busy kitchen. "She has us set up in the private dining room."

"Your mother works here?" Cat asked, surprised.

"No," Rick answered with a smile. "Everyone calls the owner Mama."

But Cat didn't hear his response. She'd lost her train of thought the instant a man stepped through the doorway at the end of the short hall. Holy Chippendales! The guy was drop-dead-gorgeous. She stood speechless as he approached the threesome - wearing a grin that was probably illegal in several states. The man playfully punched Colt in the arm before giving Cat his full attention.

"I see you've found Tinkerbell," he stated, continuing to grin.

"Cat, this is my friend and partner, Gib."

Cat extended her hand to him. "Sorry about all the trouble."

"There's no such thing as trouble if it involves a beautiful woman." Gib accepted the hand she offered. The twinkle in his eye should have been a warning. Still, she was surprised when he used that hand to reel her in and plant a kiss firmly on her lips. The audacious act had her laughing before Colt could snatch her back. Charm oozed from the man's pores. His thick, blond mane was gathered at the base of his neck with a rawhide tie. A small ruby stud winked at her from the lobe of his left ear. Lashes most women would kill for framed his gray eyes. A wolf, she thought, and suspected that description probably wasn't far from the truth.

"Take her off your radar, Gib." Colt said, anchoring her to his side.

The possessive gesture wasn't lost on Gib. "It's about damn time," he said, wondering what was so special about this woman that had Colt breaking his self-imposed vow of celibacy.

Colt reached the door to the private dining room but stopped short of entering when he heard voices rumbling on the other side. He shot Gib a questioning look but it was Rick who answered.

"Just open the door, Captain. The cavalry has arrived."

As COLT STEPPED into the room, six men immediately stood at attention, simultaneously executing a crisp salute. Colt couldn't believe his eyes. Each man had served with him at one time or another – and he had not expected to see any of them again. Instinctively he returned the salute but before his arm could drop back to his side, the closest man pulled him into a brotherly embrace.

A distress call had been sent out, Cat thought as she watched the emotional reunion, and these men had answered it. She should have felt like an intruder but Gib and Rick had stayed at her side. Gib draped an arm leisurely over her shoulder while Rick's palm rested in the small of her back - both silent gestures that welcomed her into this band of friends. After the backslapping and name-calling came to an end, Colt turned in search of Cat. Those crystal blue eyes were beaming when they met hers and if his smile could have gotten any broader, she thought, it would reach his ears. He held out his hand, inviting her to his side.

CAT WAS DOING her best to field all the names and comments being thrown at her when a short, round woman burst into the room pulling a cart overflowing with aromatic food.

"Gibson!" the woman yelled.

"Yes, Ma'am?" Gib smiled. Mama always used his given name when she demanded his attention. She mothered every unattached male on the island and particularly liked to give Gib a hard time.

"Stop flirting with the pretty lady and come help me like a good boy," the woman commanded in a voice as rich in Italian as the food before her.

Gib rounded the table and touched the robust woman's cheek with a kiss. "I wouldn't dare flirt with her, Mama. She's with Colt." The announcement got the reaction he'd expected. For a big woman, Mama was across the room in the blink of an eye, holding Cat at arm's length.

The woman's close scrutiny was unnerving yet there was warmth flowing from her that Cat guessed put everyone at ease. Her short, wavy brown hair was streaked with gray. The wrinkles that etched her broad face indicated that she laughed — a lot. Rich, brown eyes sparkled with interest and amusement. The big woman's perusal was long and slow. The devil finally took hold of Cat's tongue. "Would you like to check my teeth while you're at it?" she asked, exposing her pearly whites in a Cheshire grin.

Mama snorted out a laugh as she gathered Cat into her softness. "She's the one," Mama stated emphatically looking at Colt.

"She's the one," Colt confirmed. He wasn't surprised by her quick summation. Mama had an uncanny way of knowing when someone showed up with his or her life's partner. How she knew was anybody's guess but the odds makers in Vegas wouldn't stand a chance betting against her.

"She's small," she said, gazing up and down the length of her, "but she give you healthy children."

"Now wait just a damn minute," Cat snapped.

"And she has a temper," Mama proclaimed, obviously impressed.

"I'll say," Rick agreed.

Mama glanced at the hand she still held and stroked the road rash on Cat's palms. The scratches from her fall to the mall's sidewalk were healing but the damage was still evident. Cat tried to pull away but Mama held tight.

"How she get this?"

"Somebody wants her silenced."

"And these handsome men are here to keep her safe?"

"Yes, ma'am," he answered, his pride evident. "I guess they are."

Mama nodded emphatically then shoved Cat back into Colt's arms, apparently satisfied. "Eat!" she ordered with a flair then exited the room with the now empty cart.

· · ·

ANTIPASTO, garlic bread, pasta, sauces, and bottles of wine, covered the checkered tablecloth. The food, along with bad jokes and amusing stories, was passed around the large table. Cat couldn't remember the last time she'd enjoyed sharing a meal as much as this one.

Colt was still having trouble believing these men, the James Gang, were here. He hadn't seen any of them in the years since he'd left the Army. Some for longer than that. Yet here they were, ready to go to battle for a man who didn't deserve their allegiance.

During the meal, he'd been surprised how quickly Cat, a self-professed loner, had fallen in with his friends - listening intently to their stories, laughing at their terrible jokes and matching their colorful language. What he wouldn't give to be here, *with this woman and these friends,* for reasons other than the one that had brought them together.

When the dishes were finally cleared the conversation turned to more serious matters. Cat sat quietly, listening to Colt recap the events of the past few days. It sounded like a bad plot from a cheap novel. She still had problems believing it was real.

"Our first priority is Cat's safety," Colt summarized. "Once we're certain of her security then we can work on finding the client and his intended target."

Rick had already compiled a short list of celebrities and dignitaries who lived on the islands. It consisted of a couple of best-selling authors, a former U.S. President as well as a former head of the CIA. The last two had enough security around them on a full-time basis that Rick felt they could be eliminated – at least for now. Tomorrow, he was expecting a report from FDLE identifying other prominent Southwest Florida residents who could be considered potential targets. Jason Waters had been successful in getting that much help.

The other angle Colt wanted to pursue was the real possibility that the target was, or would be, a visitor to the island. For security reasons, some resorts routinely notified the local authorities when they expected prominent guests but a few felt it a breach of privacy to do so. The team would need to contact resorts and hotels along the Southwest Florida coast to ask about any high caliber visitors that were currently staying in the area or were scheduled to arrive in the near future. The list of places where people could stay was extensive and Rick hadn't had the time to work on it because he'd been tied up following Bookman's trail – which, so far, had led nowhere.

"I'll continue to work on the list of residents," Rick stated, "but I could use some help with the resorts and hotels."

"Get us the info," Kevin Slawter volunteered. "Adam and I will get started on it in the morning."

Colt looked at the two men. Kevin had served with him during his twelve years in the Special Forces. He'd learned to trust the advice of the analytical thinker. He had also learned to appreciate his wicked sense of humor.

Adam Lightfoot, on the other hand, was the quiet member of the team - and the best in the business when it came to explosives. His Native American coloring often had him mistaken by other units as Afghani. But they were never able to use that feature to their advantage because, unlike the locals, the kid couldn't grow hair on his face worth a damn – which provided endless fodder for amusement among his teammates. The research would be boring work for these two but you wouldn't know it by their demeanor. If it helped to meet the team's objective, they never hesitated. Colt knew that was true of each man in the room.

"Use the department's name if it helps when you're making calls," Rick added. "As far as anyone's concerned, you're under contract to the Sanibel PD."

Bill Campbell and Jesse Martinez volunteered for the first shift at guard duty. They had arrived earlier in the day and had used the time to familiarize themselves with the grounds surrounding Colt's property. That fact hadn't surprised Colt. Both men liked leading the charge.

Bill was a marksman. He hadn't had the formal training of a Special Forces sniper but the number of enemy kills to his credit was noteworthy. Colt had recommended him for the Ranger's sniper school before their last mission together. He wondered if he'd been accepted.

Jesse was the creative one of the group. Bases they'd been stationed at were made pretty damned comfortable as a result of the Martinez touch. During one tour Jesse had commandeered a hot tub. No one knew how he'd come by it and everyone was smart enough not to ask. The base had all the amenities of a friggin' spa by the time they'd rotated out.

Almost in unison, Steve Brody and Don Volpe yawned. Colt decided it was time to call it a night. All the men could use some rest but these two, in particular, needed some sleep if they were going to be effective. They'd been in South America when Rick had reached them. They'd quickly arranged leave, getting on the next flight back to the states. Colt was aware they hadn't slept in the last forty-eight hours except for the few minutes they'd managed on the flight north.

If there had been a highway across the Strait of Florida, Colt knew that Steve would have been behind the wheel - and would have probably beaten the plane back. If the term "wheel man" were still in fashion then it would apply to the solidly built soldier. Brody could maneuver a vehicle through any type of terrain, be it mountains or cities - and at speeds that would make a NASCAR driver cringe.

Don had been their resident geek. Probably still was, for that matter. Like the others he was trained for combat but his true talent was computers. Given enough time Colt guessed he could hack into anything.

"Is there an extra computer I can use?" Cat asked as they stood. "My I-pad is toast and I want to check local on-line business magazines as well as the archives of the business and society sections of the local papers."

She could read Colt's unspoken question. "The suit that guy was wearing cost a bundle. My money says he's an executive, a member of society - or both. If I'm right, he may have had his picture in a local publication at some point."

"But you didn't get a good look at him," Colt reminded her.

"No, I didn't. And, yes, it's a long shot. But I might spot something in a photo that will strike a chord – size, weight, or posture." She looked at Colt, and sighed. "I need to do something. I'm not going to sit around all day doing nothing."

"We've photographed a number social and business functions in the area," Gib suggested. "Maybe there's something in our studio files."

"Can I start on them in the morning?"

"I'll set it up first thing."

COLT LED the caravan of vehicles back to his place. With the exception of Rick, who had some work to finish up at the station, the rest of the team was behind him. Those who weren't on watch tonight would be bunking at Gib's. Colt glanced over at Cat. She'd been staring out the passenger window since they'd left the restaurant.

"You okay?" he asked. He'd been surprised she hadn't been more vocal about their plans to keep her under wraps. Her silence worried him.

Cat turned toward him. His sharp masculine features were accentuated by the lighting from the dash. "You expected a fight on this, didn't you?"

"Your movements are going to be restricted - and we both know how much you like taking orders."

"Arguing would have been tacky. Your friends have gone out of their way to help. I won't make things difficult for them."

Colt pulled up behind the studio. "Does that mean you'll do what I tell you from now on?" he asked, smiling.

She huffed a "you wish" then reached for the door handle before stopping, remembering the need to wait for the required escort.

By the time Colt came around the vehicle, Adam and Kevin had joined him - semi-automatic pistols in each man's hand. They surrounded her as they went up the stairs. Adam stopped to check around the doorframe before nodding an all clear. Cat had no idea what he was looking for and figured it was probably just as well. They were overdoing the bodyguard routine in her opinion and almost said so but when she noted their stern expressions she decided against it.

The others had remained at the base of stairs, all eyes scanning the vicinity, until Colt unlocked the door to his unit. Then, in unison, they picked up their gear and headed up the steps to stow their things at Gib's. Not a single word had been spoken since their arrival. It was as if they communicated by telepathy.

"I'd like to walk the grounds with you before anybody hits the sack," Colt addressed his former team members who were now gathered in his living room. "You'll stay with Cat until I get back?"

Gib nodded.

"I can make up the bed in your office," Cat suggested when the men passed through the kitchen where she was starting a pot of coffee. "There's no point in everyone crowding into Gib's." The place had two bedrooms. The second one doubled as an office but for the occasional guest – which everyone who lived in Florida eventually had - Colt had installed a Murphy bed.

The corners of Colt's mouth twitched up and she'd have sworn his eyes actually twinkled but he didn't say a word. If this was a test of her telepathic capabilities she was failing miserably.

"What?" she asked.

"They need their rest," he explained as he approached her.

"Yes," she answered slowly – eyeing him with suspicion. Obviously, she was missing something. "That would be the purpose in sleeping."

Colt continued to smile. How the woman could be such a hellion in bed but so naive in matters of intimacy surprised him. Maybe that was one reason he found her so appealing. Leaning close so only Cat could hear, he whispered, "You're a screamer."

21

Gib lounged on the sofa with his feet propped on the coffee table. He'd been talking non-stop since they'd sat down. 'Glib', Cat decided, might be a more appropriate nickname for the man. She was convinced that her first impression of him was dead on. He was a charmer of Olympic proportions but in spite of his playboy persona she could sense the depth to his character. His presence here, as well as his concern for his friend, spoke volumes. Cat found it easy to like him. Still, the conversation faded to the back of Cat's mind as she looked toward the rear of the unit again. Gib tapped her arm. "I must be losing my touch if I can't hold my own against a door."

"Sorry," she said, managing a smile.

"He's fine, Cat," he stated, all joking aside. "Those guys know what they're doing."

"That obvious, huh?" She offered him a grateful look. "While I appreciate your company I am sorry you got stuck with the babysitting duties."

"What? You think I'd prefer being outside with a bunch of sweaty guys to sharing a room with a pretty woman?"

"I imagine you could find something else to do." Or *someone* else, Cat was tempted to add. If not for his allegiance to Colt, she guessed that he would rather be sharing an entirely different type room with another woman at the moment.

"It's weird," she admitted softly as she looked toward the kitchen again. "I've never been the clinging type - prided myself on being the opposite, actually. But suddenly I find myself feeling lost when the man leaves the room." Cat's eyes grew heavy while she considered the significance of that statement and the fact that she'd just confessed the astonishing fact to a man she'd met only hours before.

"She's asleep," Gib announced softly as he met Colt in the kitchen. "I couldn't talk her into hitting the sack. She insisted on waiting up for you. Stubborn, isn't she?"

Colt looked into the living room where Cat was curled up on the sofa. "Once she gets something in her head it'd be easier to turn a tank than to change her mind."

Gib heard the admiration in his friend's voice, "And you love it."

"Yeah," he admitted with a smile, "I do." He took another look at the sleeping woman before stepping back into the kitchen with Gib. "She's had it rough. It's toughened her."

"Rick gave us the rundown on Montgomery."

"Did he also tell you that her dad used to beat the crap out of her until she managed to escape him?" Since Cat had no idea where her father might be, Colt had shared that ugly history with Rick as well. Although he thought it unlikely, the information might have proved relevant. As it turned out, they were dealing with a professional killer so her personal history didn't factor into her current problems.

"Son of a bitch," Gib muttered. He delighted in members of the opposite sex. Damn near worshipped them. He couldn't abide anyone who would abuse a woman.

"I don't think he's an issue anymore but Montgomery's a different story." He turned to Gib. "When this is behind us I plan to find the bastard and have a little talk with him."

The invitation was clear. "Just let me know when."

CAT DIDN'T BAT an eye as Colt carried her into the bedroom and laid her on their bed. *Their* bed – not his, he thought. He'd made up his mind on the return trip from the Keys that she wouldn't be going back to the Panhandle to live. As soon as this chaos was behind them, they'd head upstate, pack her things and move her in with him. Oh, she'd argue and he realized he was looking forward to that debate. But she belonged here with him. He was coming dangerously close to slipping into what Cat referred to as his caveman persona. He'd have to be careful how he presented his plan.

Cat stretched against the cool sheets. "I fell asleep."

"It would seem so," he said as he started to unbutton her blouse. "Let's get you out of these clothes."

"You're always trying to undress me. Why is that?" she asked, now fully awake.

"Apparently," he said as he slipped her jeans over her hips, "you need a reminder."

Sometime later, sweaty and thoroughly replete, Colt rolled on to his back and laughed. "I told you that you were a screamer."

"Me? I'm surprised the guys aren't knocking the door down after that shout out."

"Believe me, Kitten, they know the difference."

She snuggled up against him, absently running her fingers over his chest.

"You're a very lucky man."

He touched his lips to her hair. "Yes, I am."

She swatted him playfully. "I'm talking about your friends."

He thought about the men who had gathered at Mama's tonight. "I still can't believe those guys are here."

"Why not? It's obvious how they feel about you. Why wouldn't they be here?"

Colt stilled. Judgment day, he lamented. Throwing the covers aside he sat on the edge of the bed, resting his head in his hands. This conversation was long overdue. He'd known all along that he couldn't ask Cat to be a part of his future without telling her about his past. Knowing it and doing it were two different things though.

As he stepped into his jeans he tossed Cat her robe. His robe actually, but since the first time she'd wrapped it around her, it seemed to hold her scent. He no longer thought of it as his. "We need to talk."

Cat clutched the garment to her chest as she watched Colt lumber from the room. An overwhelming sense of sadness lingered behind. What could have happened to cause him such pain?

She found him sitting in one of the overstuffed chairs in the living room. She realized it was the first time she'd seen him occupy one of the armchairs. He'd always taken a spot on the sofa. She suspected that was because he could tuck her up against him. Apparently, he felt the need for some distance tonight. She noted he'd already consumed half a bottle of beer, although guzzled would probably be a more accurate description.

"I could use a cigarette," he said with a smirk, "and I've never smoked." Instead he titled his head back and finished off the bottle.

Cat studied his silhouette. Backlit by the light he'd left burning in the kitchen, you could easily see his muscles knotted with tension.

"Colt, are you sure you want to talk about it?" Whatever *it* was.

"Hell, no, I don't want to talk about it but that doesn't mean you don't need to hear it. I should have told you sooner. It will probably change things between us." And that thought, he admitted, was the reason his brow was covered with sweat. He'd accepted the fact that he'd have to live with the consequences of his failure but if it cost him Cat…

"I don't believe that," Cat stated firmly. The loyalty of his friends and the respect he'd quickly earned from Jason spoke volumes. They all knew his history. Whatever this was about, it was a cross only he felt the need to bear.

Too restless to sit, Colt found his way to the window. Though the blinds were drawn, he still sought out the darkness. "During my last tour…" he started, and then had trouble finding the words. It took every ounce of courage that remained but he turned to look into her eyes. "Innocent people died because of me."

Well, that was certainly putting it succinctly, Cat thought, but she knew it wasn't that simple and she didn't consider for a second that Colt would intentionally harm guiltless people. "Explain," she said curtly, "because I don't believe you went on a killing rampage."

"Just as bad." He hadn't spoken of that night since he'd opened up to Gib. His friend had needed to know the type of person he was getting for a business partner. When Colt had finished his telling of the events, Gib had simply told him he might want to rethink things then turned back to the blue prints they'd been discussing. Now Colt looked into the eyes of the woman he loved and tried to judge her reaction as he told the horrid truth.

"We were on patrol, checking out local villages. We'd visited this particular village a number of times. Brought candy to the kids. Played soccer with some of the older boys. Met with the village elders. These people didn't like the Taliban. I'd have bet a year's pay they wouldn't have anything to do with them. The intelligence backed this up. Still, we were cautious. We were always cautious. You learned not to take chances even if the villagers were friendly."

"What happen?" Cat asked when Colt went silent.

"We followed protocol. Studied the village and surrounding area from a rocky outcropping. Children played. Women washed clothes. Men gathered in discussion. Everything looked normal. But as we approached on foot, I realized that something was off. Yes, the children were playing but there was no energy to their play - no laughter. The adult men stood together in apparent conversation but the gesturing and animation that normally accompanied their debates was missing. Almost simultaneously, I noticed there weren't any of the older boys - no young men, in sight. I had just signaled my men to halt when one of the children – a young girl - broke away from the others. Barreling toward us she shouted a warning to take cover. She was gunned down for her efforts." Colt could still see the determination and fear on the child's face as she ran toward him. A face that still visited him in the middle of the night.

"Oh my God." Cat fought back tears as she asked, "I

can't imagine how horrible it would be to witness the death of a child but how is it your fault?"

"Not *a* child, Cat. *Children*." He saw the shock then the unspoken question on her face. "No, not one of them dead by our hands yet my hands are still covered with their blood."

"I don't understand."

"The whole thing was a Taliban trap. Somehow they'd known a patrol would be coming by. They'd snuck into the village the night before taking the young men hostage. The villagers were given a choice - cooperate or every boy would die. The people of the village had been told how to act, what to do, when the time came." Colt forced himself to breathe. He hated reliving that day. Hated even more that he had to share the ugliness with Cat.

"When things didn't go according to their plan, the enemy adjusted. They didn't waste ammunition on us. Instead, they ordered us to surrender. Shoved a couple of the boys they'd been holding hostage out into the open then shot them in the back. The killing would continue, they shouted, until we gave up our arms. That wasn't going to happen. We're trained for hostage situations but this one was unique. Everyone was so spread out." Colt's stomach tightened as he relived the moment when he knew more would die before they could put a stop to it. "Bill and I immediately took out the boy's shooters. But the hostages weren't being held together. It took time to locate them all. Too damn much time." He turned to Cat. "Children were slaughtered. Parents died protecting their young. I can still hear them crying out to us. Begging us for help."

Cat couldn't imagine the horror of what he'd witnessed. "But you did help. You did stop it. How many lives did you save that day?"

"No one should have died. No one! It was a set up. I should have known!"

"How?"

"It was my job to know! I should have questioned the intelligence."

She joined him at the window and took hold of his hand. She wasn't surprised that his palm was covered in sweat. "Finish the story, Colt."

"Not much more to tell. There was an investigation."

"You were cleared?"

"Yes."

"Yet you resigned?"

"I didn't trust my judgment after that. Why should anyone else? Innocent people died that day."

Cat wished she were big enough to knock some sense into him. He'd done nothing wrong but let something eat at him that wasn't his fault. Yes, innocent people had died. Shamefully – sadly - it happened all too often. But Colt had placed all the blame on his own shoulders. God, what a burden to bear. And in this case - an unnecessary one.

"Do you remember when you carried me up here after the attack at the mall? Do you remember what I told you then?"

What the hell was she talking about? It wasn't likely he'd ever forget the events of that day but what did it have to do with this?

"Let me refresh your memory," she continued. "*Get over yourself!* You are not responsible for me. You were not responsible for the lack of intelligence you received. You are not responsible for everything that goes wrong in this world. Get it? No matter how close you are to shit when it happens it isn't always within our control to change the outcome. You did everything you could to stop it, didn't you?"

"People are dead - because of me!"

"That's bullshit!" She shook her head in disbelief. "They're dead because terrorists used children to lure good, honest men to their deaths. They're dead because religious fanatics forced us to chase them halfway around the world. They're dead because evil exists - even in remote Afghan villages."

"Do you think if you hadn't shown up that day that those children would still be alive? The Taliban would have just waited for another opportunity, another patrol, and you know it. And because you and your men are good at what you do you stopped them that day. You stopped them before they had the chance to try the same tactic again and even more innocent lives were lost."

"Should you have known? Did you have reason to doubt your intelligence? No, or you would have questioned it. You placed your faith in a system that you trusted – a system that had worked in the past - just as I trusted the courts to put that bastard, Montgomery, away. You told me it wasn't my fault those women had been assaulted. That it was the system that had failed them. Well, you're no more culpable than I was."

Colt stared at her not sure how to react to her anger.

"Is that the reason you cut yourself off from your friends?" Of course it was, she immediately realized. "You're an idiot. You know that, don't you? I'd give my right arm to have friends like those men in my life. Don't you think you've been wearing that hair shirt long enough?"

"They suffered through one of the most horrid days of their lives because of my decisions. I don't deserve their friendship."

Cat couldn't help it. She actually rolled her eyes. It was hard to understand how someone so intelligent could be so dense. "They're not just your friends. They love you." She saw him flinch. "Yeah, I know. Not exactly a manly term but that's what I saw tonight. They believe in you. Those men came from God knows where on little notice, willing to stand between me and a bullet - because of you. They don't know me. They came because of you. What do you call that if not love and trust?"

She was livid now. "You surprise me, Colt. I didn't have you pegged for someone who would wallow in self-pity. You're right about one thing, though. This does change things between us. I refuse to load any more crap into that backpack of guilt you seem to be so fond of carrying around. What happens if everything you do isn't enough to stop Gravestone from getting to me?" She held up her hand, silencing him. "Are you going to condemn yourself because you weren't smarter, faster or stronger than the bad guys? Well, here's a news flash for you - I'm taking that possibility off the table. As of this second I am no longer your responsibility. I'm outta here."

Sure, her chances of surviving this mess were significantly better with Colt and his team in her corner but she'd be damned if she'd add to his already overloaded conscience. Besides, she was used to going her own way. She'd manage. She'd have to.

Colt followed her down the hall then stared as Cat stripped a pillowcase off one of the pillows and began stuffing it with her belongings. "What do you think you're doing?" he asked, dismayed.

"A little slow in that department, too, Colt? It's called packing."

"You can't go," he said, his voice cold.

"The hell I can't," she snapped back. "When will you get it through that thick skull of yours that I don't take orders from you?"

"You said you'd stay."

"I've changed my mind. I'll take my chances." She stopped, locking eyes with him. "*My* chances, Colt. *Mine!* I'm responsible for me. You are not. Can't you understand that concept?"

Cat slammed the bathroom door shut before Colt was halfway across the room. He thought about forcing his way in but he had enough sense remaining to know strong-arming Cat wasn't going to work. What the hell was he supposed to do?

He dropped heavily onto the bed. Cat's reaction had blindsided him. She hadn't offered consolation as so many of his friends and family had done. She hadn't held him accountable. Instead she was several degrees past furious for his assumption of blame.

Then she'd thrown his own argument back in his face. When Rick had told her that Montgomery had attacked and raped those women, she'd initially seen the assaults as her failing. She'd been ready to place the responsibility for them squarely on her own shoulders for not being successful in putting that asshole away. She'd had no more control over the judicial system than he'd initially had over the enemy that day. She'd quickly been able to recognize that fact. Maybe she was right – maybe he was a little slow.

"Cat? Can we talk about this?" he asked loud enough to be heard through the still closed door. When it opened a minute later his heart sank. Now dressed in jeans and a t-shirt she pulled the stuffed pillowcase behind her.

"Would it do any good?" she asked. "Beating yourself up over what happened serves no purpose other than to make you miserable – it never has and it never will." Her anger had dissipated as she'd cleared the vanity of her things. Emotionally exhausted, she sat down beside him. The pillowcase settled at her feet.

"You're the first person to accuse me of self-pity. I accepted it as..."

"As what? Penance? You have no reason to do penance. I may not have known you long but I know you well enough to be convinced that you did all that you could that day. Your friends know that, too, or they wouldn't be here. It's past time you did. If you feel the need to atone for something why don't you do something positive instead of punishing yourself?"

He looked at her curiously, "Like what?"

Cat didn't have to think hard to come up with a suggestion. "Find an orphanage near that village. I understand they're all over Afghanistan. See what can be done to make things a little better for the children there."

Colt stared back at her. Had he been so wrapped up in his own guilt that he'd been blind to something so simple? A slow smile spread across his face. "We could do that."

Cat grinned when she saw the spark return to his eyes. "I know we could." And she knew just the guys to reach out to for help.

Cautiously, Colt lifted her "luggage" off the floor. "Does that mean you're staying?"

The odds of getting through this without his help were slim but that wasn't the reason she wanted to stay. She simply wanted to be with Colt. Until she'd met him, she hadn't been aware that anything was missing in her life. She'd been relatively happy. The few relationships she'd been involved in had been comfortable but never serious. When they were over – there'd been no harm, no foul. This was different and, she finally admitted, worth the risk.

"Do you want to help me unpack?"

"I'd rather help you undress," he said, smiling.

22

Feeling better than he had in years, Colt stood at the entrance to his kitchen rubbing a towel against his damp hair. Last night the woman currently standing at the stove, adeptly flipping hotcakes, had told him that he was a lucky man. He would no longer argue that point. Even with the dark cloud currently hanging over their heads, he still couldn't remember the last time he felt this damn good.

As he crossed the room, he acknowledged Jesse and Bill who were seated at the corner table, then wrapped his arms around Cat's waist. Pulling her back against him, he waited until she finished turning the pancakes on the griddle then tipped her head up and settled his mouth on hers.

Colt took his time, relishing the taste of her. When he finally released her she was flushed, hot and breathing heavily. The kiss had been both possessive and searing - and in full view of two virtual strangers. She wasn't accustomed to public displays of affection and the two men in the corner were grinning at her like Cheshire Cats.

"Did I embarrass you?" Colt asked, watching the color rise in her cheeks.

"Not in the least," Jesse piped up.

"You'll get used to them," Colt said, trying to reassure her when her color deepened.

"Yeah, we grow on you," Bill said.

"Like a fungus," Jesse added.

Cat glanced up at their infectious grins and gave herself a quick lecture. She had no reason to be embarrassed. If she had succumbed to her desire to make love to Colt on the kitchen table there might have been cause. They'd just shared a kiss - a deep, demanding, toe-tingling kiss. She glanced at the three men and could see their eyes sparkle with mischief. They'd discovered a weak spot and they knew it. She'd better develop a thick skin and fast.

"Any problems last night?" Colt asked, turning his attention to his friends.

"Other than fighting off those bloodsucking vampires you call mosquitoes, it was quiet," Bill informed him.

"What are the chances we could set up a blind in that jungle next door?" Jesse asked, indicating the neighbor's yard.

The lush tropical garden would be an ideal place to keep an eye on his property. The sniper would probably think so as well which was all the more reason to hold that terrain. "I'll talk to them but I don't think it will be a problem." In any event, Colt needed to make the Copeland's aware of the situation. He might suggest that they take that trip they'd been talking about to visit their daughter and grandchildren in Atlanta. He didn't want to see them caught up in this mess.

Bill and Jesse finished their breakfast then headed to Gib's to get some sleep. Alone, Colt turned his full attention to Cat as she worked. She seemed comfortable in his kitchen. Apparently, she had a domestic side. He wondered how many other facets there were to this woman he had yet to discover. He'd seen her fight like an alley cat, put a couple of FBI agents in their place and make love to him with such passion that he felt it to his core. She didn't realize it yet but he intended to spend the rest of his life exploring all the things that made her Cat.

"We need groceries," she told him as she set a stack of hotcakes along with several strips of bacon in front of Colt. "I assume shopping isn't on my list of approved activities?" His scowl confirmed the assumption.

"I'll get a couple of the guys to make a run to the store. Why don't you put together a…"

She slapped the grocery list on the table along with most of the remaining cash from her wallet. Normally, she'd reel at the notion of being stuck in the kitchen cooking for a bunch of men so she was surprised that she was actually enjoying this portion of her captivity.

Colt folded the cash and tucked it back into Cat's hand. "Thanks, Kitten, but Jason insisted on wiring money for expenses."

Wouldn't that be just like Jason? "I'll thank him later but I still want you to keep this. Please? Tell the guys to buy some cigars or beer or something they'd enjoy. My treat. I need to do this, Colt."

Colt clasped her hand and tugged her down until their lips met. He understood her need to contribute. She wasn't one to depend on others and having others carry the load for her didn't sit well. They wouldn't spend her money but she didn't have to know that just yet. "I'll tell them."

THEY MADE A GOOD TEAM, Colt decided, when they managed to clean up the kitchen without getting in each other's way. Afterward, he took Cat down to the studio. Gib had set up one of the computers so she could view pictures in a slideshow format. He'd already uploaded hundreds of photos and there would be more when he and Adam returned. Gib had several professional photographers they wanted to visit on their way to stock up on groceries. That should keep Cat busy for at least a couple of days. While he didn't think her search would yield results he welcomed anything that would keep her mind off her confinement.

Before he left to meet with Rick, he spent a few minutes with Kevin who was already working the phone, contacting hotels and resorts from the list Rick had supplied. Kevin would be Cat's shadow until relieved.

THE SILENCE that accompanied him on the way to the police station was a stark reminder that Colt was alone for the first time in days. Since his last tour he'd craved solitude but in a very short period of time he'd grown accustomed to having Cat at his side. He liked having her close enough to touch. Close enough to see those big brown eyes sparkle with laughter or her ears turn red with temper. He figured that he was probably a little sick but he couldn't deny the way he felt when she was near.

When Colt arrived at the police station, he found Rick in his small office, scowling at his computer monitor.

"What's going on?"

"Nothing. Not a goddamn thing." The list Rick had received from FDLE had added nothing to what he already knew. "I was hoping FDLE would give me a name that would send up red flags but they couldn't add one single person to the list I'd already developed."

"Any chance one of them could be the target?"

"Not likely. The local authors might have a critic or two but I can't imagine anyone disliking their writing enough to hire a hit man. Our former President has secret service protection. Besides he won't be back in the area until Thanksgiving and the ex-CIA chief has more spooks around him than the Haunted Mansion at Disney World. No one's getting to him."

"Could FDLE be holding back?"

"For what purpose? There's no reason for them to keep that kind of intel to themselves."

Colt couldn't argue that point. "What about the guy that tried to grab Cat at the mall? Any word on him?"

"Nothing. You know as well as I do that he was probably chum before the day was out. Nobody could screw up that badly and live to tell about it - not based on what we know about that organization."

While Colt took some pleasure in picturing the bastard as shark bait, alive he would have been a lead. "Where'd they find somebody like that anyway? They're supposed to be professionals and he had amateur written all over him."

"Subcontractor would be my guess. I just can't believe a fuck-up like that worked for this group. They're too careful."

"Or he had nothing to do with our current problem."

"Don't open that can of worms, Colt. We can't keep the lid on this one."

Wasn't that the truth? "If you're right then maybe we can interest them in subcontracting again."

Rick knew where this was heading. "It would be highly unlikely they'd try it again. I wouldn't be surprised if there was a standing order to kill anyone who considered it," Rick said, not entirely joking.

"What about one of your old collars? Is there anyone

here or in Chicago who might have a way of getting somebody with my skills a contract with the organization?"

"If the FBI can't infiltrate the group what makes you think we could arrange it? Besides, contrary to what you believe, your history is too damned clean for you to be suspected of going over to the Dark Side."

Rick's editorial comment reminded Colt of his conversation with Cat the night before. "I told Cat about Afghanistan last night."

Rick didn't know what to say. It was the first time he'd heard Colt mention the country since his return. Whenever Rick broached the subject of that last mission, Colt would shut down. Now he was voluntarily talking about it?

"And?" he asked hesitantly.

"She was furious. Almost walked out."

"Cat?" Rick couldn't believe he'd misjudged her that badly.

"Yeah, she was pretty damned pissed that I had blamed myself for what happened."

Rick was shocked into silence a second time. "*Had?*" He couldn't believe that Colt had actually used the past tense. He'd been in Chicago when the dreadful mission occurred but he'd heard every detail from guys that were on the scene that horrible day. The deaths of those children and villagers did not lie at Colt's feet. If anything, his actions had saved lives that otherwise would have been lost. They'd taken out the enemy then began triage while they waited for Medevac to aid the survivors. One of those injured was a toddler, a little girl no more than three years of age. Colt had carried the child in his arms as he continued to comb the village searching for the wounded - his large hand remaining tightly wrapped around her tiny arm, stemming the flow of blood. She'd survived but the remainder of her family had been lost. Too many had died that day and no one had been able to dissuade Colt of his culpability. Had Cat finally reached him?

"To paraphrase," Colt continued, "I could either learn the difference between guilt and grief or she was leaving before she added to my guilt complex. Watching her shove her belongings into a pillowcase while she tore into me about self-pity and god fantasies was an awakening. You become a quick learner when you see your future walking out the door."

"A pillowcase?" Rick laughed. Self-pity and god fantasies? Man, he wished he'd been there to see that.

Now that the crisis had passed, Colt could find humor in the scene. "I'm not sure our combined forces could have stopped her if she'd followed through on her threat to leave. She had one hell of a head of steam built up." Then he added solemnly, "We're going to find an orphanage near that village. See what we can do to help them."

Rick nodded, "I imagine she'd have the connections. Let me know what I can do to help."

"Connections?" Colt asked, surprised. "Why would Cat have connections to orphanages in Afghanistan?"

Rick realized immediately that Cat hadn't shared information with Colt that Jason had so proudly passed on. His friend's ringing cell phone saved Rick from answering the question.

"Hang on," Colt said to the caller after listening for a couple of seconds. He handed the phone to Rick. "It's Kevin. Apparently there's some big conference coming up at the South Seas Resort."

After getting Kevin's rundown on what he'd discovered, Rick tossed the phone back to Colt. "Let's go," he said as he headed toward the door. "We just went from having no targets to having a boat load of them."

23

R ick had not met the new head of security for South
Seas Resort and he was beginning to wonder if he
ever would. They'd been waiting for him to make an
appearance for the last thirty minutes. Ralph Cordella was
aware they were waiting. Rick had overheard his assistant
call to advise him of their arrival. Apparently, he wasn't in
any particular hurry to make their acquaintance.

It was customary for the resorts located on the two
islands to notify the Sanibel PD when a large or important
event was going to take place. Unlike Sanibel, Captiva was
not an incorporated city and, therefore, fell under the jurisdiction of the Lee County Sheriff's Office but the majority
of Captiva's visitors had to travel the length of Sanibel
through Blind Pass to reach this island. Because of that
fact, Sanibel authorities were normally kept abreast of any
significant event on the island.

The luxurious South Seas Island Resort covered the
northern tip of Captiva. It was by far the largest resort on
either island. Since Rick's arrival on Sanibel, he'd seen
more dignitaries pass through its doors than he'd seen in all

his years in Chicago. The tropical islands were a magnet for the rich and famous. Now, it appeared, in a few weeks, politicians, celebrities, environmentalists and businessmen would be descending on the resort. Any one of them could be the target. If Kevin hadn't picked up on the resort's evasiveness and kept pushing, Rick still wouldn't have known about the event.

Colt paced the perimeter of the office where they'd been sequestered, his patience just about gone. This place might hold the answers they'd been looking for and some jerk was keeping them waiting like kids in a principal's office. He was considering going on the offensive to hunt the guy down when the office door opened. A tall, thin, reed of a man quickly took a seat behind the desk. His salt-n-pepper hair had Colt estimating him to be in his late forties or early fifties. After taking his time to pull up something on his computer, he finally acknowledged their presence.

"I don't see where we had an appointment."

Rick dropped his badge on the computer keyboard. "I don't need an appointment. We're here to ask you some questions regarding the environmental conference that's scheduled to take place here in a couple of weeks."

"And why is it any of your business?"

Rick put on his best public servant face. "Perhaps you're unaware that both the Sanibel PD and the Lee County Sheriff's office are generally notified of large gatherings. Especially those when people of prominence are in attendance." Rick had checked with the Sheriff's office on their way to Captiva and confirmed that they had not received any notice of the upcoming conference.

"I was made aware of the previous practice. The Sheriff's office will be notified in due time. As for the Sanibel police, what happens at this resort doesn't concern them."

Rick's eyebrows rose. "Have you spoken with your General Manager about your decision to keep us out of the loop?"

"As head of security it's my decision to make."

Rick knew he was wasting his time. It was obvious he wasn't going to get anywhere with the pompous ass but he made the attempt anyway. "I'd like a list of those attending the conference. We have reason to believe that one of the attendees may be in danger."

"You can't expect me to release that information. Our guests value their privacy."

"Do they value their lives?" Colt snapped.

"I think we're done here," the security chief said, rising from his chair. "If you'll excuse me, I'm already late for a meeting."

Rick quickly blocked the man's path. "Can we assume that most of the attendees will be arriving at the resort via private or rental cars?" There were three ways to access this part of the island - by boat, helicopter or, as most did, via the two-lane Sanibel-Captiva Road that passed through Sanibel.

Cordella eyed him suspiciously. "Why are you asking?"

"You might want to warn your guests that there may be traffic delays around the time of the conference. I expect that we'll be setting up a sobriety checkpoint at Blind Pass starting on... What was the date the conference is scheduled to start?"

"You wouldn't dare."

DESPITE THE WALL they'd hit with Cordella, Colt was in good spirits when he pulled up behind his unit. Rick's threat had rattled the man but instead of folding, the stubborn SOB had ordered them from his office. Still, they were making progress and the thought of seeing Cat again went a long way toward lifting his mood.

As he entered the kitchen, the sight before him made him smile. Slices of bread topped with sandwich meat, cheese, lettuce and tomato covered the countertop. Cat was making a last pass, topping off each sandwich with another slice of bread in the makeshift assembly line. Adam and Gib sat at the table, nursing beers. He acknowledged his friends while making a beeline for the woman at the counter. Then he did what he'd been thinking about doing since he'd left her this morning. Dipping his head, he covered her lips with his. His aggravation at Cordella, his worry about Cat's safety, all his concerns disappeared as he feasted on her mouth. Only the sound of someone clearing their throat reminded him that they had an audience. He nipped at her lip one last time then stepped away before he was tempted to carry her off to finish what he'd started.

"I figured you'd all be downstairs," he commented as he opened the refrigerator to retrieve his own beer.

"We talked Cat into making lunch," Gib explained but Colt knew there was more to their presence than filling their stomachs. No one would be leaving Cat alone.

"Kevin's still downstairs if you're looking for him," Cat added.

"Did he tell you guys that he might have found the key to our mystery?" Colt told them about the upcoming conference at the South Seas Resort.

"I went out with a girl who works in their Marketing Department," Gib said as he reached for his cell phone.

"Is there anybody on the islands you haven't dated?" Colt asked, smiling.

"Cat," Gib said grinning, "and I'm working on her."

Cat eavesdropped on the conversation between Gib and his friend at South Seas Resort. What she heard reinforced her assessment of his charm. The man had it in spades. God, if she could just find a way to bottle it, she'd be a rich woman.

"See you shortly," Gib said, ending the call. He eyed the tray of sandwiches still sitting on the counter. "Do you plan on sharing those, Tink?" he asked, using the nickname he'd tagged her with the evening before. "I may need the fuel."

Cat shook her head as she placed the platter of sandwiches on the table in front of the men. "I wouldn't want to be responsible for your loss of stamina."

WHILE GIB WAS OUT "DOING" public relations, Colt worked in his home office trying to dig up information on Gravestone. He had settled Cat in the studio to view more event photos. Kevin and Adam were downstairs contacting the remaining hotels on Rick's list. The South Seas Resort event looked promising but to assume they'd found their target area would have been a fool's assumption. A meeting of that magnitude could also provide the perfect distraction a professional killer needed. Until they had confirmation of their suspicions, they'd continue to check other options.

Colt struck out with regard to finding substantiated data on Gravestone. That didn't surprise him considering what the Feds had revealed. There were numerous references on the Internet to the organization but none could be classified as anything more than urban legend.

Abandoning that angle for the time being, he researched and found several job posting sites that looked promising. Despite Rick's opinion to the contrary, he'd decided to market his skills with a rifle. He suspected that most individuals seeking similar work through these sites were honest individuals looking for legal but high paying security jobs. However, if Gravestone recruited using any of these sites, they just might take the bait.

He finished placing his embellished job history on the web then began surfing for information about the conference. Holy Terra was the organization hosting the three-day event. They were a relatively new, but powerful, not-for-profit environmental group. The founders, a Catholic bishop, a noted scientist and a rock star, made such odd bedfellows that their partnership attracted considerable media attention. The group appeared to be extremely adept at using that attention to their advantage - building a very large and active following in a short period of time. They'd also become quite skilled at using their celebrity status to raise awareness about issues affecting the environment.

Considering the group's expert use of the media, Colt was surprised to find only a passing comment about the South Seas conference. Apparently, it wasn't open to the general public. That led Colt to wonder if the caliber of attendees was so high that security was an issue. Before he could investigate further, his cell phone buzzed.

"I just got off the phone with the South Seas' employment office," Rick started in. "I went around Cordella and scanned a photo of Bookman to their Human Resources manager. We hit pay dirt. Bookman was a new hire using the name, Mark Leighton. He was scheduled to begin orientation on Monday and would have started work in Guest Services the following week – the week before the opening of the conference."

Pay dirt was right. They were obviously on the right track. Colt informed Rick of Gib's attempt to get a list of attendees.

"As soon as he gets back, call me." Rick paused for a

minute. "Now that we have something concrete on Book-man, the FBI will be back in the picture as fast as their nondescript sedans can get them here. I figure we have anywhere from three to twelve hours before they descend on us en masse."

"The conference could be cancelled when the organization gets wind of the threat."

"The Feds will do everything they can to make sure that doesn't happen. They've been waiting a long time for an opportunity like this."

"Still, the hit could be called off if Gravestone thinks the target is compromised. That could take Cat out of the crosshairs."

"You know as well as I do that that's unlikely unless the contract is time sensitive and they miss their window of opportunity. Then yeah, maybe. But we don't have any idea if they're on a timetable. There's also the possibility that they might make the attempt regardless of the security. If they do, whether they succeed or not, our problem still exists."

"Things are going to get pretty hot around here and I can't see them letting this become their Waterloo." Colt found it hard to believe they'd take the chance of exposing the organization. They'd gone to extremes to keep it under the radar.

"If it were my team, I'd agree. I'd cut my losses, fold up shop and get on the first plane out of town but these guys have a reputation to protect. We don't know enough about them to guess to what extent they'll go to maintain it. Even if they call off the hit on their main target, the contractor may still see Cat as a threat and keep her contract in place. Speaking of which, did anything happen today that I should know about?"

"Nothing. But I'd be surprised if it stayed this way for

long. We gained a little breathing room with the trip to the Keys but they've had enough time to regroup."

"Do we need more backup? I can make some calls."

Rick had reached almost every active and non-active member of Colt's Special Forces team. The squad that was currently in place was made up of the friends who had been able to make immediate arrangements to leave. Others had to clear their schedules and were now on stand-by.

"Let's hold off, we might need them later."

Cat couldn't suppress a chuckle when Gib let himself in through the kitchen late that afternoon. He was grinning as he held up a flash drive for her to see. She suspected the information on the stick wasn't the only thing he'd gotten his hands on.

"I see you got lucky," she said as he snatched a slice of carrot off the cutting board.

"Gentlemen never kiss and tell."

"I was talking about the list."

"No, you weren't," he winked. "Good. I didn't miss dinner," he said. "I'm starving."

"Let me guess. Running low on fuel."

"Gib! Get your ass in here and leave Cat alone," Colt called from the living room.

"Afraid I'll steal her away from you? I could, you know," Gib baited.

"I just don't want her ruining dinner."

"Hey! One more crack like that and you'll be chopping these vegetables," she threatened Colt from the doorway.

"I've already got an assignment. I'm grilling the steaks. Remember?"

"No, you're not," she grinned. "Your friends spilled the

beans regarding your culinary skills. Don is working the grill tonight. You, Captain, are doing dishes."

Colt was laughing as she disappeared back into the kitchen. Would there always be this good-natured teasing between them? God, he hoped so.

His upbeat mood evaporated a short while later, though, when Rick appeared at the kitchen door holding an arrangement of bright spring flowers. Colt snatched the bouquet from his friend's hands. "Those aren't for Cat, are they?"

"Well, they're certainly not for you."

"Why are you bringing her flowers?"

Rick raised his eyebrows at the snappish tone. Was his friend jealous? How surprising, he thought – and entertaining.

"Because you didn't?" Cat quipped, hoping to lighten Colt's obvious foul mood.

"If you wanted flowers, I'd have bought you flowers."

Cat stared at him. What was his problem, she wondered? She seriously considered telling Colt where he could shove his attitude but she suspected any comment would only serve to fuel whatever was suddenly eating him. Instead she slipped the note from the tiny envelope peeking out from the bouquet. Rick had scrolled *Thank you* across the simple, white card.

"For what?" she asked, perplexed.

Watching Colt squirm was a rare experience - one that Rick found himself perversely enjoying. Then he remembered the reason behind the gift and sobered.

"Afghanistan," he simply stated. Cat was obviously confused by the response but out of the corner of his eye, Rick saw Colt's tension visibly ease.

. . .

THAT NIGHT'S dinner conversation was limited to a discussion of the names connected to the conference. Colt knew his men would latch on to the project like pit bulls until a solution was apparent. They'd need that tenacity because this would be no simple job. At least fifty names on the list warranted some attention, although only ten qualified as high value targets. Each possible target would have to be researched. Tonight's session was to narrow down the targets and from there determine who might want him, or her, dead. Colt and Rick agreed to split the HVT's and work them. They consisted of state legislators, an actor, several environmental activists and a couple of scientists. The team would handle the balance of the names.

Cat left the guys to brainstorm while she made a fresh pot of coffee. She didn't plan on volunteering to help with the conference research. Instead, she wanted to continue to explore the photos she'd been weeding through. She knew that the team saw her task as busywork. Something to keep her mind occupied. And, as far as that went, it was working but she still believed it might pay off.

The man she'd seen on the beach had money and, the more she thought about it, arrogance. His clothes told her that he was in a high tax bracket but his posture spoke volumes, as well. In spite of being a bit shorter than his companion, he had virtually loomed over Bookman. His stance was intended to be intimidating. At the time, it didn't strike her as odd. But if this mystery man was conversing with a known killer then his body language told her that he was either stupid or thought himself superior. The trick would be to recognize him in a photo after having only seen him for a few minutes. But with the right picture at the right angle she might get lucky. A bellow from the other end of the unit yanked her from her thoughts.

"Cat! Would you mind getting your butt in here and explaining this?" Colt might have posed it as a question but it was not a request. "*Now*, Cat," he added.

She threw the dishtowel down, both literally and figuratively, as she stormed through the living room. She was oblivious to the stunned look on the faces of the men she passed on her way to Colt's office. "Who the hell do you think you are ordering me around?" she shouted in response.

Rick immediately got to his feet and followed her down the hall. He admitted it was probably a little perverted but he was looking forward to watching the two of them go head-to-head again.

"Seems to me a wise man would be heading in the opposite direction," Gib commented but fell in to step with Rick.

"What? And miss the fireworks?"

The two men, now accompanied by the rest of the group, reached the doorway to the office. Inside, Colt was pointing an accusatory finger at the computer's monitor while he glared down at the woman before him. Cat was being true to form. Instead of backing down as a women might do facing a large, visibly angry male, she was on her toes, doing her best to get in Colt's face.

"Who are those guys?" Colt demanded. He'd gone to his office to scan copies of the conference information. When his screensaver disappeared, Cat's mailbox stared back at him. What he saw left him cold.

Cat glimpsed quickly at the monitor. What was with Colt tonight? First, getting surly about the flowers Rick had given her and now this? She'd been responding to emails just before dinner and had forgotten to log off. Not that it was a big deal. The correspondence was easily explained but she'd be damned if she'd do it now.

"Those emails are none of your business. What gives you the right to read my mail?"

"I didn't read a single email," although he'd been tempted, "but I sure as hell saw who was sending them." And he didn't like what he'd seen. Military addresses filled her inbox.

"And why is that a problem? You have something against Marines?"

"I do if those Marines are writing to *you*." He was jealous. He was actually jealous. The admission, as well as the depth of the emotion, stunned him. Had he ever been jealous before? Certainly not to this extent. Sure, he'd been annoyed when Rick appeared with those flowers but he'd quickly dismissed that as guilt. But these guys...? Who the hell were they?

Not the least bit intimidated by the large, surly male, Cat leaned in closer. "Who am I allowed to associate with, Colt? No, wait! I know. You can make it simple for me. Draw up a list. It shouldn't take you long. I'm sure it will be a short one."

Her insinuation that he wanted control over her and whom she had as friends wasn't lost on Colt but he wasn't ready to deal with that accusation. Possibly because she might be right so he ignored that warning bell.

"Are you going to tell me who those men are?"

"Are you accusing me of something?"

"Answer the damn question, Cat."

If she hadn't been so furious she would have laughed. The man was all but beating his chest.

"Listen up, Tarzan. I do not have to explain myself - or my friends - to you. Not now – not ever!"

The sea of men parted as she sailed out of the room. She didn't need a sixth sense to know that Colt was right behind her. "Back off, Colt!" she warned him. "I've had all the macho crap I can stand from you in one day."

Furious and in need of a place to cool off, she resumed her march toward the rear of the unit. The small gym in the studio was just the place to work off some steam.

"Gib!" she hollered. Gib immediately appeared at her side. "You're taking me downstairs while that Neanderthal contemplates the definition of trust."

"She's not going anywhere."

Cat spun on Colt so violently that her arms literally flew away from her sides. Rick would later swear that the temperature in the room dropped to match her freezing stare.

"The hell I'm not."

She turned her attention to the group of slack jawed men, "One of you escorts me downstairs or I'm going through that door *alone* and hitchhike back to my car."

24

Rick sat in one of the armchairs watching Colt navigate his way around the furniture. He'd been circling for a landing for the past thirty minutes. Apparently, he still had some fuel to burn off. The rest of the guys had departed with Cat. She'd be safe with them while she calmed down. Rick had already learned that she tended to cool off as quickly as she heated up. But, man, could she get hot. She'd take off like a rocket when the right button was pushed. Colt had obviously found her launch code.

She'd done a pretty good job cracking Colt's store of emotions wide open, as well. Prior to Cat's arrival on the island Colt had been making headway, slowly returning to the world of the living. But the minute she'd walked into his life – bam! Feelings he'd buried - and a few he may have never experienced – were fighting their way to the surface. Colt was struggling against the onslaught. Add the stress of a killer stalking Cat and you had a volatile combination. Rick wondered if he shouldn't feel a little sorry for his friend. Nah.

"Tell me," Rick asked as he extended his leg, blocking Colt's progress around the room, "did that outburst have its intended effect? "Because if your aim was to chase her away, I'd say it worked like a charm."

Colt didn't know where to direct his anger. What the hell was going on with Cat and those emails and what was she thinking walking out like that? He knew he hadn't helped matters by grilling her on the topic. Then there was Rick who'd been sitting there smugly, apparently enjoying the current situation. Colt considered wiping the look off Rick's face when his comment suddenly sunk in.

"Fuck."

The corners of Rick's mouth ticked up. Houston - The Eagle has landed.

"What the hell set you off?" his friend asked, genuinely curious.

Colt dragged a hand down his face as he slumped into a chair. "I was jealous," he reluctantly admitted.

"Believe it or not, with my superior powers of deduction, I was able to come to that conclusion on my own. The question is why?"

"Why?"

"Yeah, why? What happened to unleash that green-eyed monster? In all the years I've known you, I don't think I've ever seen you make a bigger ass of yourself."

"You're the one who started it. Showing up with flowers..." Colt stopped the accusation mid-snarl, realizing how childish he sounded. "Sorry. That was out of line."

"Damn straight it was. That whole argument with Cat was even further out of line. Do you honestly think she'd cheat on you?"

With her sense of right and wrong? Not a chance. Colt shook his head.

"Then what got into you?"

"Hell, I don't know." And he really didn't. He'd been trying to figure that out since she'd walked out the door. "First you show up with flowers. Something I should have done," he quickly added. He understood the reason behind Rick's gesture but it ate at him that he hadn't been the one responsible for the sparkle the thoughtful act had brought to her eyes.

Then there was the fact that he'd had Cat virtually to himself since the day they'd met. When it hit him that she had friends – worse yet, male friends - outside the circle he'd created for her, he'd felt vulnerable. What if she didn't stay with him when this was all over? What happened if she decided to go back to her world? "Then I saw those emails..."

"Those emails you're so worried about are from troops stationed in Afghanistan – and, I imagine, a few other God-forsaken hell holes around the world. Jason told me that for the last few of years Cat's been befriending servicemen and women who don't have much in the way of family or friends – writing to them, sending care packages..."

Colt felt like he'd taken a blow to his gut. "Why didn't she say something?"

"You'll have to ask her but I am willing to bet she'd have explained if you'd just asked instead of acting like a – what did she call you? Oh, yeah - a Neanderthal."

"I'm a fucking idiot."

"That too."

"I'd better get downstairs and apologize."

"Apologize? Hell, you need to grovel."

Wasn't that the truth? Before he made it out of the room, though, Cat came through the rear door flanked by Gib and Adam. She'd obviously spent her time away working off her anger. Her skin glistened with a thin layer of perspiration. Soft curls that had escaped the scrunchy thing she used to tie up her hair lay damp against her neck. She gave Rick a quick smile but ignored Colt as she passed through the room.

Shit! Still, he turned to follow her. Gib and Adam stepped into his path. Resigned, he raised his hands in defeat. "Okay. I admit it. I screwed up. Now let me go talk to her."

"Did we say anything?" Gib asked, standing his ground. "Besides, I promised Cat I'd keep my mouth shut." Then, despite the promise, Gib made his opinion of Colt's earlier behavior clear. Colt listened to the uncustomary tongue lashing in silence. He couldn't argue with Gib because he was right and any discussion would only prolong their stay. He needed to talk to Cat - although he wasn't at all sure what he was going to say to make things right.

After a few threats to his manhood the men departed leaving Colt to face the music. He found Cat in front of the same computer that had set off the chain of events. Colt watched from the doorway as she silently responded to one of the emails, click *Send* and then turned toward him. "Hi," she said, smiling.

A single word. A single expression - and everything was right again. "Cat, I'm…"

She held up her hand, stopping him. "Read this," she said, opening one of emails. "It's from an Army Sergeant stationed in Afghanistan."

Colt laid a kiss in her hair, grateful that he hadn't screwed this up. "It's not necessary, Cat."

"This isn't a test, Colt. I'm asking you to read it." She touched the hand that rested on her shoulder. "This," she said, pointing to the screen, "is important to me. But there's been so much going on that, with the exception of responding to a few emails, I've had to put it aside. I wasn't hiding anything. I just didn't think to mention it. Once I calmed down, I could see where it could be misinterpreted."

She turned, her dark, round eyes trapped his like laser beams. "That still doesn't excuse your behavior and if you ever pull the kind of crap on me again that you did tonight, I will leave. Do you understand?"

He gently pulled her to her feet, smiling at her ferocity. "Yes, ma'am. You have my word." Then he covered her mouth with his.

He deepened the kiss, asking for more. As he caressed, then suckled, Colt reached behind her and lowered the Murphy bed from the wall. Gently, he pushed her down on to the mattress and reverently removed her clothing. Leaving a trail of kisses, he gradually made his way down the length of her body, until he could taste the heart of her. She was still shuddering from the effects of her release when he nudged her legs apart and slipped into her warmth.

SOMETIME LATER, Cat gathered up the clothes that had been so quickly discarded and tossed Colt's shorts to him. "Get dressed then start reading," she ordered, pointing to the monitor. "I'm going to take a shower. Alone," she quickly added when she noted a prominent part of his anatomy spring back to life.

When she returned to the room Colt still sat at his desk - a grin on his face. He'd read the emails. Most were from young men but there were a few from women. Colt had been surprised to see a couple of officers and a Major among her correspondents. All were thanking her for simple things that made their tour, or their troop's deployment easier – a special magazine, drink mixes that replaced electrolytes they lost in the savage heat, a favorite snack that reminded them of home. Some of the messages were from guys that obviously didn't have, or hear from, family or friends and relished the opportunity to correspond with someone who worried about them. A few soldiers asked for little trinkets or candy to pass out to children in orphanages who suffered so terribly as a result of war. Colt had also briefly checked out the website Cat had used to find these troops.

"I wish I'd known about programs like this when I was on tour. There were always a few guys who didn't get mail. It sucks trying to survive in those hellholes but when you think nobody gives a shit whether or not you come back, it makes it almost impossible." He held her close. "Thank you, Kitten, for understanding that."

"I'm glad you approve because I could always use some help."

"Whatever you need..."

She stared into those crystal blue eyes and felt her heart tumble. She suddenly knew that all she needed was right in front of her.

25

O ver the next few of days, Cat settled into a comfortable routine. When she wasn't preparing meals, she was viewing photos. She'd looked through hundreds of photos with no success and she still had hundreds to go. And while she might have been frustrated with her lack of progress, she could never complain about being lonely. Contrary to what the men believed, she was fully aware that it was no coincidence that she was never left alone. Their concern was appreciated but she wasn't used to the constant championship. She craved a few moments of solitude and freedom but refused to complain. These men had left their homes and jobs to come to her aid. Hopefully, they'd get to the bottom of this soon so everyone could return to their former existence.

Everyone, that was, with the exception of herself. This morning she'd received official notice, via email, that she no longer had a job. Downsizing, they'd claimed. Bullshit, she'd been tempted to reply. The AG's office couldn't be happy with the kind of attention she was garnering. The FBI and FDLE, along with a host of local authorities would all have made inquiries about her. It was a no-brainer to figure out they didn't want someone with a target on her back showing up for work. She'd be putting others at risk which, she agreed, was unacceptable. She just wished they'd been honest about it instead of sticking the "downsizing" label on it.

Under different circumstances she might have put up a fight. Perhaps requested a leave of absence instead of the layoff but as she'd already decided not to stay on after Jason left and her "downsizing" came with a nice sever-ance package, she decided not to kick up a fuss. Choose your battles wisely she'd philosophized when she spoke to Jason earlier that day. He hadn't seen it that way. In protest, he'd submitted his papers for retirement – weeks earlier than planned. He'd be back in West Palm with the love of his life as soon as his cases were reassigned.

The receipt of her electronic pink slip prompted Cat to notify her apartment manager that she would not be renewing her lease. She told herself the decision to move was her choice but somehow it felt pre-determined. When had she lost control of her life? Well, duh – maybe the day she witnessed two men conferring on the beach?

Cat didn't tell Colt about the loss of her job when she saw him at lunch. Why, she wondered, had she consciously withheld that rather significant bit of information? Then it dawned on her that what to say and to whom were deci-sions she still had some control over. Once she assured herself that she could still flex those independent muscles she felt a bit better. She'd tell Colt tonight.

COLT HAD SPENT most of the day chasing information on one particular conference participant. A keynote speaker, to be more precise. State Senator Martin Lucas was scheduled to address the conference on the consequences of building near environmentally sensitive areas. Many developers considered land that bordered wildlife preserves, wilderness areas and other similarly protected lands, to be ideal places to construct resorts.

But a recent study conducted by a state university had backed Lucas' claim that this practice was hazardous to those lands. Lucas had introduced a bill in the Florida Senate that would require a buffer zone around all protected places. Lobbyists representing developers, contractors and a slew of other industries that might be affected were coming out of the woodwork to oppose the bill. Industry representatives from Florida, as well as other parts of the country, were descending upon Tallahassee. The fear was that if this bill passed it would set a precedent that could eventually become the law of the land. Colt had downloaded a copy of the proposed legislation. Barring any amendments to water it down, it was a powerful bill.

To no one's surprise it had the backing of virtually every environmental group. When Lucas had initially introduced the bill, most of his fellow legislators would not endorse it. That, however, was changing. The study had not only showed how such developments were hazardous to the fragile environment but how the loss of those environments affected the bottom line of the State's biggest industry – tourism. Now, with Lucas spearheading the effort, there was a good chance the bill would pass the Senate during the next legislative session.

However, if Lucas was no longer in the picture, Colt suspected the legislation stood little chance of getting out of committee. Opposition to the bill was still powerful. Not many politicians seeking re-election would be willing to become a target of the lobbyists opposing the bill - not like Lucas was doing. He didn't seem to have a problem with drawing their fire. In fact, he appeared to enjoy it. Colt had left messages for him at his office in Tallahassee and his home district.

Colt pushed back from his desk, ready for a break when Rick strolled in. "The Feds have arrived," he announced.

"What took them so long?" Although Hernandez and Morgan had returned days ago, they'd come alone. A fact that had surprised both Colt and Rick.

Rick shrugged, then grinned. "The resort is swarming with them. Cordella is freaking out from what I hear."

Anything that irritated that pompous ass was good news as far as Colt was concerned. He picked up his notes and looked at Rick. "I've got an HVT that looks very promising," Colt started, then spent the next hour with his friend discussing what he'd found.

BY LATE AFTERNOON everyone had once again gathered in Colt's apartment with the exception of those on sentry and Gib, who had left for a photo shoot that had been impossible to reschedule. Cat had immediately missed his jokes and the constant teasing. Gib's absence also re-enforced her mounting concern about the personal and professional lives these men had put on hold to protect her.

Dinner was served, as it was most nights, buffet style. The guys piled their plates high with the chicken and rice dish she'd prepared then settled down in the living room to continue their discussion. Gib returned in time to finish off the casserole.

After dinner, Cat successfully chased everyone out of the kitchen so she could have a rare few minutes to herself. While she put things away, she thought about the volumes of photos she had yet to view. She couldn't believe the number of social functions that were held in the area. In Tallahassee, the large number of gatherings wouldn't have been unusual. Lobbyists were known for throwing parties and there were a lot of lobbyists. But this area rivaled that social scene. And as a result, it was taking much longer than she'd anticipated getting through the shots they'd gathered for her. Thinking she could put in another hour or two with the photos, Cat headed for the door and then froze. If she went downstairs, Colt would insist that someone go with her.

He'd nailed one thing early on, having her movements restricted grated on her. The only time she could enjoy some fresh air was on her trips to the studio and those were rushed and always with an escort. It probably wasn't all that much fun for the guys to be saddled with her either. Each day she felt more and more like a kid sister who required a fulltime babysitter. She released her grip on the knob. She was in no mood for a babysitter tonight.

Deciding to check her emails instead, she headed toward the office. Cat passed the guys as they were heading toward the rear deck to enjoy their nightly cigar. She was glad that Colt was able to spend time with his buddies. He had a couple of years of catching up to do she thought as she dropped into the desk chair and powered up the computer. All thoughts of the men vanished as Cat stared at the screen. Why the hell hadn't she thought of this before? She didn't have to work downstairs tonight. All she needed was one of the flash drives Gib has prepared and she'd be good to go up here. That request didn't feel like near the imposition as needing a bodyguard. Or so it seemed until she neared the rear of the unit and heard the laughter emanating from the deck. The minute she stuck her head out the door their mood would shift. She knew it and she had no intention of spoiling their fun. The photos could wait until tomorrow.

She grabbed a soda from the fridge then snatched a bag of pretzels off the counter. In doing so, she inadvertently knocked a set of keys to the floor – a set that included keys to the studio. After only a moment's hesitation, she picked them up and rushed toward the front of the unit. She'd be back before they missed her.

26

The humid night air reeked of smoldering cigars but the pungent, smoky haze was filled with pleasant memories for Colt. Not all the time he'd spent in the mountains of Afghanistan had been horrible. There had been nights when he and his team played cards and polluted the atmosphere until dawn. He'd swept those memories under a rug in his attempt to block out anything to do with those tours. Thanks to Cat he was now recalling some of the better times. He smiled. Maybe he'd cut his time with the guys short tonight and show her a little of his appreciation. Snuffing out his cigar, he turned to say good-night to his friends. He never got that far.

CAT TURNED off all the lights at the front end of the unit to prevent any of it from spilling outside then stepped onto the front deck. Freedom. It made her feel a little giddy and strangely nervous. As she reached the top of the stairs the reason for her nervousness suddenly became clear. Logic, which had been absent only minutes ago, returned in a flash. What a friggin' moron! The front of the studio below was fully illuminated just as it had been every night since her arrival. How the hell had she forgotten that bright fact? If she continued down the stairs, her personal hit man couldn't ask for a more perfect target. Not only that, if she was dumb enough to continue playing the role of a duck in a shooting gallery, she wouldn't get past the studio's alarm system. Since she had yet to be alone on her forays downstairs, she hadn't paid any attention to the security code. Her escorts had taken care of that little detail. She'd been so focused on the end goal of retrieving the flash drive that she'd neglected to analyze the trip. A silent voice screamed at her to get her ass back inside – now!

Instinct had her crouching as she turned back. At the same instant, the wood railing above her head splintered into toothpicks. Cat was already throwing herself to the deck, shielding her face with her arms when a large, hard body covered hers. Colt.

Above the roaring of blood in her ears she could hear the heavy clamoring of feet racing up the front staircase. "Go!" someone shouted. Colt rolled to his feet, sweeping Cat into his arms as he moved. Using his body as a shield, he carried her past Rick who was on one knee by the front door - his weapon drawn. God, what had she done?

"Are you hurt? Were you hit?" Colt demanded in tense, rapid fire as he carried her down the hallway.

"I'm okay. I'm okay." Damn! Her stupidity could have gotten someone killed. Still could, she realized.

"Make sure she's not hurt," Colt said as he dropped Cat into Gib's outstretched arms. "Keep her away from the doors and windows," he added then turned back toward the front door.

. . .

EYEING the woman he now held, Gib asked, "Are you sure you weren't injured?"

She nodded. "You can put me down."

Gib let her feet drop to the floor but kept his arm around her waist. In spite of her attempts to conceal it, she was trembling. He wasn't at all sure that her legs would hold her.

"What the hell were you thinking going out there?" He was angry. Not an emotion he was accustomed to. He rarely raised his voice and never at a woman. But damn it, she'd scared the hell out of him. And Colt? Gib had seen the color drain from his friend's face when Don had called from the blind next door to tell him Cat had just exited the front of the building.

Cat knew she deserved this dressing down and the one that she was sure would follow. What *had* she been thinking? Obviously, she hadn't been thinking at all.

"I was just going to grab a flash drive..." she began. Her first instinct was to rationalize her actions but there was no legitimizing the lapse in judgment that put these men at risk. Raking her fingers through her hair she looked anxiously toward the front door. What if one of them got hurt – or worse – because of her actions? "Stupid, stupid, stupid!"

Gib knew that the insult was self-directed. She'd be kicking herself if it were anatomically possible. "You didn't know anyone was out there," he said, his anger slipping away.

She began to pace, her frustration mounting. "God, I hate this! I could take my life being fucked up. Been there, done that..." The words came tumbling out as her pacing increased. "I lost my job today. Did you know that? No. Of course you didn't. I haven't told anybody. My problem. Not yours. How the hell did I go from being an independent, self-sufficient woman to being a fucking albatross? It's not right. Your lives shouldn't be screwed up because I was in the wrong place at the wrong time. Why the hell did I have to pick that beach on that day? What if something happens to one of you because of me?"

Gib knew he'd have to put a halt to her ramblings the minute he saw tears beginning to gather and with those big eyes she could probably shed buckets. "I've got to warn you, Tink, I'm not very good with weeping women."

The comment brought her up short. "A Lothario like you? I would've thought you'd be used to them." But, then again, what man was ever good with tears? She didn't care for them much either especially when she was the one shedding them. "I'd like to wait in the bedroom," she told him. If she couldn't hold it together then she'd prefer privacy when she fell apart.

Gib didn't argue but insisted on inspecting the room - making sure the windows were locked and the blinds drawn tight. When he returned to the hall, he shoved a handful of tissues at Cat. "Don't turn on any lights and stay away from the windows or Colt will have my ass."

What a sad sight she made, Gib thought, as she closed the door behind her. Stress, fear and worry had extinguished the fire that usually brightened those eyes. It killed him to see them filled with tears. He hadn't had the slightest idea how to handle them so he'd taken the coward's way out and let her retreat. When the door latched shut, Gib lowered his frame to the floor and settled in to guard Cat's sanctuary.

27

As soon as Colt exited the building, he and Rick quickly made their way down the steps while Rick briefed him, "No sign of him since he took the shot. Jess and Bill are sweeping the sides and back. The others are over there now," Rick said, indicating the thick stand of brush and trees where the single shot had originated.

Colt wanted this bastard but his experience told him that the guy was long gone. Still, they had to be sure. As soon as they'd crossed the road they split up. Rick circled wide, heading north, while Colt skirted the dense thicket to the left. They'd work their way from the edges of the brush toward the center where Don and Kevin had started their search. The plan was to flush him out in the unlikely event he'd stuck around.

Saw palmetto and sea grape grew thick on this particular strip of Periwinkle Way. A bike path ran between the street and the brush. The natural vegetation had, for the most part, been left undisturbed. Only plants that might become a safety hazard for bicyclists were cut back. The residents prided themselves on keeping native plants in place whenever possible. In addition to the conservation value, it also gave the tourists a feel for the natural Florida as they cycled their way around the island. Normally he'd applaud those efforts but tonight he was cursing them.

The air was still except for the calliope of insects and the not-too-distant sound of the water slapping against nearby seawalls. It was a testament to his friends that he couldn't hear them as they searched the vegetation for the shooter. The silence also told him the gunman was just as good or gone.

The sound of a Jet Ski cranking up answered that question. Shit. There'd been no way for them to cover the nearby canals and the shooter most likely knew it. Colt took off in a dead run through the underbrush toward the water. He could hear the small vessel heading out toward the Gulf though he couldn't see it through the darkness created by the cloud-covered moon.

Colt turned to face Rick as he exited the brush. "I alerted the Coast Guard," Rick said pocketing his phone. For all the good it will do, he thought. The guy had an escape plan. The shooter would switch to another mode of transportation long before the authorities arrived on the scene.

"How long has this guy been waiting out here to take a shot at her? Why didn't we spot him?" Colt asked, his frustration obvious.

"Colt, we've checked this area regularly but we can't cover every inch of brush every minute. And what were the chances that he'd be in the perfect position to take a shot at Cat when she slipped out? We didn't expect her to pull a stunt like that. Why would he? The man is not only skilled but lucky."

"What the hell got into her? What do I have to do? Tie her up?" Colt's heart had stopped when Don called him. If she hadn't turned back when she did there was a good chance that the killer would have hit his mark.

"We're talking about Cat here. I don't think you'll win too many points with that kind of thinking."

"I'm more concerned about keeping her alive than winning points," he said as he stormed back toward his unit.

WHEN COLT RETURNED to his unit, he immediately spotted Gib sitting on the floor in the hallway with his hand resting on the gun at his side. He didn't see Cat.

"Where is she?"

"Relax. She's safe," he said indicating the bedroom. "I take it you didn't get the guy?"

"Took off on a jet ski," Colt informed him, turning his attention back to the closed door. "Is she okay?"

"Physically, she's fine. Emotionally, I'd say she's a bit rocky at the moment. She's expecting you to tear a few strips off her hide."

"She could have been killed."

"At the moment she's more concerned about your safety than her own." Gib lowered his voice. "Give her a break, Colt. She knows she screwed up and she's pretty down on herself at the moment. Called herself an albatross." Gib raised his hands in defense. "Her word, not mine. Did you know she lost her job?"

News of that omission cut at Colt but he quickly brushed it off. "She wasn't going back there anyway," he rationalized aloud. He'd already decided one way or another he'd convince her to stay.

"I'd bet she'd have argued that with you but it's a moot point now. The decision has been made for her."

And that summed it up, didn't it? Something else had

been taken out of her control. She'd lost her freedom, her independence and now her job. She'd spent more than half her life forging her own way and she was now being forced to rely on others.

"Thanks, Gib," Colt said as he turned toward the bedroom.

"Go easy. She's in a shitload of hurt right now."

Colt didn't acknowledge his friend's concern. His attention was already focused on the woman waiting on the other side of the door. A jolt of alarm shot through him as the light from the hall filtered in framing an empty bed. Darkness enveloped the rest of the space.

"Cat?"

From the corner of the darkened room an almost childlike voice answered, "Are you okay? Was anyone hurt?"

He let go the breath he was holding and turned toward the sound of her voice. "I'm fine. We're all fine."

She was huddled on the floor next to his dresser - her knees pulled to her chest, her arms wrapped tightly around them. Crouching in front of her, he took one of her hands in his. "What are you doing down here, Kitten?"

She shrugged. "It just seemed like the right place to be." She couldn't explain it but something had drawn her to the spot. So there she'd sat tucked safely away while the men outside risked their lives to keep her that way.

Colt resisted the urge to lift her off the floor. Instead he settled down next to her his back against the wall.

"I'm so sorry, Colt. I never meant to put any of you in danger."

"What the hell got into you?"

"A severe case of idiocy? I didn't think about the consequences until I set foot outside. I realized my mistake a second before you appeared." And a bullet whizzed by my ear, she thought. "I guess that answers the question as to whether I'm still a target."

"You thought that had changed?"

"Wishful thinking on my part. I'd hoped once they saw you and your friends that whoever was out there had taken off."

He wasn't sure which misconception to correct first. The team had known the sniper was still stalking Cat. The guy was good at avoiding them but they'd found evidence of his existence. Colt's mistake was in believing he should keep that bit of information from her. He'd tell her about their findings later. Right now, another issue took precedence.

"They're your friends, too, Cat. None of them think of you as a burden."

"Sounds like I need to have a little chat with Gib. He shouldn't have said anything." Cat sighed, letting her head drop back against the wall. "Every one of them, including you, had a life before I showed up."

Colt brought her fingers to his lips. "You are my life, Cat. Don't you know that by now?"

She closed her eyes. "This thing... Us. It scares me," Cat admitted, opening her eyes to meet his. "I haven't had any experience with... with this sort of relationship. I don't know how to do it right."

"Ah, Kitten, I don't think there is a right or wrong way." He dusted kisses against her quivering lips as he lifted her off the floor. At some point, she'd stopped fighting him on the carrying issue for which he was grateful. He loved the feel of her draped across his arms. She'd been custom made for them.

Laying her atop the comforter, he kissed the scrapes from her fall to the deck while he gently removed her clothing. He stroked her silky hair, suckled her small, perfect breasts and made love to every inch of her exposed skin until he felt her release. When she lay replete, he shed his clothes, stroking her back to the edge of ecstasy before slipping inside her warmth. His invasion took her over the edge and he rode her through another round of spasms.

When her tremors slowed he began the dance of the ages, savoring the feel of her gloving him. In spite of his intent to take it slow, his rhythm quickened. When he felt her tighten around him, it triggered a climax so intense he wondered if he'd survive it. His heart clamored to break through his chest while his lungs screamed for air. His muscles finally uncoiled and he collapsed on top of her. Fingertips gliding across his shoulders brought him back to reality. He propped himself up on his forearms and looked his fill. "You alright?"

"I am now." She smiled, stroking his chest then suddenly pushed against it. "I need to see the guys. I owe them an apology."

"No. You don't," he said, forcing her gently back against the mattress. "But if it'll make you feel better, you can do it tomorrow."

She glanced at the clock. When she saw the hour she flopped back against the pillow. "Tell me. While Gib was being so talkative did he mention that I've officially joined the ranks of the unemployed?"

"He did," he answered. He wanted to ask why she hadn't shared that fact with him but she'd been pushed enough for one day.

"After that bit of news, I called my apartment manager and told her I wouldn't be renewing my lease."

"Would you happen to be looking for a place to stay?"

"No promises, Colt. Not until this mess is finished."

He relaxed a bit. She hadn't said no. Making a decision of that magnitude was difficult enough under the best of circumstances, especially for someone with an inherent need for independence. Colt's gut told him she wasn't going anywhere so he could wait for her to come to that realization on her own.

"This shit won't last forever," he assured her.

"It better not or I won't have to worry about a place to live. They'll put me in a padded cell. I don't know how much longer I can stay locked up before I start banging my head against…" She snapped her mouth shut when she realized that she was whining again. "Sorry. You keep me safe. I shouldn't be complaining."

"Don't be sorry. I want to know what's going on in there," he said, tapping her forehead.

As he crawled in bed and pulled Cat close, his cell phone rang.

"What?" he asked Gib sharply, wondering what else could happen tonight? The line of his mouth softened, and then curled slightly as he listened. "I tied her to the bed and beat her to within an inch of her life. Didn't you hear the screaming?"

He smiled at something Gib said. "Tell them she's fine," he said as he stared into those big brown eyes. "No," he corrected, "tell them she's perfect."

As he set the phone on the nightstand, he explained, "Gib was elected to make sure you were okay. For an albatross, the guys seem to care a great deal about you."

She relaxed as he cradled her head against his chest, "I plead temporary insanity brought on by a severe case of cabin fever," she said touching her lips to his bare skin.

"Go to sleep, Kitten." With a feather touch he stroked her temple, coaxing her into slumber. He listened as her breathing slowed and exhaustion overtook her. From the beginning Colt knew that confinement would be difficult for this fireball. Her independent streak coupled with her love of the outdoors was in direct conflict with the world she'd been forced to live in since their return to the island. But she hadn't objected and he was so focused on solving this mystery that he hadn't noticed the effect it was having on her.

Halting her trips to the studio would be the prudent thing to do but he couldn't bring himself to shrink her confines any further. If anything, he'd like to find a way to expand them. To give her some of her freedom and control back. The question was how to do that and still keep her safe?

28

C at stood under the needle-like spray of the shower, letting the heat penetrate muscles that seemed all too happy to remind her of last night's up-close-and-personal meeting with the front deck. The tight muscles, she suspected, weren't only due to her fall but her pent-up anger. She had no life or future as long as some bastard was standing in the wings waiting for his chance to take her out. Well, she was done being passive. It was time to make some changes to her current situation.

The first item on her agenda was to cancel all future pity parties. Last night she'd experienced her first bout of self-pity since she'd left her childhood home. She didn't like the taste it left in her mouth.

It was also past time she went on the offensive. She'd have to drop the Rachael Ray routine for a while and focus solely on the photos. If the bastard's picture was in there somewhere, she would find him. A little less time socializing and homemaking and a little more time viewing photos and she just might find the guy before her hair turned gray. Each member of the team was competent in the kitchen. Even Colt could manage reasonably well. No one would starve if she retired her chef's hat for the time being.

Her next idea was going to be a little bit harder to sell. Colt wasn't going to like it. Hell, who was she kidding? He was going to go ballistic when she suggested they use her to draw out the gunman. No one had to tell her what she was thinking was risky but it was also logical. She'd certainly gotten the shooter's attention last night. Their current line of investigation could take forever. If they found Gravestone's target it still wouldn't guarantee a trail back to the client. And the client was the key. Even if she could identify him through the photos they would still need to tie him to Gravestone.

Contrary to the old saying, Cat knew there was little honor among thieves. In her years working with Jason she'd discovered that most felons would sing like mockingbirds if it aided their own personal cause.

Currently, the guys were holding a mostly defensive posture while protecting her. However, if they did what they were trained to do – hunt – then maybe, just maybe, they'd get the bastard. The idea of playing a goat tethered to a stake didn't exactly appeal to her but she trusted Colt to put together a plan that would work. However, there was no such thing as a perfect plan and that would be reason enough for Colt to nix the idea. She'd yet to come up with an argument she thought might convince him but she was determined to find one.

The room was full of sunlight and men when Cat entered the kitchen as was usual for this time of day. Only Rick and the two guys on sentry were missing. Apparently, Adam and Steve had pulled that duty this morning. Colt was leaning against the granite countertop, one foot crossed leisurely over his ankle. He held a cup of coffee in one hand. As soon as he saw her he extended his free arm, inviting Cat to his side.

She accepted the invitation, and the coffee he offered, then looked into the faces the others in the room. "I want to apologize for that stunt I pulled last night."

Colt tugged her closer. "It's okay, Cat. They're good."

Don was grinning, "Yeah, it was fun. Besides, I don't remember ever seeing Colt turn so white."

"Oh, I don't know," Bill chuckled. "What about that time in Katmandu when we dared him to eat those... What were those things?"

Smiling, Colt raised his hand to call a halt to the conversation. "That's enough. Cat hasn't eaten yet."

"And I'm not going to. I want to get an early start." She laid a kiss on Colt's cheek and turned to the group. "Can one of you take me downstairs?"

She wasn't entirely surprised by the bewildered expressions across the room. It was her habit to spend some time visiting with the guys while preparing breakfast but today she was on a mission.

Kevin was the first to recover. "We were just heading down that way," he said, tapping Bill on the arm.

"You're on your own for lunch," she added, grabbing a couple of containers of yogurt from the refrigerator. "I plan to work through it."

As soon as the door closed behind them, Gib turned to Colt. "What's up with Tink?" he demanded. "You said she was okay."

"What the hell are you talking about?" The implied accusation didn't set well with Colt though he had to admit he was a little mystified by Cat's behavior, as well. She'd seemed almost anxious to escape. Her unfinished cup of coffee sat on the counter. And this was the first time that he could remember that she'd asked to be taken downstairs.

Normally, she would wait until someone was ready to leave.

"Tink." Gib stated, pointing to the door she'd just exited. "She didn't make breakfast or discuss lunch like she does every morning. She barely said a word. What did you do to her?" he asked, emphatically.

"I didn't do a damn thing."

"I bet she's just shook up a bit," Don suggested, attempting to play the role of peacemaker. "That was a pretty close call last night."

"Or maybe she's not feeling well," Jesse suggested.

Gib snapped his fingers. "PMS." He looked expectantly at Colt. "It's her time, right?"

"Her time for what?"

"You know…"

The light in his brain blinked on when the reference to 'PMS' finally registered. "How the hell would I know?"

"Trust me," Gib assured Colt, "You'll know."

Of course he would - which brought up another issue.

"Did you pick up the stuff she'll need for that?"

"You're kidding. Right?"

"No, I'm not kidding. You know she can't leave to go shopping."

"Well, I am not shopping for those supplies. She's your… your… whatever you call her. You can make the run."

"I wouldn't know what to buy." It was a lame excuse and Colt knew it.

"And what? I'm an expert?"

"Okay, okay. What about one of your lady friends?" Colt asked, hopefully. When Gib pulled out his phone and began scrolling through his numbers, Colt added, "Whoever you call, I don't want them coming around here. We have enough to deal with without putting a Good Samaritan in danger."

A grin spread across Gib's face as he waited for his call to be answered.

In spite of telling himself that he was worrying needlessly, Colt still took frequent breaks to check on Cat. With each of his visits, though, she grew increasingly irritated. When he tried to coax her upstairs for lunch, he'd have sworn she'd hissed at him. Maybe Gib was on to something.

Colt prided himself on not being a stupid man and, therefore, finally took the hint. He spent the rest of the afternoon in his home office cruising the information highway for anything he could find on Lucas and his bill. The more he read, the more Colt was convinced that Lucas was the target. When calls to the Senator weren't returned, Colt finally resorted to contacting Jason. There'd been an agreement among the group that they would play that card only when absolutely necessary. Jason had been generous with his money and influence. No one wanted to abuse either but when all else failed, it was time to bring in the big gun.

Not surprisingly, Jason was anxious to help. "I don't know Lucas personally but I know him by reputation. He's honest. A little naïve when it comes to the games they play here which is refreshing. I'll track him down and have him get in touch with you. You think he's our target?"

"He's the best candidate we have so far. The question is - does he have any enemies angry enough, or feeling threatened enough, to go to these extremes?" They hadn't come up with any other people on the list of conference participants that held as much promise as Lucas. The team was still following up leads but Colt was concentrating on Lucas. He needed those names.

"Considering the ramifications of his bill, I wouldn't be surprised if there wasn't one or two willing to give it serious consideration."

After Jason and Colt had finished their discussion about Lucas, Colt broached another subject. "When did you last talk to Cat?" He wanted to be sure Jason was aware of what had happened the last night before he heard it from a third party. Colt was pretty confident that Cat hadn't shared that information with her boss or Jason would have picked up the phone long ago.

"A couple of days ago. Why?"

Colt recognized the concern in the attorney's voice. "She's fine but a sniper did manage to take a shot at her last night." He had no intention of telling Jason just how close the bastard had come to hitting her.

"What the blazes happened? I thought you were supposed to be protecting her!"

Colt understood Jason's anger. He was still furious with himself. Jason listened patiently while he recounted the events doing his best to reassure Jason that Cat was fine and nothing like that would happen again.

"Not much you can do when she sets her mind to something." Jason admitted. "How's she handling things, otherwise?"

"She's acting different today. Distant. We can't get her to take a break – not even to eat."

"Sounds like she's got her teeth into something. She's done it before. Don't let it worry you." Jason ended the conversation with a promise to find Lucas and put him in touch with Colt before the end of the day. Less than an hour later, Colt got the call.

"This is Martin Lucas. I understand you've been trying to reach me," the Senator said when Colt answered.

"I have, Senator. Did Jason Waters explain why?"

"He gave me the abridged version. Said you'd fill in the details. I have to tell you this whole thing sounds bizarre. If Waters hadn't been the one to call me I'd have put it off as a joke."

Which was probably why none of Colt's calls had been returned. "There's nothing funny about the attempts on Ms. Storm's life."

"Agreed. All right, you've got my attention. Tell me what you know and if I can help, I will."

Colt recapped the recent events and theories, spelling out his reasons for believing Lucas might be a target. He was impressed with the Senator. The man didn't dismiss him. Instead, he asked intelligent questions throughout the conversation.

"I can't fault your logic, Mr. James, but I can also envision several other scenarios that could explain the presence of these predators on your island. Besides, I'd prefer to think I don't have someone gunning for me. Literally, that is."

"Understandable, Senator. But right now you're the strongest possible target we've unearthed."

"Why would they wait until the conference? They could make an attempt on my life anywhere. At any time."

The same question had occurred to Colt. "Perhaps someone wants to send a message to others with similar agendas. The conference will be well attended by environmentalists, legislators and those friendly to the cause, as well as activists. If this is about your bill, there'll be a lot of people present to receive the message."

"But that sort of logic could backfire. I could be

labeled a martyr and the bill passed in my memory although I'd prefer to avoid that scenario."

"This guy isn't thinking along those lines. In his mind, you're an obstacle. One he wants out of the way. And Gravestone isn't concerned about those repercussions as long as they can stay in the background and collect their fee."

Apparently Lucas had heard enough, "What do you need from me?"

"The names of people and organizations that might benefit if you were out of the picture. Copies of any hate mail or death threats."

When Lucas didn't respond immediately, Colt added, "The information will stay with us, Senator. No one else will see it."

"That's not my concern. Waters vouched for you. That's good enough for me. I was debating whether or not to back out of the event. Would that help?"

"It might delay things but I doubt it will change anything. They'll just wait for another opportunity."

"If your theory is correct then I agree with that supposition. However, if I cancel, might that pull them off the island and away from your friend?"

Colt's respect for the man went up a notch. "Thank you, Senator. But Cat is a target because of what she saw, or rather, whom she saw. Whether you're here or not won't change that fact. We need to find that man. Those names might be the answer."

"I'll have my staff get you everything we have."

Colt breathed a sigh of relief.

"I'd appreciate being kept informed," Lucas added.

"Of course."

"My aide will be in touch with you immediately. He's

easier to reach than I am but don't hesitate to contact me directly if you feel it's necessary."

Within the hour Colt had received a phone call from Lucas's aide followed by an email with the Senator's personal cell number and the names of individuals and organizations that the Senator's staff considered less than happy with their environmental stance. Not surprisingly, the list was long. Obviously, green wasn't everybody's favorite color.

"Now who has their nose to the grindstone?" Cat asked from the doorway. She'd been standing there watching him concentrate, studying the papers on his desk while furiously scratching notes on a yellow legal pad.

Colt looked up to see her leaning against the doorjamb. He'd bowed to Cat's wishes, leaving her alone for the remainder of the afternoon. Now he was sorry that he had. Creases etched her forehead and those beautiful brown eyes were no longer round but pinched. "Are you okay?"

"Why does everyone keep asking me that question today? Do I look that bad?" From the time she'd walked through the studio door this morning, everyone had been making inquiries about the state of her health in one variation or another. Colt had seemed overly concerned about it. It was for that very reason she wasn't going to tell him that she was fighting a nasty headache. She figured they'd go into panic mode based on the level of concern they'd shown today. The headache was her fault. Working without a break and little food or caffeine was risky behavior with her history of migraines. But that history was ancient and today she'd finally felt like she was getting somewhere with the photos so she'd kept at it. The pounding in her head was the price she'd paid for the progress of the day.

Colt was smart enough to know there wasn't a safe and still honest answer to her question. Something was off but he decided not to press. He crossed the room and brushed the hair from her face. "Just checking. You done for the day?"

"Yeah. It's hard to believe the number of events that go on around here. When do they have time to get anything done?"

"There's no shortage of wealthy people living in the area. For some of them, social and charity events are all they do."

She rolled her shoulders. "I'm going to take a hot bath. I'm still a little sore." She recognized his look of concern. "Stop worrying. Between last night's tumble and sitting at that computer all day my muscles are just a little stiff."

She popped a couple of aspirin and slipped into a steaming bath. After a long soak, Cat felt marginally better. As she dressed she could hear the men chatting in the other room. Do guys 'chat' she wondered or was that a word only attributed to women? The back door slammed shut interrupting that line of thought. It was immediately followed by a shout from Gib.

"Tink! You have a visitor. Get your butt dressed and get out here. Better yet, don't get dressed and get your butt out here," he teased.

Cat was smiling at Gib's continuous attempts to get under Colt's skin until she spotted Rick. He waited for her in the middle of the living room holding a large brown shopping bag - and looking extremely uncomfortable. As soon as he saw her he closed the distance between them, shoving the bag in her direction. "I threw in some choco-lates. My sisters say you can't have one without the other," he whispered.

Curious, Cat peaked inside the bag and immediately

understood his unease. In addition to several brands and types of chocolate, the bag was filled with a variety of feminine hygiene products. What had possessed Rick to bring her tampons? And what was she supposed to say? "Ah, thank you?"

From the time the delivery had been left at the front desk with a note that Cat needed the items, every member of the department had taken great pleasure in ribbing Rick. Based on Cat's reaction, she hadn't been the one behind the request. "You didn't arrange for these to be dropped off at the station, did you?" Rick asked.

Gib's hoot of laughter answered the question. "You son of a bitch," Rick muttered, turning toward the guilty party. Gib, however, was already halfway out the door.

29

When they sat down to dinner that evening Gib had managed to avoid the threatened beating – although there'd been some serious roughhousing at the base of the stairs. Cat discovered that the subject of her cycle had come up as a result of the deviation from her routine that morning. Of course, to the male way of thinking that could only mean one thing. It also explained the numerous inquiries about her health. She decided to be flattered by their concern rather than embarrassed by the subject.

After the meal, though, the lighthearted conversation was put away along with the dishes. The men gathered in the living room, or the war room as Cat thought of it, to review the information received from the Senator's office. Colt had mentioned that Lucas was developing into a prime target but because she'd had her head buried in her own project today, Cat hadn't been aware that he'd been moved to the top of the list. The FBI had been advised of their theory when Rick touched base with them that afternoon. Agent Hernandez had taken their suspicions seriously. The Feds were moving to increase security around Lucas. FDLE had also been brought up to speed and two of their agents would be joining the Lucas "staff" prior to the conference.

With the Senator's safety out of their hands, Colt wanted his team focused on identifying the client. The materials the Senator had sent were extensive and it would require all of them to sort through the possibilities. County Clerks' websites would have to be searched for building permits that backed up to protected lands. Purchases of large tracts of land located near protected areas would need to be researched as well. Although it would add to their workload, Colt didn't want to limit this avenue to the names provided by Lucas. The Senator likely had enemies he wasn't aware existed.

In addition, an Internet search needed to be conducted for the individuals and companies suggested by the Senator. Large-scale developments were frequently mentioned in trade and news publications prior to a permit being issued.

"I'll take that one," Gib volunteered. "That'll free up one of you for the public records search."

"I'm finally nearing the end of my project," Cat told them. "I should finish up sometime tomorrow then I can help Gib." She'd had no luck so far and, she reluctantly admitted, odds were that wouldn't change but she wanted to finish what she'd started.

"I plan on visiting SWF Communities and Island Resorts tomorrow." Colt had immediately recognized the two local companies among the names of businesses Lucas had provided. He wasn't surprised that the two largest developers in the area were unhappy with the proposed legislation.

"How do you plan to get in?" Gib wondered.

"I'm sure I won't be the first photojournalist to show up at their doors without an appointment." Colt had already talked to a couple of magazines he'd done work for in the past. Both publications had offered the use of their names if he needed his story corroborated.

Tasks for the following day were divided up and ideas kicked around. Cat listened intermittently. Her thoughts kept returning to her idea to draw out the shooter. She'd yet to come up with an argument she felt could win Colt over but, she admitted reluctantly, it was unlikely she ever would. She could drop the idea and avoid the inevitable argument or jump in with both feet. She jumped in. "Wouldn't it be to our advantage to catch the guy who took a shot at me last night?"

Colt eyed Cat suspiciously before asking, "What are you getting at?"

"Let's say we get to the point where you're confident you've identified the person who placed the contract. How do you plan to tie him to Gravestone or to the contract on me, for that matter? Bookman isn't around to point any fingers and the authorities aren't going to arrest our suspect based on my description of him." She turned to Rick for confirmation. "Right?"

"No. Your description is too vague for an arrest warrant," Rick agreed, then quickly added, "but that doesn't mean he couldn't be brought in for questioning."

"You're not going to do that. You'd be giving him notice that he's being watched and if he's as high powered as we suspect, his lawyer will have him out before he opens his mouth." Cat had been around attorneys long enough to know they wouldn't let him say a word. "Unless he's an idiot he's not going to admit to anything. And I don't think this guy's anywhere near stupid."

"Are you suggesting we stop looking for him?" Colt

asked. Why was Cat dancing around her point? Normally, she wasn't one to muddy the waters.

"No. But if we caught the shooter…"

"You're assuming our intent is to take him alive," Steve injected.

Cat raised her eyebrows at the oldest member of the team. Not that Steve was old. He only had a couple of years on Colt but he was constantly harangued about being the old man of the group. The few silver strands of hair that were making inroads at his temples made him fair game as far as the others were concerned. She realized that the sniper had unknowingly signed his own death warrant when he accepted the contract on her. Scanning the room she could see they were all thinking along the same lines.

Deciding it was probably prudent to ignore Steve's commentary, particularly with an officer of the law in the room, Cat continued, "Let's say we were able to do both - *capture* the shooter *and* identify the client - we'd have a tidy little package for the Feds. It's not unusual for one suspect to give up the other if they smell a deal." She continued quickly. "I'm going on the assumption that they've met. Since the contractor arranged a meeting with Bookman, I'm guessing there's a good chance he wanted the same connection with his newest hire. There's also the added possibility that the gunman could lead the Feds back to Gravestone."

Colt had considered a similar idea but hadn't been able to devise a plan that he thought would work so he'd dropped it. The guy outside was an expert and they didn't have enough trained manpower to flush him out – not with the amount of territory they'd have to cover. The only other alternative would be to set a trap and since the bait would have to be…. Suddenly he understood why Cat was being so evasive.

"Don't even think about going there. We're not using you as bait to catch the son of a bitch." He waited for Cat to deny that was her intent. Instead she glared back at him before turning to the others in the room in search of an ally. Not surprisingly, the men remained silent.

"Colt, just listen…"

"Forget it." He snatched his empty coffee cup off the table and headed to the kitchen. He didn't need any more caffeine but he had to move or he'd start slamming things. He could feel his nerves dancing across his skin. What the hell was she thinking? Was she insane? How could she think he'd even consider such an idiotic idea?

"I will not 'forget it.' Don't turn your back on me, Colton James. I want to discuss this."

He turned around and found himself facing one very angry woman. Well, he wasn't feeling very sociable himself. "Of all the stupid, harebrained…"

"Stupid? Are you calling me stupid?"

"No - just your plan."

"You haven't heard my plan."

"I don't have to hear it. Only an idiot would think…"

Silence descended upon the room. He didn't need anyone to tell him that he'd screwed up again. Not only had he effectively dismissed Cat's idea but Cat herself. Colt looked at his friends and then the door knowing his team would follow the silent request.

"Hold on a second," she countermanded as the men collectively rose to their feet. "Can any of you honestly say that the idea hasn't crossed your mind?"

Rick looked from Cat to Colt and back again. Sure, he had considered it but had quickly dismissed the thought. Every man in the room knew that Colt would never agree to put Cat in that kind of danger and not one of them could blame him. "Cat, you can't expect…"

"Yes, I can. Look, I know you're not comfortable with the concept. Hell, I'm not excited about the prospect myself but it could work…"

She stopped. The expressions on the men's faces told Cat all she needed to know. There was no point in wasting another breath. None of them would go against Colt. Deep down she'd known it would be a lost battle before she'd began. She pressed fingers into the center of her pounding forehead. Spots were now dancing in her field of vision. Her headache was back with a vengeance. Without saying another word she left the room in search of a dark, quiet place. She'd be fighting another type of battle for the next few hours.

As HE MADE his way through the unit checking to make sure the doors and windows were secure, Colt admitted that his relationship skills were a bit rusty. He wondered if those skills would be any better if the circumstances were different—if Cat's life wasn't hanging in the balance? He quickly dismissed the idea. It was just the natural protective instinct that every man possessed which had kicked in. Nothing wrong with that. Even so, his response to her suggestion had been insulting. He'd have to figure out a way to make it up to her even though he'd had every right to lose his temper. She'd been asking him to set her up as a sacrificial lamb. What the hell had she expected?

Convinced that she had been the one who'd overacted, he decided to give her time to cool off before attempting to make things right. He settled down at his desk and began pulling up information on the developers that he would be visiting the next day.

A vast majority of South Florida's upscale, planned communities were the product of SWF Communities.

While those developments were built for year-round and seasonal residents, the company had recently become a player in the resort market. The founder of the company, J. F. McLaughlin, was a prominent citizen who was active in local politics and had been a major fundraiser for the previous White House Administration. That support had been rewarded with an appointment as Ambassador to Scotland. During his time in the UK he had relinquished the helm of his empire. Though he was now back in the States and on the Board of Directors of SWF, he'd stayed away from the day-to-day decision-making process of the business. Regardless, he would still have a large economic investment in the company.

It was the new Chief Executive Officer, however, that drew Colt's interest. Unlike most CEO's, J. J. Williamson wasn't a golden boy but a roll-up-your-sleeves, get-your-hands-dirty, kind of guy. He'd started at the bottom. Literally. His first job was on one of SFW Communities' many construction crews as a laborer. He'd rapidly made foreman and then supervisor. During that time he obtained a degree in business. Eventually, he found his way to the corporate offices where he'd quickly climbed the ladder to the top floor. Once in Administration, nothing seemed to stand in his way and now he was the CEO. The guy deserved kudos for his drive but he also bore a closer look. It would be interesting to hear what the rank and file had to say about their boss.

The second company, Island Resorts, appeared to be exactly what their name implied – a resort developer. From what Colt could tell, the Lucas bill would take dead aim at them. Many of their developments backed up to public lands. That isolation was one of their selling points. How many projects did they have in the planning stages that might be affected by the proposed legislation? There was no one single individual that drew Colt's attention but Island Resorts would appear to have a great deal to lose if the bill passed and, therefore, would require a little more scrutiny.

Colt shut down the computer after checking the email account that he'd set up for responses to his gun-for-hire posting. Not surprisingly, nothing significant had developed on that front but that didn't mean Gravestone wouldn't still take the bait. Tonight, however, he was glad they hadn't. He didn't have the energy to deal with it. A couple of years out of active duty and he was getting soft. Or was he just getting too old for this kind of thing? Last night's events along with the issues that had come up today had worn him out. Besides, he wanted some time with Cat. Hopefully, he'd given her the space she'd needed to calm down. She'd been uncharacteristically quiet since their blow-up.

As soon as he entered the bedroom he knew something was wrong. The bed was empty, although it was obvious that she'd spent time tossing around on it. He switched on the bedside lamp and quickly scanned the room thinking she might have retreated to the corner where she'd found refuge the previous night. The room was empty.

Nerves on end, he quickly went through the unit, forcing down the panic that was clawing its way to the surface. He was certain she hadn't left the building. The guys on guard would have contacted him immediately if she'd stepped outside.

He returned to the bedroom. Something was off. Then he realized the bathroom door was closed. They were both in the habit of leaving it open when it wasn't in use. No light escaped from beneath the door but still… It was the only place he hadn't checked - and it would be the last place he'd look before he called for backup.

He found her curled up on the oversized bath mat.

She'd been ill. He'd nursed his share of overindulgent, scared and sick recruits to recognize the odor of vomit. "Cat? What's wrong?" he asked, dropping to his knees beside her.

"Migraine," she whispered.

Her head rested on a towel she'd stuffed beneath it. A damp washcloth was pressed to her eyes by her forearm. When he reached for her fisted hand, he was surprised to find it as cold as ice. Her skin was pale as paste. When he tried to lift the arm that shielded her face, she held it in place.

"Don't!" she whispered sharply.

Colt savagely raked his fingers through his hair. He'd led men into battle but he didn't have a clue what he was supposed to do for one small woman.

Cat was in agony. She'd forgotten how painful a migraine could be and couldn't remember ever having one this bad. It had been so long since she'd experienced an attack that she'd failed to recognize the warning signs. Damn. She'd thought she was done with the killer headaches. Still, being a cautious person, she always packed her prescription painkillers when she traveled – just in case. Unfortunately, the pills were among the casualties the night her cottage had been ransacked.

She tried to ignore the man looming over her. It was taking all her concentration to avoid another bout of retching. There was nothing left in her stomach but that hadn't prevented the repeated attempts to purge itself and with each attempt the pain in her head intensified.

"Go away," she begged. "Please?" There was no way she could deal with this torture and a worried man.

Her condition scared Colt. Even after the attack at the mall, Cat had shown spunk and temper. This thing had incapacitated her. Ignoring her moans of protest, he carried her to the bed. Did she actually expect him to leave her on the bathroom floor? Grabbing the comforter, he pulled it over her frigid body in an attempt to warm her and shield her eyes from the light that was obviously causing her pain. Once she was tucked securely against him he called Gib.

"I need to get Cat to the hospital. Just listen," he said firmly when Gib started blasting him with questions. "She says it's a migraine. Tell the guys to do whatever it takes to get us out of here safely and quickly. And keep the noise and lights to a minimum," he added.

Colt held her close for what seemed like an eternity while his friends did what they did best. Instinctively, he wanted to rush out the door with her in his arms but the team needed to secure the area first. Even then, they were taking chances.

Gib entered the room a short time later. "How's she doing?"

"She's been better. We clear to go?" Colt asked, tossing aside the cover. He immediately regretted the sudden move when Cat flinched.

"If you are," Gib answered, staring at the small woman curled tightly against Colt's chest. She was pale and tense. No wonder Colt had sounded so anxious. Gib gently shook out a large swath of heavy, black material that had been draped across his shoulder.

"I grabbed one of our backdrops," he explained to Colt. On the rare occasion when they did studio portraits it served as one of their backgrounds. "I thought it might help to block out some of the light. Steve and Adam are in the Jeep," Gib continued as he arranged the cloth over Cat. "They'll be out front by the time we get downstairs. Don says we're good to go."

"Kevin and Jesse?"

"They'll be creating a little distraction out back then meet up with us at the hospital."

The Jeep appeared as promised just as Colt reached the bottom step. "Do you know the way?" Colt asked, sliding into the rear seat with Cat.

"I assume the guy I'm following does," Steve answered, pulling out onto Periwinkle Way.

Colt hadn't noticed the flashing lights up ahead. He'd been totally focused on Cat. Not paying attention could get her killed. Thank God his friends had his back. "Rick?"

"No. This guy's uniform. Rick's bringing up the rear," Adam answered as he turned around to look at the bundle in Colt's arms. "She gonna be okay?"

Colt lifted a corner of the backdrop and Cat immediately buried her face deeper into his chest. Dropping the cloth back in place he cradled her head gently against his chest. "She has to be," he said softly.

WHEN GIB ENTERED the hospital's Emergency Room with Rick they found Colt pacing the waiting area. "Where's Cat? Why aren't you with her?" he demanded.

"We're not related." Colt spat out the explanation he'd been given by hospital staff when told to leave the room. He'd carried Cat to an examining room but he'd been quickly dismissed when the staff discovered he wasn't family. He'd started to argue but abruptly stopped when Cat visibly cringed at the sound of his raised voice. Besides the debate would have delayed her treatment.

"She's alone?" Now Rick was on alert.

"Strickland's with her." That statement managed to soften the lines etched across Colt's brow. The officer who had escorted them to the hospital had stuck by their side since their arrival. Whether it was by Rick's request or instinct, Colt didn't know or care. He was just grateful that the man had followed him through the double doors because when he'd been pressured to leave, Strickland quickly sized up the situation. He told the staff that their patient was under police protection and that he would not be leaving her under any circumstances. Colt suspected not many people questioned the large black man. The officer's size was intimidating. His demeanor even more so.

Rick slipped his badge from his waistband as he walked toward the security desk. "Let me see what I can find out."

While they waited for word, Colt circled the waiting room trying to force his attention on the security situation. When it came to protection, the hospital emergency room was a logistical nightmare. Even tonight, when it was relatively slow, the place was crawling with people. They'd never be able to secure it without a contingent of men. The only alternative was to stick close to Cat. Strickland wouldn't have a problem doing that but, damn it, Colt should be the one by her side.

It looked like he might just get his wish when Rick returned a few minutes later with one of the ER physicians.

"How is she?" Colt asked the doctor when she was still halfway across the room. Sarah Abiaka was embroidered on the white lab coat above the hospital's name. Colt couldn't help but notice that the woman was stunning. She was tall with high cheekbones and straight black hair, which was gathered in a clip at the base of her neck. He'd spent enough time in the area to be pretty certain she was of either Seminole or Miccosukee heritage.

Dr. Abiaka glanced from Colt to the group of anxious men who had gathered behind him. "She's going to be fine. It looks like a severe migraine but we're going to run a couple of tests to be sure there's nothing else going on."

"It's just a precaution," she added immediately in an effort to quell the concern that flashed across their faces. "Once they're done with her in Radiology we'll give her something for the pain then send her home. She'll probably sleep for the next 12 hours and she may be a little weak for a day or two so don't let that worry you."

"What happened? What caused it?" Colt asked.

"For various reasons, some people are prone to migraines. As to causes, they can be triggered by a number of things depending on the person. Food and stress lead the pack. Ms. Storm told me she has a history of these types of headaches but hasn't had one for quite some time. That's encouraging."

Colt shot a worried look down the corridor where they'd taken Cat. He hadn't found much about the evening that could be considered encouraging.

"She'll be fine. I'll see that she has a prescription before she leaves in the event she gets hit with another one but I'm not overly concerned at this point. If they become more frequent, though, she should see a neurologist."

"I want to see her. Now," Colt added.

Dr. Abiaka almost smiled at the order she'd just been issued. "They'll be taking her to Radiology in a few minutes. You can stay with her until then."

It wasn't necessary to have Cat's cubicle pointed out to him. Strickland was planted in front of the drawn curtain like a tall, dark oak. They acknowledged each other with a simple nod before Colt stepped inside the small space. His heart stilled. *Don't worry. She'll be fine.* Hadn't the doctor just told him that?

But Cat looked as pale as the sheets she lay upon. Those beautiful eyes were covered with a warm compress and someone had tucked an airsickness bag under her hand. He was relieved to see she hadn't made use of it.

Colt knew the instant she was aware of his presence. A tight smile crossed her lips.

"Hey, Kitten," he said taking her outstretched hand. It was still so damned cold.

"Looks like I discovered the secret to getting out of the house," she quipped softly.

"Not funny, Cat. You took ten years off my life."

"Sorry."

"Why didn't you tell me you were hurting?"

"I've always dealt with these things myself."

"You're not alone anymore, Cat. Accept that fact," he state firmly, then softened as he asked, "How's the stomach?"

"They gave me a shot for the nausea."

"Good. Now hush." It was obvious that she was struggling with the conversation. "The doctor said we can take you home after they take some pictures of that thick head of yours."

"We?"

"Everyone's here with the exception of Don and Bill. And we picked up a new guy. Wait until you meet Strickland. You look like a Munchkin next to him."

Just then Colt heard the officer's deep voice questioning some new arrivals. "I think your ride is here," he said, brushing her forehead softly with a kiss.

As he stepped outside to give the attendants room to maneuver Cat out of her confined space, he turned to the officer. "I appreciate your help."

"No problem."

Colt glanced down the corridor filled with medical personnel, patients and their families. "This place makes me nervous as hell but I didn't see that I had a choice. She needed help that I couldn't give her." And that had torn Colt up inside.

"You did the right thing," the big man assured him. "She's been a real trooper," he added. "I haven't heard a single complaint out of her. I respect that. If you need any further help, Rick knows how to reach me."

Strickland turned and followed the attendants down the corridor. Colt waited until they disappeared around the corner then headed toward the lobby to update his friends.

IT WAS another hour before Cat was discharged. Colt had been holding her hand when a nurse finally gave her an injection for the pain. It was a relief when he felt the tension drain from her body as the drug took hold. He carried her out of the ER over the objections of the hospital staff. He'd played by their rules. Now they could live with his. She was in his arms and that's where she would remain until he got her home.

The trip back to Sanibel was as uneventful as the ride to the mainland. As a precaution, however, Rick had additional cruisers waiting at the studio for their return. If anybody had any ideas about targeting Cat on the trip up the stairs, the police presence would, hopefully, discourage it.

The island city had yet to balk at providing assistance when Rick called for backup. But around the clock coverage would have stretched the small force beyond its limits. Colt's team was acting as the first line of defense. The current arrangement had worked out well for the small municipality.

While they'd waited at the hospital, the idea of moving Cat to a different location had been suggested, discussed and dismissed. They all felt that it was better to hold familiar territory. As he carried Cat up the stairs for the second time since their fateful meeting, he admitted that she had been right about drawing out the sniper. Her logic was solid and they couldn't keep up this cat and mouse game forever. He just wasn't sure he could plan an operation that required her to be the bait.

Surprisingly, it was only a little after midnight when Colt finally put Cat to bed. It seemed like an eternity since he found her curled up on the bathroom floor. Now, thankfully, she was resting. He wanted nothing more than to crawl in next to her and pull her close but he had some things to discuss with the guys.

After helping himself to a beer he dropped into a chair and faced the group. "Gib, I'd like to switch assignments with you tomorrow. I'll stay with Cat and do the legwork on the computer if you'll visit the developers and see what you can find out." Colt had wanted to talk to people face to face. As a trained interrogator he knew how to read the "tell" signs people unconsciously gave off. But the individuals he'd planned to question weren't suspects and Gib had a natural talent for reading people. His partner could handle the job and that would allow Colt to stay near Cat in case she needed him.

"I'm surprised you didn't tap me for that in the first place. Charm's what you need for a job like that." Gib wiggled his eyebrows. "Cat says I have it in spades."

A throw pillow sailed across the room in Gib's direction. When his head came up, he saw that his comment had had its intended effect. Colt cracked a small smile for the first time since his call for assistance.

"God, I'm beat." Colt let his head fall back against the chair. "And if this is rough on me what's this been like for her?"

"He's really starting to piss me off."

All heads turned toward the normally quiet Bill. Adam and Jesse had relieved him and Don of their watch as soon as they'd returned. Instead of bedding down, though, they'd come to check on Cat.

"Who?" Rick asked.

"That bastard who's taking pot shots at our little lady. I was really hoping he'd show himself tonight when you guys took off."

Colt could imagine what Bill would like to do if he had the guy in his sights. Colt could easily understand his anger but Cat had been right when she said the shooter was of more use to them alive than dead. The men knew it as well. They were just frustrated. He looked at Rick. "When Cat asked you about setting a trap, you sidestepped the question. Had you considered it?"

Trust had always bound Rick and Colt together. They'd made a good team because they knew they could rely on each other. Neither played head games. Rick answered him with the honesty his friend would expect.

"I did."

"Yet you didn't bring it to the table for discussion." Colt scanned the room. "None of you did. Why? Because it wasn't feasible or because you thought I'd object?"

"Of course you'd object." Rick answered for the group. "And none of us wants any harm to come to Cat."

"But could it be done?"

"If properly planned? Yes. You know it could."

"Wait a minute." Gib had been listening to the exchange thinking he was missing the joke. He now realized that they weren't kidding. "You guys can't be serious!"

"You think I like the idea?" Colt asked him. "But Cat's right. Fingering the client won't be enough to end this nightmare she's trapped in any more than eliminating the sniper would. As long as the client is willing to pay the price, there will be someone just as eager to collect the fee."

"Identifying the client isn't enough. We need to connect him to Gravestone and a contract for hire," Rick elaborated. "If Cat's theory that the two men have met is correct, and I agree that there's a good chance that it is, then we have our connection."

"What makes you think he'd talk?" Gib couldn't believe it would be that easy.

"He'll talk," Steve assured him.

Rick chose to ignore the comment. As a law officer, what Steve was insinuating was cause for alarm, but silently he agreed with him. "We're not talking about some religious fanatic who's willing to sacrifice his life for a cause here. This guy's a cold-blooded businessman. He'll cooperate when the alternatives are presented to him."

"Rick?" Colt looked up from studying his hands. "I'd like you to work with the team to develop a plan."

"You're the tactician."

"I'm too close to this."

"All the more reason for you to take the lead. You won't leave anything to chance where Cat's safety is concerned."

COLT STOOD BY THE BED, just watching Cat sleep - if you could call her drug-induced state sleep. Whatever it was, it was preferable to the pain she'd endured earlier tonight. Her breathing was now steady and most of her color had returned. He debated bunking in his office or on the couch so he wouldn't disturb her but what if she woke during the night and needed something? He laughed at himself. Who was he kidding? The truth was he needed to be with her – to know that she was safe. Stripping down to his briefs, he crawled under the covers and gently tugged her into his arms.

30

If Cat's bladder hadn't been pressing the issue she would have rolled over and gone back to sleep. She felt like she'd been drugged. Well, duh. That was one powerful shot they'd given her. Blinking a couple of times to clear her vision she focused on the bedside clock. It was after noon which explained her urgent need to pee.

Slowly, she raised herself up to a sitting position. No pain. No nausea. No dizziness. All positive signs. Easing out of the bed she tested her legs. She felt weak as a kitten – no pun intended – but otherwise not too bad.

After she answered nature's call she decided she had enough energy remaining to wash her face and brush her teeth. Both were begging for attention. The thought of a shower sounded heavenly but that would have to wait until she was a little steadier on her feet.

Colt appeared as she was splashing water on her face. He stood in the doorway, arms across his chest, scowling. She was getting used to that look.

"What are you doing up? You're supposed to be in bed," he grumbled. He wasn't sure whether to be relieved or concerned when he'd heard her moving around.

"I'll be done in a minute," she stated, ignoring his question.

Colt flashed a quick smile. She was back to being her obstinate self. He could finally relax. Leaning against the long granite countertop, he waited.

"How's the head?"

"Lucky it's still attached."

"The doctor said you'd probably sleep for a couple more hours."

"And that's exactly what I plan to do," she said as she slipped by him.

"Can I get you anything?" he asked as he pulled the covers over her shoulder. Guess not, he thought. She'd already drifted into a peaceful slumber.

COLT MUNCHED on a sandwich while he rummaged through the cabinets trying to find something resembling soup or broth. Cat would be hungry when she woke up. He figured it best to keep her menu light. He wasn't having any luck, though, so he called Rick.

"Can you pick up some soup for Cat before you head over this way?"

"I'll make a stop at Mama's for some of her cure-all minestrone. How's Cat doing?"

"Better. She was up for a few minutes but she's sleeping again."

"She'll be fine, Colt. She's tough."

"As nails," Colt added but just a quickly his mind flashed back to the picture of her on the bathroom floor. That image would haunt him for a long time to come.

"Have you heard from Gib?" Rick asked.

"No, but I wasn't expecting to. Something up?"

"I just had a brief conversation with the head of security at SWF Communities," Rick told Colt. All calls coming in to the Sanibel PD regarding Cat, or any member of the team, were being routed to Rick. "They wanted to know what we could tell them about Gib."

"That sounds promising."

"Could be. Could be they're just normally cautious."

"What'd you tell them?"

"The truth. That he's a respected photographer on the island."

"From my research, I get the impression that a rift has developed between the Board and the CEO. It appears to be tied to the Lucas legislation."

Colt had decided to start his research with the local developers then broaden his search. Not surprisingly, he found several articles where both companies expressed concerns about the bill. But it was SWF Communities that was proving to be the more interesting of the two.

"You got something that links them?"

"Couldn't get that lucky. But an article in last month's *Florida Trend* reported several of the Directors want SWF to abandon its entry into the resort market and stick with planning residential communities. They sighted the proposed legislation as the reason. Williamson was rather outspoken in his disagreement. Apparently he doesn't believe that the bill is going to pass."

"And he believes that because…?"

"He didn't elaborate – at least not in that article. I'll call Gib. See if he can troll for a few answers while he's casting a net."

. . .

THE NEXT TIME Cat awakened she felt closer to normal. A shower, then some food, she decided. Colt poked his head into the bathroom while she was showering. The fact that there were no comments about joining her told Cat he was still in mother hen mode. Just as well, she needed nourishment before she'd have the strength for those kinds of activities. When she finally walked into the living room seven pair of eyes locked on to her like heat seeking missiles.

They looked so concerned. No one had ever come to her aid like these guys had. She'd never perfected the art of expressing her feelings and was afraid if she opened her mouth to tell them how much their actions had meant the tears would start to fall. So, in lieu of words, she made her way around the room embracing each one. Gib, of course, made a production out of the show of affection by laying a wet, sloppy kiss on her mouth. She was laughing by the time she reached Colt.

"You, sir," she gave him a quick wink, "will get your reward later but accept this as a down payment." As she often did, she tugged at the collar of his shirt to bring his head down to her level. She nibbled on his lips then took the kiss deeper. The others in the room were forgotten until someone let out a "whoop."

Colt was the first to break away but his gaze never left hers. "Sit," he said, coaxing her down to the floor in front of the coffee table. "You need to eat."

She didn't argue. She'd emptied the contents of her stomach well before the trip to the hospital and after sleeping for half a day, she was starving. Kevin appeared carrying a large bowl of steaming, aromatic soup. He sat the dish, along with a basket of bread, in front of her. She reached for the spoon then froze as she glanced at the laptop that was sharing the table with her dinner. A photo stared back at her.

"Who's that?" she asked, pointing to the screen.

Several guys turned their attention to the pretty girl centered on the computer screen but Gib was the one that responded.

"That's Kim. She was my escort at SWF Communities. I just finished downloading the pictures I took today."

"Did you get her number?" someone asked.

"What do you think?" another joked.

Colt ignored the banter. Instead he concentrated on Cat. Resting a hand on her shoulder he could feel the tension that now gripped her. "What is it? Do you recognize her?"

"Not her," she said, pointing to the man in the background of the shot. "Him."

"That's J.J. Williamson, the CEO," Gib replied.

"Do you have any more pictures of him?" she asked anxiously. But she was already scrolling through the shots.

"Yeah, I'm sure I do."

She released the computer to Gib. He quickly found a second photo of Williamson. Silence drifted over the room while Cat studied it. "Any more?"

Gib quickly found two more photos. The CEO was not the main subject of any of the shots so none of them had a full frontal view of the man but that didn't matter. What she was looking at was his general appearance and bearing. His size and coloring were spot-on but what screamed to her was his presence.

"Is that him?" Colt asked, leaning over her shoulder, studying the last photo.

"It's him," she answered.

"You're sure?"

Solemnly, Cat turned to Colt, "I'd bet my life on it."

31

Cat's identification of Williamson had surprised everyone but her. She'd been looking for him for so long she figured it was about time he'd turned up. "Where the hell has he been?"

"What do you mean?" Rick asked.

"Those pictures that I've been going blind over. If he's such a big shot, shouldn't he have been at one of those functions?"

"From what I gathered today," Gib volunteered, "he's not much of a socializer."

"What else did you discover?" Colt asked.

"I got the standard PR story about his rise from the construction site to the executive suite but couldn't get any personal info on the man. It was pretty obvious, though, that his staffers don't care much for him. That struck me as odd at first. You'd think they'd respect a man who came up through their ranks."

Cat looked at Gib with understanding, "But then you saw him."

Gib nodded. "And overheard him. The feeling is

mutual. The man doesn't think much of his subordinates, which goes a long way toward explaining the negative vibes I picked up every time his named was mentioned. Apparently, he's forgotten his roots and the people he's passed on the way up resent the hell out of it."

"Did you hear anything about his reason for believing the Lucas Bill was doomed?" Colt asked.

"The people I spoke with either couldn't, or wouldn't, elaborate and I didn't want to sound any alarms by pushing the issue. They did repeat Williamson's conviction that the legislation wouldn't pass but the responses sounded rehearsed to me."

"How the hell does this guy succeed?" Cat asked no one in particular. "He's smart, I'll give him that, but he doesn't have an Ivy League background. Obviously, he hasn't developed many social connections. Apparently, his people skills are almost non-existent. How does a man like that rise to the top of a large corporation and stay there?"

"We need to find out everything we can about him." Rick directed the next comment to Gib. "We need his schedule. You did get that girl's number, didn't you? Maybe she can help us."

Letting out an exaggerated sigh, Gib pulled his phone from his pocket and headed out of the room. "What I have to suffer through for you guys."

Cat turned to Rick. "You don't plan to question him, do you?"

Rick thought about that for a second. "I don't think that would be our best move..."

"Because it would tip our hand," she finished. They'd already discussed the possibility but nothing had changed to turn it into an advantage for them.

"I'd rather not alert the FBI just yet, either," Colt

added. He didn't want the Feds questioning Williamson before they had a plan in place.

A small laugh escaped Cat's lips. "Damn, and I was looking forward to witnessing my first clusterfuck."

After an instant of stunned silence the room burst into laughter. It was so easy to forget this petite woman's rapier tongue. Pulling her back against him, Colt smiled into her hair. He knew the smart-ass remark was Cat's way of letting the team know she was going to be fine.

"What's next?" she asked.

"Bed." The guys would be more comfortable discussing the upcoming topic without the subject of it sharing the room. "You need sleep," Colt clarified when she gave him an impish grin.

Definitely still in mother hen mode, Cat thought. Would she ever get used to someone fussing over her?

"I'll get there shortly. I was taking care of myself long before you came along."

Colt lifted Cat to her feet. She was definitely feeling better if she was snapping at him. "We have work to do," he told her as he pointed her toward the hall.

"And what? The little lady will get in the way?"

Colt could see the storm clouds gathering. Tread carefully here, he told himself.

"Cat? Please?" he implored as he extended his hand - a peace offering as well as a request. He relaxed slightly when she took it.

Colt leaned against the bathroom's door jamb watching Cat ready herself for bed. He didn't think he'd ever get his fill of this woman. How in God's name was he supposed to develop a stratagem that would put her life in further jeopardy? Tactical specialist or not, he wasn't at all sure he was the best one to devise a plan. So many things could go wrong. One mistake... He shook his head to clear it. With a mission before them, he should have spent the day drafting different scenarios to debate with his team. Yet not a single option had made it to the pad on his desk. Avoidance. He'd been playing that game all day. But now his time was up. Putting a name to the client had started the clock ticking.

Peaking over the plush towel she was using to dry her face, Cat studied Colt's expression in the mirror. "Are you going to tell me what's going on? Why you're so uptight?"

Her question didn't surprise him. Cat had been doing a good job of reading him since that first day on the beach.

"You just got out of the hospital," he answered a little too quickly. He wanted to have the details worked out before he told her about their idea. He was convinced she needed to rest and if she knew what they were working toward he suspected she'd get little of that.

"Bullshit."

"You've had a rough couple of days..." he started to explain.

"Fine," she snapped, cutting him off. Men! Did he think she was blind or just plain stupid? Well, if he didn't want to talk about it then she couldn't think of damn thing she wanted to say to him.

Colt took a step back as she stormed passed him. What the hell had pissed her off? And she was definitely pissed.

"What's got into you?" he asked, approaching the bed.

"Excuse me? You want to know what's eating me but the subject of what's got you tied up in knots is off limits? Do you see something wrong with this picture?"

"I'm not 'tied up in knots'. You just need your rest."

"And I said, 'fine'." She rolled away from him.

Shit. If he didn't settle this he knew damn well he wouldn't be able to concentrate on the task ahead. It was going to be difficult enough without the added distraction.

The mattress sagged as Colt sat down next to her. She waited but when he didn't speak, she finally turned to face him. The muscles pulsed in his forearms as he tightened his fists.

"What do you want from me, Cat?" he asked.

"An honest answer. Is that too much to ask?"

He looked into those big brown eyes. He could see that steel backbone returning but she'd given him such a scare. He hadn't lied when he said he wanted her to rest. She'd need to be at one hundred percent when the time came to lure the gunman out and it looked like that time was quickly approaching.

"We weren't prepared for you to ID the client tonight," he admitted to her.

"You weren't expecting me to identify him at all."

The corner of his mouth ticked up. "Yeah, well, I was wrong, wasn't I?"

She let his confession slide. "So what's the problem? I'd have thought you'd all be dancing for joy at the breakthrough."

"It moves up our timetable. We figured we'd have a couple of days before we narrowed down the suspects. We'd planned to use that time to develop an offensive operation."

"What sort of offensive operation?" When the answer to her question didn't come fast enough to suit her, she added, "Don't make me hurt you, Colt."

Despite his somber mood, a smile tugged at the corner of his mouth before it quickly sobered. "Setting a trap for the gunman."

Cat stared at him. She'd have bet her precious Roadster that the subject would never come up again.

"If you've changed your mind..."

"No! No, I haven't changed my mind. You just surprised me."

"As much as I hate to admit it, you're right on that point, as well. The shooter is the thread that binds everything together. If we can get him, the whole thing could unravel."

Cat wanted to explore the subject further but first she had to deal with the coiled bundle of nerves sitting next to her.

"That still doesn't explain why are you so tense."

"The hell it doesn't! We're talking about using you as bait! Making you a target for a professional killer. What if something goes wrong? What if something happens to you?"

Cat threw back the covers and scooted on to Colt's lap, pressing her head to his chest. She could hear his heart racing. She stayed in his arms, wishing she could absorb some of his worries. Wishing she could give him back some of the confidence that he'd lost in those mountains of Afghanistan. When his pulse finally slowed, she lifted her head and stared into those intense blue eyes.

"I'll go along with whatever you decide." She pressed her finger to his lips preventing him from interrupting. "But I know you can pull this off *and* keep me safe. Don't let what happened in that village cause you to doubt yourself any longer. No one here will second-guess your instincts. Those guys out there would follow you through the gates of hell. They trust you, Colt. I trust you." She sealed the promise with a kiss.

Colt took the strength she offered. Lapped it up like a thirsty animal. He wasn't sure he deserved the faith she bestowed on him but he knew damn well he would not let her down. When she attempted to deepen the kiss, he pulled back. If he didn't stop now, he might not get to the planning session tonight.

"You really do need to get that rest," he said, smiling. "Things will start to move quickly."

She cocked her head, questioning the remark.

"Once we start investigating Williamson, there's a chance he'll figure out someone's on to him. If he does..."

"He'll want to ramp things up," she finished, thoughtfully. "It's one thing to wonder if a witness might be able to identify you. It's another thing all together to *know* that she can."

"I thought we'd have a couple of days to develop and fine-tune an operation. We can't assume that we'll have that kind of time now."

"Then I guess you'd better get your ass out there and get busy."

32

A fter several hours of brainstorming and with more than just an outline of a plan in place, the team took a break. With the exception of Kevin and Don, who had disappeared into the lush landscaping to relieve Jesse and Bill, the guys had gathered on the rear deck nursing both beers and cigars.

Colt leaned against the railing, listening to his friends razz one another. It was customary for the crew to blow off some excess energy this way. The only difference now was the addition of Gib and his partner was holding his own among this band of soldiers - fielding barbs and needling as though he'd been doing it for years.

Colt could now admit to himself how much he'd missed this camaraderie - the bad jokes, the bullshitting - the friendships. It would seem he owed Gib another debt. Being AWOL for the photo shoot at Lighthouse Pointe had started a chain of events that brought them all to this place, this time. He'd found old friends and, he reflected sentimentally, lost his heart.

He stared out into the thick vegetation wondering if

the sniper was out there watching them. They all agreed that their prey was talented. Even with the team's focus on guarding Cat, they'd done their share of tracking these past few days. A couple of times they suspected that they'd come pretty damn close but they had yet to lay eyes on the bastard.

At one time Colt had speculated that there might have been more than one gunman sent to accomplish the task. No one, no matter how good, could keep up twenty-four seven surveillance indefinitely. Eventually, a person would lose focus, forcing a mistake. A slip up of that kind could be fatal. A professional would know that.

But Colt was convinced that Gravestone wouldn't commit two men to do the job of one. Especially to rid themselves of a witness they currently had little reason to suspect could lead back to them. The more people targeting Cat, the better the chance that one of them would be caught. No, the assassin assigned to this detail was confident that if Cat slipped away he would be able to locate her. Colt figured the bastard was probably enjoying the game. Not for long, though. The hunter was about to become the hunted.

Rick's phone chimed again. Text messages had been coming in steadily since he'd placed calls to the team members who had remained on standby. At last count, four men were on the way and Rick was confident that number would increase. By the time Gib returned tomorrow with Williamson's itinerary, Colt and Rick would have two units set up. Rick's team would focus on Williamson while Colt's squad would catch themselves a killer.

But he was getting ahead of himself. The sprint to the finish would begin in the morning. Tonight he needed to shut it down for a while and get some rest - or not - depending on how Cat was feeling.

33

Cursing, Cat swatted at the blaring alarm clock. Who the hell had set the damn thing anyway? Half asleep, she slapped it several more times to no avail.

Colt reached for his cell phone. He couldn't blame Cat for being disoriented. When he returned to the room and found her sleeping his intent had been to let her rest. But then she'd snuggled her tight little ass up against his groin and he hadn't been able to keep his hands from wandering to places soft and warm.

"What do you want?" Colt snapped. Maybe there was time to pick up where they'd left off in the wee hours of the morning.

"Do you plan to get this show on the road sometime today?" Gib inquired.

Colt zeroed in on the clock that Cat had attempted to pulverize. Shit! He couldn't remember the last time he'd slept this late. "Is the coffee ready?" he asked, throwing back the covers on his way toward the shower.

"It will be as soon as we let ourselves in." Gib was tempted to add "again." As was their custom, the guys used their key to enter through the kitchen but retreated when they realized the couple remained in bed. While it might be fun riding Colt about his now active love life none of them would intentionally intrude upon it.

"Get it started. I'll be out in ten minutes."

Leaning back under the pelting spray, Colt allowed the hot water to wash away the cobwebs. There was a lot to be accomplished today. It had been a long time since he'd readied himself for a mission and this one was twofold. He smiled, realizing he was looking forward to it.

"I thought we'd be environmentally friendly and save water," Cat said, stepping into the spray.

She had watched Colt's very firm backside disappear into the bathroom, reminding her of their lovemaking of the night before. He'd been gentle, still worried about the state of her health. Well, she wasn't made of glass and she knew of a very interesting way to make that point.

"As enticing as that sounds, Cat, you might want to rethink the suggestion. The guys are out there and they could hear a pin drop."

Her eyes sparkled and her smile broadened as she lowered herself to her knees in front of him. Closing her fingers around his growing erection, she whispered, "Then I guess you'll just have to be very, very quiet."

COLT WAS HAVING difficulty keeping the silly grin off his face. Cat had surprised him – *again*. She'd teased, tasted, and tempted. She may not have a lot of experience when it came to seduction but she had one hell of an imagination. Only sheer will had kept him from shouting when she finally opened for him.

"I overslept," he offered in response to the curious looks that greeted him in the kitchen a good deal more than ten minutes later. The roomful of cocky grins told him that his friends didn't buy his story.

"I *did* oversleep," he repeated but his teeth-baring grin did little to convince them.

"Anybody hear from Rick?" he asked, quickly changing the subject.

"Yeah, he called while you were *sleeping*," Steve grinned. "Jack and Troy will arrive within the hour. That's the last of them. They'll meet the others at the station."

The additional men were being directed to the police station where Rick was assembling his group. If their plan was to succeed, it was critical that the assassin not get wind of the reinforcements.

"Alright then, let's wrap this up."

34

C at ducked into the kitchen just long enough to get her morning shot of caffeine. She had no intention of inserting herself into the current topic of conversation. She'd leave the planning to the experts.

Besides she wanted to start to work on a personal project today. It was way past time for her to make some decisions about her future. Which brought her back to the original reason for her trip to Sanibel —where to live and how to earn a living.

Where to live was the easy part or at least it was now. Cat had made so many trips to Sanibel Island that she'd lost count. Something about this enchanted isle kept calling her back as if it wasn't finished with her. Perhaps it was the same magic that had drawn a troubled Colt here. She wouldn't be surprised to learn that there were mystical creatures in the surrounding waters that lured injured souls to these shores so they could be mended. She chuckled at the silly thought but there was no denying she always left here feeling restored. So here she would stay because the island, and Colt, wanted her.

Never before had she felt drawn to someone like she was to this man. She might not need *a* man, but she needed Colt. God, what a terrifying admission. She hadn't run from anything since her sixteenth birthday and wasn't going to start now.

So with that decision made, it left her with one more to puzzle out – a source of income. What did she want to do? Actually, that wasn't a fair question. She knew what she *wanted* to do. Operating a gardening business appealed to her more than it ever had. These last couple of weeks served as confirmation that life, was indeed, too short. The big question was could she do it?

It was a complicated question that would require some serious research. The plan today was to spend time doing just that. Before she dug in, though, she wanted to talk to Jason. He was her friend and mentor and the one who had first planted the "seed" in her head - that she get out of an office environment and into the earthly one.

Oddly enough, her love of plants and gardening sprang from Jason and Ellie. Years ago, on a visit to their home in West Palm Beach, she found herself puttering beside them in their flower garden. She discovered that she had an innate talent for working with plants. What didn't come to her naturally, she learned from spending countless hours at nurseries asking questions from the experts. She'd eventually taken more structure classes and earned the designation of Master Gardener. Jason frequently kidded her about the title because she lived in an apartment with no place of her own to garden.

As it turned out, that wasn't a problem. Word got around about her horticultural skills so she rarely had a free weekend. Instead she'd find herself designing planting areas for co-workers, volunteering at community gardens or digging up someone's yard - and loving every minute of it.

Jason and Ellie should both be in West Palm now, Cat figured. Ellie was to begin her cancer treatments sometime this week. Jason still had some work to finish up in Tallahassee but he would be dividing his time between both locations until his business at the Capitol was finished. Cat picked up the phone.

"Cat. Are you okay?" Not surprisingly, Ellie had answered Jason's cell. He had ignored Cat's request to withhold information from his wife. Cat argued that the woman had enough stress in her life and Cat didn't want to add to it. But Jason had refused to keep his wife in the dark. They'd never kept secrets and he wasn't going to start now. Besides, he told her, Ellie would know something was up and that would worry her even more.

"I'm fine. The question is — how are you? You start your treatment soon, don't you?"

"This afternoon. When are you coming for a visit? You've got to see all the hats I've found. I'm going for a vintage Elton John look this time. It might bring a little attention to this nasty disease. Make a few women think about getting screened."

Bless Ellie. Cat swore she'd invented the recipe for making lemonade. If there was a more optimistic person on this earth, Cat hadn't met them yet.

Jason and Ellie had not been blessed with children. That revelation had initially seemed unfair to Cat - that such a nurturing couple hadn't had a gaggle of kids to raise and love. But Ellie hadn't seen it that way. She'd once told Cat that if she and Jason were meant to have a brood then they would have had them. Instead she took it as a sign that she was put on this earth for another purpose. She'd found that purpose in volunteering and raising money for kids in need. It was her passion. She headed up numerous charities devoted to the care, education and well-being of children.

"I'll be there as soon as I can."

"We'll go on a hat safari. Speaking of heads, how's yours?"

"Fine."

"You don't need to take that tone, Cat. You have no reason to be upset."

"Colt shouldn't have worried you. Nothing is going to happen, not with him hovering over me."

"Won't argue with that. We've talked, you know? I like him. Besides," she added with a chuckle, "he's *hot*."

Cat snorted out a laugh. "How would you know that?"

"He sent a photo of the two of you in Key West. You sure picked a good one, sweetie. So, are you going to stay there – with him?"

"God, Ellie… It scares the hell out of me," she admitted.

It was Ellie's turn to laugh. "Falling in love should be easy compared to what you've been through these last few weeks. Relax, Cat, and enjoy it. Taking that tumble with the right man will be the best trip of your life. Trust me on that one."

And she would know, Cat thought. "I guess I'll find out." Because it was too late to stop the fall.

"It's obvious that he loves you." Ellie could hear the affection in Colt's voice whenever she mentioned Cat. "He hasn't said the words, has he?" Ellie continued when Cat said nothing. "That's not surprising. You wear your independence like a shield, young lady. You might consider taking the first shot at that announcement. Surprise him. Here's Jason. You be careful."

Cat thought Ellie had handed the phone off to Jason until she added, "We love you, Cat."

Ah, crap. Why did Ellie have to go and say that? She knew Cat wasn't good at the mushy stuff.

"You two done blabbing?"

Cat instantly smiled. Jason to her rescue.

"It would seem so since you've snatched the phone away from your beautiful wife."

Jason chuckled at Cat's retort. The moment she'd walked into his office to interview for the job as his secretary, the two of them had hit it off. She was quick-witted and smart. He would miss their daily sparring.

"Everything okay there?"

"Everything's fine. I'm sure Colt will give you details when he reports in," she jibed then turned serious. "I wanted to talk to you about something else - starting that business."

"You're finally going to do it?"

"If I can get a push off this ledge I'm stuck on, yes."

"Then consider yourself pushed."

"Gee, Jason, is that all there is to it? Damn. If I'd known it was that easy I'd have done it years ago."

"Cat, you don't need a push. You have brains, tenacity and talent. You've been stashing money away for years and you know you have at least one investor, namely me, waiting in the wings. So stop hedging and just do it. How many times do I have to tell you that?"

Cat smiled into the phone. "Believe it or not, Jason, you didn't have to tell me this time."

"Pardon?"

"But if you're in the mood to do some cheerleading," she continued, "Give me a minute and I'll see if I can find some pompoms."

"Very funny. If you didn't call for a dose of encouragement, what did you want?"

"To bounce some ideas off of you and to get some free advice."

"Why didn't you just say so?"

They spent the next hour kicking around some startup ideas and getting Jason's input on the legal technicalities involved. Toward the end of the conversation Colt stepped into the office.

"Hang on a minute." Cat smiled at Colt. "It's Jason. Would you like to give him your report now or wait until later when I'm not listening?"

Her voice was so sweet it would have made a diabetic cringe. Obviously, she wasn't happy about his updates. No surprise there. Colt had known Cat wouldn't like his regular conversations with Jason and Ellie. Tough. They cared about her. What he could safely tell them, he would. If Cat was expecting him to be penitent, she was the one in for a surprise.

"Later," then added, "when you're not listening." So he wouldn't miss it, he remained focused on those eyes. He wasn't disappointed when he caught the quick flash of temper.

Cat bit her tongue when she saw the grin creep across his handsome face. Point to Colt, she acknowledged, but not the match.

Ending the call she crossed the room, allowing Colt to pull her into his embrace. "You shouldn't worry Ellie," Cat scolded him.

"I have a feeling that woman can handle just about anything. If I didn't know better, I'd think you were related." His lips touched her silky hair. "I'm looking forward to meeting her."

"I promised her I'd get over there soon."

"And we will. It won't be much longer, Cat. We're in the home stretch."

Colt stepped back. He had to leave. They were waiting for him at the station. He should have left an hour ago, but with only a few details remaining on this end of the mission, he'd wanted to wind things up here before heading out.

"I'll be with Rick. Call if you need me."

Cat's eyes sparkled with mischief. "There are six big, strapping men out there. What would I need you for?"

Suddenly, she was backed up against the wall. Colt's mouth covered hers, determined to wipe the grin off her face. But when her lips parted in surprise, his tongue swept in. Tightening his hold, he plundered her mouth. His fingers stroked her throat just before they found her breast. Her sigh of submission fueled the fire burning inside him.

He might have taken her up against the wall if the nails digging into his back hadn't pulled him out of his lust-induced state. Damn, what this woman could do to his senses. He'd meant the kiss to be a clever comeback to her teasing remark but he'd quickly lost himself in her surrender. Holding her at arm's length, he asked, "Does that answer your question?"

Stunned by the voracious kiss, Cat could only nod her head. Game, set and match to Colt, she conceded.

35

Cat's bewildered look was still trapped in Colt's head when he arrived at the police station. Her expression had been priceless and worth the discomfort of his straining erection. Fortunately, he had the problem under control by the time he'd gotten off the phone with Rick. He'd called his friend as soon as he'd pulled out of his drive to let him know he was finally on his way. His reputation for being punctual was taking a beating since Cat arrived on the island.

When he reached the conference room, Colt paused in the doorway to look at the men who were gathered there. For the second time in just a few short weeks, Colt wished he were meeting these friends and comrades under different circumstances. But the reason couldn't be helped and if it didn't exist, these guys wouldn't be here. He was glad they were.

Troy MacKenzie sat on Rick's right. He was known as "Hollywood" by the team because of his movie star good looks. Much like Gib, Colt didn't think there was a woman on the planet that Troy couldn't charm. He'd led their fire support team during the time he served with Colt. The man had an uncanny ability when it came to targeting the enemy.

Next to Troy was Jack Grovont. Colt had immediately recognized the shadowed face under the tattered Stetson. The hat was fitting since the man was a cowboy - literally and figuratively. Born and raised in Wyoming, Jack worked on the family ranch until September 11, 2001. On the morning of September 12, he was waiting outside of the Army recruiting office in Cheyenne when they unlocked their doors. Colt had often speculated that being raised in the West gave Jack his natural ability to track – that or he was part bloodhound. If Jack couldn't find the sniper, chances were he couldn't be found.

Gene Shannon's red hair was longer than it had been when Colt had last seen the tall Irishman but it was still as bright as a copper penny. "Red" was an electronics wiz. He also possessed the hearing of an owl. With Jack and Red on his tail, the sniper's elusive days were numbered.

Tommy Banks, Manny Ramirez and Craig Bukowski leaned against the far wall returning their former commander's assessing look. The Three Musketeers, Colt mused, but kept the thought to himself. He was only aware of one open attempt to tag the three with the names of Alexander Dumas' fictional characters. Taking offense to being compared to men in tights, they'd made their displeasure clear. The comparison was never again resurrected fearing one's ability to procreate would be in serious jeopardy. The three men were a team within a team. They were so attuned to each other that it was eerie even by Ranger standards. Individually, they were dangerous. Collectively, they were deadly. In hand-to-hand combat, Colt would bet the proverbial farm that they could not be bested.

"Who's out saving the world if you're all here on this island?" Colt asked from the doorway.

Rick swore he felt the air in the room move as the group let out a collective sigh of relief. There wasn't a man present who hadn't known of Colt's struggle to deal with the ramifications of that disastrous mission. At one time or another, they had all tried to help. But because their presence only reminded him of what he'd been trying to forget, they'd reluctantly given him the distance he'd requested but only after Rick had arrived to become their eyes and ears.

What Rick had found when he landed on Sanibel was a man who had begun to pick up the pieces of his life. Initially, the improvements were subtle. While Rick gave Colt credit for the lion's share of his emotional reconstruction there wasn't a member of the team that didn't feel they were in Gib's debt for the lifeline he'd tossed to their friend. Although Gib would never admit to it, Rick didn't believe the ponytailed, ladies' man had been looking for someone to join him on a photo shoot the day he'd met Colt. He very much doubted a day taking pictures had been planned at all. But Gib possessed an unusual ability to read people and Rick suspected he'd read Colt like a book that day. Now Cat had stumbled into Colt's life. Rick was convinced that she was the guide he'd needed to navigate the final leg of his journey home. Everyone gathered was aware of those facts but seeing the transformation was entirely different than hearing about it.

"We're leaving that to the young guys," Jack Grovont commented, rising to greet his former commander.

"Christ, if you're old then I must be ancient," Colt said, smiling.

For the second time in just a few weeks, Rick allowed himself the pleasure of watching old friends greet each other. A clasp of hands. A brotherly hug. A slap on the back. Each one rekindling the connection that they all feared had been lost.

Then, as if no time had passed between them, everyone settled in around the conference table and listened as Colt brought them up to speed and outlined the strategy they'd finished earlier that morning.

Gib joined the group as the briefing was winding up.

"Nice lunch?" Rick asked with a grin.

"I'll only admit to a productive one."

As introductions were made, Gib surreptitiously slid a notebook across the table toward Colt. The action told Colt that the information acquired would, among other things, contain data that would allow Don to do some creative hacking. The two men had agreed this morning that if Gib were successful in getting that key info, they'd keep those details from Rick. It was highly unlikely that Don would be discovered snooping in areas considered off limits by the authorities but if his hand did get caught in the metaphorical cookie jar, Rick could honestly claim that he had no knowledge of the act. Plausible deniability.

There was also an unspoken agreement that Rick would be elsewhere when they apprehended the sniper – as Colt now had no doubt that they would. Answers would need to be obtained before the authorities were called. If Rick were present, he'd be required to take the bastard into custody, read him his rights and then wait for his lawyer to show up. Nothing would be gained from that scenario except, most likely, the man's death. They all knew that Gravestone would not have a get-out-of-jail-free card and answers were difficult to obtain from a dead man. They stood a better chance of getting the information they needed before the authorities showed up.

Colt skimmed through the notebook he'd been given.

"His schedule, if you can call it that, is erratic," he commented.

"He's late for most meetings," Gib added, "and constantly moves items around on his calendar, according to Kim. I got the impression it's meant to catch staff off guard."

"Nice guy," Troy commented, sarcastically.

"He doesn't often leave the building during business hours. I understand he likes people to come to him. Holds court, you could say," Gib continued, "Other than the office, he's either at work, home or at his gym. The addresses are there along with the description of his car and his tag number."

Colt didn't ask how Gib had managed to get that information. "Red. Jack. Troy. I'd like you on the sniper detail." Addressing the three-some still leaning against the wall he said, "You're with Rick. I don't want Williamson taking a leak without one of you knowing it."

Colt turned back to Rick. "You sure you have enough men?" He was hesitant to leave Rick with only these three to cover Williamson but he didn't want to pull any member of the first team off to cover Williamson. The sniper might get suspicious if some of the "regulars" suddenly disappeared and Colt needed the three he'd selected because of their talent in tracking.

"We're covered." Rick smiled. "Strickland and Pulaski are on board."

Colt raised an eyebrow at that news. He hadn't anticipated having Rick's boss teaming up with them. "How'd that happen?"

"Pulaski claims we've been having all the fun." Rick had been giving his boss daily status reports. He considered himself fortunate that his chief had not voiced any objections to Rick focusing solely on the sniper issue. The opposite turned out to be true. Pulaski had stepped up to the plate, taking over Rick's open cases which freed him up to spend his time on the Gravestone problem. There hadn't been anything major on Rick's desk. Sanibel was the farthest place from a crime Mecca that Rick had ever seen. Only one murder had occurred on the island in the last ten years and that had been the result of a domestic dispute between two visitors. Most investigations were the result of break-ins, car thefts and fraud - and those incidents were almost non-existent during off-season. Rick had gladly accepted Pulaski's help expecting that to be the extent of his assistance. Instead, after this morning's update, his superior had offered his expertise in the surveillance of Williamson.

Rick had been surprised but welcomed his captain's assistance. The man was no novice when it came to wet work. Before getting involved in traditional law enforcement Pulaski had done some undercover work for the U.S. Government. Rumor had it that the time was spent with the CIA.

"Do you think that's a good idea?" Colt knew and trusted Pulaski. He had no issue with his help. But there would be times during the operation that they might skirt the boundaries of law. He didn't want Rick's career on the line.

"He and Strickland are limiting themselves to surveillance. I've been assured that both he and Strickland have recently come down with a sudden and severe case of tunnel vision."

Another unspoken agreement, Colt mused. If Rick was comfortable with the arrangement then Colt wasn't going to argue. He rose to his feet. "Okay. We're outta here. I'll see you in the morning, Rick."

"Try to be on time," Rick quipped.

36

Colt wasn't only on time but arrived early the next morning. He had managed to slip out of bed without awakening Cat which would have had the potential of making him tardy again. There had been no reason, other than a selfish one, to rouse her.

The two of them had been up late discussing ideas for her native plant nursery and garden design business. Once the apprehension of starting her own business was gone, excitement flooded in. She was animated as she detailed her plans along with the issues she'd have to resolve. But watching her hands fly and her eyes sparkle, Colt couldn't do anything but smile.

He wouldn't have cared if she opened a hotdog stand on the Causeway. The bottom line was that she was staying. Short of putting a ring on her finger, he couldn't think of anything that would make him a happier man. She now seemed comfortable with the idea of making the island her home. He wondered if that comfort transferred to their relationship or if she was still skittish about making the arrangement permanent. He'd find out shortly because he had every intention of cornering her on the subject as soon as this mess was behind them.

Rick was in his office sending a text when Colt entered. "That was Manny with an update," Rick explained as he set the phone on his desk. "Let's grab some coffee and I'll fill you in."

Several cups of coffee later all hell broke loose.

37

Crushed shell rooster tailed from beneath the tires of Colt's Jeep as he tore into the lot behind the studio. Steve and Adam were standing guard on the upper deck. Gib was at the base of the stairs, pacing frantically.

"Where's Rick?" Gib glanced nervously back toward the drive.

"We're on our own," Colt shouted as he raced up the stairs. "Where is she?"

"Still in bed. She never got up this morning."

"And you didn't think that was a little strange?"

"You told us to let her sleep."

"Till noon?"

Gib let the accusatory question pass. "Same drill as before?" Gib asked as he raced up the steps after Colt.

"How bad is it?"

"Worse than the last one."

"Jeezus! No choice." He tossed his keys to Steve then plowed through the rear door. Nothing more was said. Nothing needed to be.

Minutes ticked by. Finally, Gib opened the front door.

Colt stepped out balancing his precious cargo, once again draped with the backdrop.

The Jeep slammed to a stop at the base of the stairs. Adam, who was riding shotgun, slid from the vehicle. Pressing the earpiece of his headset closer to his ear, he held up his hand – the signal for everyone to freeze. A few seconds later, his stern look vanished and he gave the thumbs up signal. Suddenly, the dense vegetation lining the far side of the drive parted and a man wearing camouflage clothing, his hands behind his back, was unceremoniously shoved from the thicket. Another push propelled him across the drive.

Colt tossed the bundle over the side of the railing and quickly finished his descent. Amazingly, it had been Gib, the only one of the group without a covert background, who had suggested the simple decoy. Knowing the sniper would gamble on a repeat of the escape plan, they'd hidden the additional team members strategically to intercept the sniper as he moved into position for a clear shot at his target. The plan was so simple that it was genius.

Colt reached the sniper and grabbed a fistful of his shirt. "I've been looking forward to this meeting," he snapped.

"I'll be out before dinner," the assassin boasted.

"Look around you. See any cops?" Colt didn't smile when that fact registered with the man. He was too consumed with anger to take any satisfaction in the worry that had briefly flashed across his captive's face.

"Get him inside." Colt told Troy and Jack, who each had a grip on the man's arm. He didn't immediately follow. He couldn't – not until he got his anger under control. The moment he'd laid hands on the bastard he'd wanted to kill him, slowly, painfully...

"Are you okay?" Gib asked.

The question, laced with concern, pulled Colt away from the visceral images. He stole a page from Cat's book and took a steadying breath. He needed to approach this as he had previous successful interrogations. This was the beginning of the end - the chance to tie things up and concentrate on a future with that fireball waiting upstairs.

"Just taking a minute to put things in perspective. Thanks," he told his friend, giving Gib's shoulder a squeeze. "Would you head upstairs and let Cat know what's going on? She's probably wearing a hole through the living room floor."

"She's not going to like staying put."

No, she wouldn't, Colt thought, but while they still suspected only one assassin the team would continue to scour the area. Only when the all clear was sounded would Cat be allowed to wander freely. Gib would have his hands full until then.

WITH HIS ANGER IN CHECK, Colt entered the studio. Troy and Jesse stood guard by the front door. Colt knew the others would be stationed strategically throughout the unit just as he knew that they would continue to wear their headsets until it was confirmed that the situation was contained. They had exchanged their cell phones for the more high-tech, efficient means of communication that Red had brought with him. With part of the team still combing the grounds it was necessary to remain in contact.

Colt approached the man now strapped to a chair with flex cuffs. Ironically, it was the same chair Cat had used during her search of photos for Williamson. The cocky attitude he'd sported outside was gone. He glanced briefly at Colt when he'd entered the room then quickly resumed his study of his surroundings. He was assessing every possible avenue of escape. Colt couldn't fault the effort. He'd do the same if the situation were reversed.

"It's a waste of energy. You're not going anywhere," Colt assured him.

"What are you planning to do? Kill me?"

"Not planning on it…" Colt left the statement unfinished. "Right now I just want to have a little talk."

Colt straddled a chair, taking a few minutes to study the man in front of him. The assassin was nondescript. Not the type to attract attention - a trait that would come in handy in his line of work. Early forties. Average height and solid build. His chestnut colored hair was cropped short. This man had "military" written all over him. Dark brown eyes, stared back at Colt. They telegraphed what Colt already knew. He was no amateur.

"What's your name?" Colt asked matter-of-factly.

Not surprisingly, the man didn't answer.

"How long have you been doing work for Gravestone?"

A quick flash in his captive's eyes had Colt smiling again. "Yes, we know about your employer and the contract to get rid of the woman upstairs. We also know about the planned hit on Senator Lucas and the name of the man who paid for those contracts. What you're going to do is tie everything up into a neat little package for us to present to the authorities."

"You must have me confused with someone who's stupid."

"Maybe I should explain what happens if you fail to cooperate." Colt rolled his chair closer. "First, we call our friends at the Sanibel PD. They arrest you for any number of violations. Doesn't have to be much. Let's say…for prowling. But instead of being *'out before dinner'* as you put it, your paperwork gets misplaced." Colt paused. "You've probably noticed that we have a few friends on the force."

"While you're waiting for the paperwork to be *found*, word mysteriously starts circulating that you're being real chatty. Maybe even bragging. Maybe one of the news stations gets an anonymous tip. How do you think your employer will react to that?"

To Colt's satisfaction the man was now visibly sweating.

"They won't believe it."

"Maybe they won't but will they take that kind of chance?"

"Why don't you just kill me and be done with it?"

"As tempting as that might be, it won't solve our problem. The contracts will remain whether you're dead or alive. We want them to disappear and we need Williamson to do that."

"Either way I'm a dead man."

"If you give us Williamson, we'll introduce you to some of ours newest friends. They have a little program called Witness Protection. It just might give you a fighting chance. Regardless, it will be your only chance. Tell the Feds whatever you'd like to get in their good graces. I don't give a damn what you say to them. But I do want Williamson and you're going to give him to me. Otherwise, you're right. You *are* a dead man."

Colt met his captive's stare allowing the killer to take his measure. Colt wasn't bluffing and he wanted the guy to know it. While he might not pull the trigger, he had no qualms about throwing this guy to the sharks.

"I don't know anyone named Williamson."

Literally and figuratively, the man had just blinked.

"Didn't think you exchanged business cards." Colt tossed several prints on to the desk then spun the chair around so the sniper could see them. "Do you recognize him?"

The dark eyes flirted from Colt to the photos and back to Colt. "You'd have to be crazy to meet face-to-face to set up a hit."

"Who says he's not? Is he in these photos?" Colt had the man by his hair forcing his attention to the pictures strewn across the surface. He waited while their captive processed his options. It didn't take long.

"I want that protection."

38

Gib's announcement that their quarry had been caught didn't do much to help Cat relax. Her thoughts shifted from concern to curiosity. What had the sniper told them? Would he give them the information they needed? The longer the inquisition went on, the more anxious she became. So when she recognized the sound of Colt's footsteps coming up the stairs, she was at the door before he crossed the threshold.

She threw herself into his arms. "You're okay." It was an affirmation not a question. She hadn't realized just how terrified she'd been for him. Gib had assured her that everyone was fine – that no one had been hurt. Still, until she'd seen him walk through the door she hadn't been able to set those concerns fully aside.

"I'm fine," he told her as he tipped her chin up and looked into those beautiful brown eyes. "We've got them, Cat. Rick just called. They've picked up Williamson."

He kissed her hard and fast. "I've got to get back." He'd wanted to be the one to tell her that the nightmare was over. "The Feds will be here any minute to pick up our friend downstairs, then I'm headed to the station."

"I'll go with you."

Colt caught her by the arm. "They're going to want to talk to you but not for a while. We may be at it for hours before you're needed. Why don't you get out of here for a bit? I'll call you when they're ready for you."

Why not? She'd been holed up too long already.

"I'll ask Gib to run me over to pick up my car when he gets back."

When his eyes darted past her to scan the room, Cat recognized Colt's protective mode. "I don't need a babysitter any longer, Colt. Gib had some things to do and I wanted some time to myself." As soon as they'd been given the all clear, Cat had chased Gib out of the building. She'd needed a little space. While she hadn't left the unit, being alone in it was almost as freeing.

At that moment Steve stuck his head in the door announcing the FBI's arrival. "Go," she said rising up on her toes to kiss him lightly.

Watching him exit the same door he had that morning when they'd been baiting the killer, she recalled the gut-wrenching fears that had gripped her then. Things could have gone so terribly wrong. It was time that she told him what he'd been waiting to hear.

"I love you," she shouted at the closing door.

Every window in the house rattled as the door flew back open and hit the interior wall. Colt was suddenly in front of her, his hands grasping her shoulders. Crystal blue eyes drilled into hers. "Say it again."

"Go?" she asked mischievously.

"Say it again, Cat." He was breaking the "no orders" rule but he didn't care. He needed to hear those words. To see her face when she said them.

"You're overprotective and bossy," she said flashing another smile, "but I love you anyway."

His mouth claimed hers. A deep, soulful kiss she felt down to her toes.

The woman picked the damnedest times, Colt thought, tearing himself away. "We'll finish this later," he snapped before slamming the door on his way out.

Cat stared after him not sure what to make of his reaction. There'd been heat, which she understood, but it was the temperamental edge to their exchange that confused her. She was still pondering that aspect a few minutes later when her cell rang.

"We need to work on your timing," Colt stated flatly.

So that was it. "You're. in a snit because you had to leave?"

"Men don't do snits. What I am is in love with you. But I'd planned something a little more special than yelling it to you as I ran out the door." He'd been planning candlelight and music. Flowers and champagne.

Cat stopped laughing. "You've told me, Colt, in a hundred different ways." She'd just been too afraid to acknowledge it.

"I love you, Cat. We're going to make this permanent."

"I love you, too." It surprised her how easy the words rolled off her tongue. "And we'll talk about the rest."

"Damn straight we will." Colt disconnected, knowing her parting shot was meant to keep him off balance. Life with her would never be dull.

THE OFFICER at the front desk stopped Colt as he entered the station. "Rick's in the interrogation room. He'd like you to observe." The man came out from behind the desk and escorted Colt to a viewing room. Some of his team had gone ahead to the station and were now crowded into the space watching the events unfolding on a video screen via a live feed.

Once the FBI had arrived, the assassin had been quickly identified as Mike Mathison. Mathison was now on his way to the Tampa FBI field office. From there, who knew where he'd end up? Colt didn't care. He'd gotten what he wanted from the man: a video and a scrawled statement summarizing the hit on Cat. The statement would never hold up in court but he didn't particularly care. This little gem was merely intended to coerce an answer or two out of Williamson. Colt watched as the sergeant handed the confessions to Rick.

The scene on the other side of the glass was surreal. It looked more like a board meeting than a police interrogation. No one wore a uniform. Rick was the only man present who wasn't wearing a jacket. In addition to Rick and Pulaski, their old friends from the FBI, Hernandez and Morgan, were present along with a man and woman who had identified themselves as agents with FDLE. Even the detective from the Lee County Sheriff's Office who'd been handed the attempted kidnapping was, surprisingly, in attendance.

Williamson, as guest of honor, sat at the end of the table. Colt recognized him immediately from the photos but actually seeing him made him realize that Cat had nailed the man perfectly. He was one arrogant son of a bitch.

The CEO hadn't been formally charged with any crime so there was no counsel present. Currently, the Sanibel PD had been given jurisdiction over Williamson as the attempts on Cat's life had been made on their turf. Colt knew, however, that the small police department had little desire to hold on to their catch. Williamson now had a target on his back the size of Rhode Island and the local cops didn't have the manpower to protect him. Once this meeting was over, Colt guessed the FBI would take him into custody as well.

"I've been extremely patient answering all your questions," Williamson addressed the group. "But I have a business to run so if there's nothing further..." he said as he pushed his chair back from the table.

"Sit down," Rick said, flatly. He pocketed the flash drive he'd been given then scanned the paper in front of him. "We're nowhere near done. You might as well get comfortable." The comment was said casually enough but the look Rick gave their guest had him retaking his seat.

"You seem to be fond of our beaches, Mr. Williamson," Rick commented while still skimming the document.

"I like them well enough," Williamson responded warily.

"Well enough to hold several meetings on them." Rick passed the confession to Hernandez, who sat next to him, then looked back at his suspect. "You met a man there several weeks ago to discuss the contract to kill Senator Lucas. It is also where, on two other occasions, you met with a guy named Mathison to arrange the death of a woman who happened to witness that earlier meeting between you and Bookman."

"I have no idea what you're talking about."

"Maybe this will refresh your memory." He reached for the confession that was making its way around the table and slid it across to Williamson. The CEO's expression sobered as he read Mathison's confession. Stalling or calculating, Rick wasn't sure. When Williamson spoke again, his arrogant tone had returned.

"This is a fairy tale," he announced, tossing the paper

back at Rick. "If that's the reason you dragged me in here then you're wasting my time," he said rising from his chair.

"Sit down!" Rick ordered this time, slapping his hand on the table. "You can't be so stupid as to think you can just breeze out of here and live to tell about it. You'll be lucky to be breathing come sunrise. Gravestone doesn't leave trails. You must know that. Mathison certainly does," Rick tapped the confession, "and he's a lot more familiar with the organization than you are. Your best hope right now is that you have some very interesting information to share with the Feds. Without it there's not much incentive to keep you alive."

Colt took pleasure in watching Williamson's meltdown. His skin turned a sickly gray as he rubbed his sweaty palms against the trousers of his designer suit. His eyes flashed to the others around the table looking for a possible ally. He was nervous but it was the set of his jaw that had Colt concerned. It telegraphed the anger that boiled within him. That anger could work against them. They wanted Williamson frightened enough to cooperate. Not shutting down in defiance.

The door to their small observation room opened and Don entered carrying a folder full of papers.

"I suspect this is just the tip of the iceberg but I think it might be enough for what you need," he said, handing the file to Colt.

Colt wasn't an accountant but a quick glance of the summary sheet Don had placed on top told him that Williamson had been doing some creative accounting, possibly some money laundering as well. The summary contained a simple spreadsheet outlining some of the transactions that had wound their way through numerous accounts and banks.

Colt grabbed the top page and headed for the door.

They'd see that the rest of the information mysteriously made its way to Hernandez and Morgan. The FBI had the forensic accountants who could dig further, deeper...and do it legally.

Rick quickly studied the printout the sergeant had just slipped to him then handed it off to Pulaski. The document slowly made its way around the room. The silence was deafening. Colt had returned to the observation room to watch Williamson. His eyes darted from one person to another as each reviewed the data. He didn't know what they were looking at but he knew it wasn't good. Finally, Rick shoved printout in front of their suspect.

Williamson stared at the sheet. Colt suspected it wasn't the numbers he was digesting as much as his alternatives. Again Williamson searched the faces in the room. He had no allies, nowhere else to go. His defeat was signaled when he dropped his head into his hands. He might as well have been waving a white flag. The men around Colt sent up a loud cheer.

After his rights were read, Williamson was offered an opportunity to call for counsel. He declined. A smart move on his part, Colt thought. The fewer people who knew about his situation, the longer he might remain among the living. Even with that, Colt knew the chances of him surviving to trial were slim. He figured he should care about that fact but, quite frankly, he didn't.

The other investigators in the room took turns asking Williamson questions. Like Mathison, he danced around the subject of Gravestone. It was evident that he wasn't sure how far up that road he wanted to travel. For the time being, he was treating the contracts as private arrangements. He admitted to wanting Lucas out of the way, believing his livelihood, and more importantly, his life depended on the environmental legislation's demise.

Williamson had played with some very bad boys and they had invested their laundered money heavily in the resort developments. He was convinced Lucas's death would keep his plans on track and him alive. The contract on Cat wasn't personal, he told them. It was just her bad luck to have been in the wrong place at the wrong time. The asshole was lucky Colt wasn't in the room with him.

"What about the kidnapping? What did you expect to gain from that?" Rick asked.

"That wasn't my idea. The man who attempted it was an imbecile."

Not only was his contempt for the kidnapper obvious but so was the use of the past tense to describe the man.

"Bookman was supposed to be a professional. The best. But the bastard got greedy and hired that incompetent lackey to keep an eye on her while he handled another job. God only knows what the idiot was thinking when he tried to snatch her. All he managed to do was put the woman and her friend on alert."

"The break-in at her cottage had already done that. Just what was the purpose behind it?" The break-in had remained the square peg in their theory full of round holes. None of them could understand why anyone would pull such a flag waving stunt.

"That's one you can't hang on me or Bookman. He didn't pinpoint the woman's location until he picked up the call about the break in over his police scanner. Instead of dealing with the woman and her friend after the police cleared out, the fool put tracking devices on their vehicles."

The hairs on the back of Colt's neck stood up. His gut told him Williamson was telling the truth. He had no reason to lie about the incident at the cottage when it paled in comparison to the other crimes he'd just admitted to. If he didn't arrange the break in then who did? And who was in the Lincoln that had tailed Cat?

Rick's thoughts were apparently in sync with Colt's because he asked, "When did you start having her followed?"

"Aren't you listening? Why would we waste our time following her when the tracking device would lead us right to her at any time?"

"What about before he tagged their cars?"

"I just told you. He didn't know where to find her until that night. He'd gotten her name when he ran her plates but hadn't pinpointed where she was staying. He'd staked out the beach the next day but she didn't show." Williamson paused. "The break-in bothered Bookman."

"Why?"

"He wouldn't say but he didn't like it."

Colt was out of his seat and heading for the door, calling Cat's cell as he went. Her phone rang then went to voice mail. He left an urgent message then tried his apartment. When that failed, he tried Gib. That call went to voice mail, as well. By the time he reached the bottom step of the station Colt had no doubt that Cat was in trouble.

"What's going on?" Steve shouted as he and the others raced down the stairs.

"I can't reach Cat."

"Could she be out of range?" Don suggested.

"Not if she's on this island." He turned to look at them, his expression grim. "Whoever followed Cat and tore up her place is still out there."

"Where do you want us?" Steve asked.

No argument. No debate. But Colt didn't have time to appreciate bonds of unquestioning friendships.

"She planned to pick up her car. I'm heading over to

the cottages. Some of you follow me, the rest of you check out my place."

Steve beat Colt to the driver's side of Jeep. "Keys," he said, raising his hand.

Colt didn't argue. Tossing the keys to his friend, Colt slid into the passenger side and attempted to reach Cat again. Unsuccessful, he tried Gib a second time. Nothing. His next call was to Rick.

"Cat's not answering her cell," he announced.

"Shit!" Rick had been afraid of that the minute Williamson washed his hands of the break in. "I've got a unit on the way to your place."

"Let them know some of the team will be joining them. I'm headed to Pat and Terry's. Gib was supposed to take her to pick up her car. I can't raise him either."

"We'll get some units out there, as well." Rick paused then added solemnly, "She's smart, Colt. She'll be okay."

Colt prayed he was right.

39

As they turned into the parking lot of Sunset Cottages, Cat couldn't help but grin when she spotted her bright yellow Roadster. Pat and Terry had told them to leave the car there. They'd taken care of it until she needed it. The vehicle was her pride and joy. Didn't matter that it wasn't new when she'd purchased it. It was a symbol of a goal she'd set and obtained. She couldn't wait to throw the top back and turn on some music. As soon as Gib's Yukon came to a stop, she jumped out of the truck and was making a beeline for her own car.

"Slow down, Tink. I want to be sure that *Hot Wheel* of yours starts before I take off," he said, walking around his vehicle to intercept her. He didn't know why but he felt uneasy. He wasn't comfortable with the idea of leaving her on her own. It would likely take them all some time to get used to her being free to roam. But all the players had been rounded up so there was absolutely no reason Cat couldn't take off and enjoy herself. Still, he couldn't shake the fore-boding feeling.

Cat didn't let Gib's snide remark about her car get

under her skin. She was in too good a mood. She rummaged through her purse for her keys and did a little victory dance when she found them but Gib wasn't paying the least bit attention to her. Instead he was focused on something over her shoulder.

"Tink, do you know that guy?" Gib carefully eyed the man who had just stepped out of the last unit. He was heading toward them and he didn't look happy.

Cat turned. Her stomach lurched as soon as she spotted the object of Gib's attention. Oh, God! Was this nightmare never going to end? Trying to maintain her composure, she slapped on a smile. "Michael," she stated flatly, hoping he hadn't noticed her momentary jolt of terror. She knew from experience his violent streak fed on fear.

As Montgomery drew closer, Cat noted the changes in his appearance. His blond hair was no longer clipped in a short, crisp business style. It was unkempt, unruly and hanging haphazardly over his forehead and ears. He'd also bulked up - too much and too quickly to be the product of physical training alone. Great. A violent man on steroids – could it get any worse? His green eyes flashed fiercely with anger. That much hadn't changed. They held the same rage they had the night he'd tried to rape her.

It took a monumental effort on her part to sound casual. "What are you doing here?"

"You're coming with me, Catherine."

His tone sent chills down her spine. But his voice wasn't the only thing that made her skin crawl. The semi-automatic pistol he pulled out from behind his back was equally terrifying.

Stay calm. Don't panic. She needed to keep her head. If Michael had been unstable before, she had no doubt that he was certifiable now. Upsetting him wouldn't help. Angering him would be even worse.

She attempted a smile but Michael didn't reciprocate. He was agitated. What was he planning to do? If he'd wanted her dead, he'd had plenty of time to get off a shot. No, he had something else in mind for her. Based on what she'd garnered from the police reports Rick had shared, it was obvious he enjoyed the punishment and humiliation he doled out. As terrifying as that was, it might give her time to get away. Unlike the other women, she had the advantage of knowing his game. She needed to play along. Buy some time.

Her immediate concern at the moment was Gib. Cat suspected that Michael wouldn't think twice about killing him. Making matters worse was the fact that Gib had closed the distance between them and had wrapped one arm protectively around her shoulder. She shrugged him off but not before Michael's nostrils flared at the perceived show of affection.

"What can I do for you, Michael?" Cat asked, stepping between the two men. Gib wasn't cooperating, though. Instead, he yanked her back to his side.

Gib was berating himself for returning his Glock to the office safe. He was a lover not a fighter. So when he'd thought all the bad guys had been rounded up, he'd gladly stowed the weapon. *Big* mistake. Gib loosened his grip when he saw Cat wince but tightened it again when she attempted to step away. There was no way he was letting her get any closer to the bastard.

"Let me go," Cat begged in a hushed, urgent tone. "I can handle Michael until you get help."

"Not gonna happen, Tink. I'm not going anywhere without you."

"Are you spreading your legs for this one, too?" Michael snarled.

"What?" Cat asked, genuinely confused.

"I saw you on the beach with Mr. Tall, Dark and Handsome. He had his hands all over you. You'd have taken him to your bed that night if my surprise hadn't stopped you. You're no better than a bitch in heat."

The pieces finally clicked into place for Cat. "You broke into my cottage!"

"You left me, Catherine. Nobody leaves me until I'm done with them. It's time you were taught a lesson." His voice dripped with vengeance and hatred.

Cat's self-control snapped. "A lesson? Is that what you were doing to those women you attacked? Teaching them a lesson?"

Gib held her back as she strained to get closer to Montgomery. She seemed oblivious to the gun pointed at them.

"You raped those women, you son-of-a-bitch! You beat them. Violated them! You're the one who needs to be taught…!" The shrill ringing of her cell interrupted her tirade. Michael's face was red with fury. The hand that had been raised to strike now reached out toward her bag.

"Give it to me."

She shoved her purse at him.

"No, you stupid bitch. Take the phone out of the bag."

Cat pretended to search for the ringing phone as she dug through her purse looking for something, anything, she could use as a weapon. Nothing. Not even a goddamn pen lay on the bottom.

"The phone, Catherine! Give me the fucking phone!" Michael screamed.

Giving up the search, she plucked the now silent phone from its pocket and threw it at him. He was quick and caught it before it hit him in the face. Her stomach clenched when he deftly began to retrieve the message that had been left in her voice mail. She knew the call had been from Colt and she didn't think Michael would like hearing anything he had to say.

She was right. His jaw clamped tighter as he listened.

"Cat, call me. It's urgent. Williamson wasn't behind the break in. You could still be in danger. Please, Kitten, call me the minute you get this." He paused and Cat prayed he would disconnect. But today was not turning out to be her lucky day after all. "I love you," Colt added before ending the call.

Michael's anger morphed into fury at Colt's parting words. Enraged, he hurled the phone across the lot. It struck the side of the nearest bungalow then dropped into the bed of yellow lantana that surrounded the building.

Gib's fear for Cat intensified. Montgomery's focus had been equally divided between the two of them but it was now fixed solely on her. Violence radiated off him like heat escaping the South Florida roads in the middle of August. Gib knew he'd run out of time. Slowly he released the hand that had encircled Cat's arm, letting it drop to his side.

Cat's stomach sank the instant she realized Gib's intent. He was preparing to jump a mad man. She knew it but couldn't think of any way to warn him off without throwing the spotlight back in his direction. If she couldn't stop him then she'd have to join him. Maybe between the two of them they'd be able to overpower the crazed bastard. Yeah, right. But she didn't see any alternative.

Being crazy didn't make Michael stupid. At the first sign of movement he took aim at Gib, the bigger threat. Cat immediately plowed forward, ramming her shoulder into Michael's rock hard abdomen. The explosion almost deafened her but it was the blow to her face that sent her

skidding backward across the lot. Pain emanated from her
cheek where the grip of the gun had made contact. When
her visions cleared, Michael was looming over her, holding
the weapon, poised to strike again. She averted her face,
anticipating another blow, and spotted Gib sprawled on the
ground next to his truck. Ignoring Montgomery, she
scrambled from between his legs.

"Gib!" Blood oozed from a hole in his left shoulder.
"You bastard," she swore at Michael. Gib was unconscious which frightened Cat more than the bullet wound.
She didn't know squat about being shot but she didn't
think the wound should have rendered him unconscious.
Then she noticed a small trace of blood on the running
board of his truck. He must have struck his head when he
fell.

"Get up," Michael ordered her.

"He needs an ambulance." Cat stayed put, pressing the
heel of her hand against the wound.

"He'll need a coffin if you don't move away from him."

The chill in his voice told her that he meant every
word. There was no question he'd pull the trigger if she
didn't do as he said. Reluctantly, she got to her feet.

"That's better. Let's go," he said, reaching for her.

The eerie silence suddenly struck her. Where was
everyone? No one had come out to investigate the shouting
or the gunshot. Granted the shot probably wasn't as loud
as the cannon's roar she'd heard when the gun went off
next to her ear but certainly someone must have heard it.
Where were Pat and Terry? The place was unnaturally
quiet and they never left it unattended. She looked toward
the office then turned back to Michael.

"Where is everyone?"

"You mean the two fags?" He laughed at her reaction
to the dated slur. He was enjoying himself now. Was that

part of his game? Get her riled up so he could knock her down?

"The three of us have become good friends," he told her. "I'm watching the place for them today. It seems the few guests they had were gone for the day and your 'friends' don't get much time away from this dump. Your timing couldn't have been better."

Yeah, it was just about perfect. Cat turned her attention back toward Gib. There would be no getting help for him while Michael was here. She figured his best bet was for her to lead Michael away before he decided to finish what he'd started. She picked up the keys that she had dropped on the ground and headed toward her car.

Michael grabbed a fistful of her tank top as she walked by and jerked her back. "This way," he said, shoving her in the direction of the cottages. "We're taking my car."

What the hell was he talking about? Was he having visions now? The only two vehicles in the lot were her Beamer and Gib's truck.

Michael didn't loosen his grip on her shirt as he steered her past the units until they reached the last cottage. She glanced up at her captor. His eyes continuously darted from her to their surroundings. She wondered if he was on something other than steroids. With her luck? Probably. Whatever the reason for his madness, she knew it was not a good idea to get into a vehicle with him assuming one existed outside his twisted imagination. Her chances of being found would plummet if he managed to get her off the island.

Could she slow things down? Buy time until Colt arrived? He would come looking for her. She had no doubt of that. Deciding to stall a bit, she stopped which infuriated Michael. He slammed his fist into the center of her back, launching her forward. Once again she found herself sprawled on the ground. This time, however, when she raised her head she was staring at the ominous black Lincoln.

"Get up!"

She'd made it to her knees before his impatience had him hauling her up the rest of the way then slamming her against the driver's side door. "You're driving." Without warning, he grabbed a fistful of her hair and yanked her back so that he could open the driver's side door. She was giving serious thought to shaving her head when he placed the cold steel of the gun against her temple.

"Move and you're dead," he said before abruptly leaving her standing between the open door and the car's interior.

The surprise maneuver offered Cat an opportunity she hadn't expected. If she timed it right she might be able to reach the brush before he could get around the big vehicle. The downside to the plan was the gun that remained pointed in her direction while he rounded the vehicle. Still, she might make it. She figured her odds of survival were better in the brush than they were in the car with him. She waited until he opened the passenger door and began to slip inside. The second he broke eye contact she took off like the hounds of hell were at her heels.

40

Steve flew down the two lane road at triple digit speeds passing other vehicles as if they were standing still. Colt didn't notice. Instead he was running through every conceivable scenario trying to find one that would explain his inability to reach Cat. He told himself there could be any number of reasons she was not answering his calls but none of those reasons explained why he couldn't raise Gib. Nor did they explain the sinking feeling in his gut that both of them were in danger.

Colt checked the magazine on his gun again. He'd been caught in a loop since he'd jumped into the passenger seat. Call Cat. Check his weapon. Call Gib. Check his weapon. He started to call Cat again and almost dropped the phone when it buzzed in his hand. Gib was finally returning his calls.

Colt put it on speaker. At first he couldn't hear anything but the wind blowing across the microphone. Grimly, he realized that it wasn't the wind but Gib's labored breathing he heard. "Gib? Where are you?" he said, praying for an answer.

"Sunset Cottages. It's Montgomery. He has Cat."

His words echoed through the Jeep. Everyone in the vehicle was familiar with the name. Upon hearing it Steve pushed the vehicle to its limit. Adam dialed Rick while Don alerted Bill, who along with Red, Troy and Jack, were en route to the cottages. Colt blocked everything out. They knew what to do. He needed to concentrate on the call.

"Where are they?"

"I don't know. They were gone when I came to."

"Take it easy. We'll find them." They had to. "How bad are you hurt?"

"Don't know. First time being shot."

Shit. "Hang on. We're turning in now."

Steve slowed down just enough to take the corner without flipping. Colt was running toward his friend before the Jeep came to a stop. Gib had taken a bullet to the shoulder but, thankfully, the flow of blood was already easing.

"Any idea how long have they been gone?" Colt asked.

"Damn it! I don't know how long I've been out." Gib's frustration was evident.

"Easy," Colt said, moving aside when Don appeared with a first aid kit. Colt quickly scanned the complex of buildings. Without a word of instruction, his friends had fanned out upon arrival.

Gib hissed when Don pressed a wad of gauze against his wound. "Montgomery's crazy. Scary crazy," Gib told them. "He was going on and on about how Cat still belonged to him. How he hadn't finished with her yet."

Adam returned, handing a banged up cell phone to Colt.

"It's Cat's," Colt confirmed. Any hope they'd had of tracking her through her phone was slashed.

"You called. Left her a message," Gib remembered. He

would never forget the rage he'd seen in Montgomery's eyes as he'd listened to the voice mail. "How long ago?"

Colt immediately understood the significance of the question. "No more than ten minutes." Meaning they were most likely still on the island. Adam called Rick with the update. They would set up a roadblock at the causeway and alert the Sheriff's Office and the Coast Guard. The problem was that almost half of Sanibel was a nature preserve. If Montgomery wanted to stay hidden there were plenty of places to do just that.

"Over here," Steve yelled from end of the row of cottages.

Colt sprinted to the last building. Next to the side of the unit sat Cat's mysterious Lincoln Town Car. Both the passenger and driver's side doors were standing wide open. Steve walked around the rear of the vehicle and popped the trunk. Colt wanted to drop to his knees when Steve indicated that it was empty. Instead he turned his attention to the ground surrounding the car.

The sandy soil reflected two distinct sets of footprints leading into the thick vegetation. No attempt had been made to conceal their tracks. The depth of the impressions told Colt that both Cat and Montgomery had been moving quickly.

"She's running," Colt stated with a mixture of pride and fear. "Steve, I want you to coordinate our team with the first responders when they get here. Update me as soon as you get hooked up." He snatched the headset from around Steve's neck then signaled to Adam. Without another word they followed the footprints into the brush.

SHORTS AND A TANK top had seemed like a good idea when she'd dressed for her drive but the attire sucked for blazing a trail through the Florida wilderness. The serrated stems of the Saw Palmettos cut into her arms and legs like teeth on a steak knife. Insects flocked to the blood still seeping from the gash on her cheek. Come sunset, which was fast approaching, they'd be feasting on every inch of her exposed skin, and there was plenty of exposed skin for them to feast upon. She'd removed her shorts and hidden them beneath a mature stand of palmetto palms. The bright red material was a beacon against the green and brown landscape. The lacey underwear Colt was so fond of didn't offer much protection against the elements but at least the muted tones didn't stand out.

Even before she broke for the woods, Cat knew that there was no way she'd be able to outrun Michael. But she stood a chance of surviving if she could lose him. Hidden by the thick curtain of plants and fueled by adrenaline, she'd crawled furiously, zigzagging her way deeper into the brush.

Her goal was simple. To stay ahead of her pursuer. Colt would be looking for her. When she didn't return his call he'd be a man on a mission. Eventually, he'd check to see if she'd picked up her car. Cat hoped it would be sooner rather than later for Gib's sake.

She reached a small clearing and crouched at the base of a cabbage palm to catch her breath and, more importantly, listen. She was having trouble getting a fix on Michael. From the minute he'd taken up the chase he'd made no effort to keep his whereabouts a secret. Thrashing through the underbrush or lobbing threats into the air, he'd made his presence and location clear. But a few minutes ago the racket had ceased and the silence that followed was more frightening than his shouted promises of retribution.

She chanced closing her eyes, directing her attention to the calliope of life teaming around her but the air rushing from her lungs was trumping all other sounds. She took several slow, calming breaths. Finally the natural rhythm of the area began to emerge. A breeze tickled the fronds of the palm trees. Turtledoves cooed and mockingbirds answered but no matter how hard she concentrated she couldn't hear her pursuer.

Her eyes flew open as something cold moved over her foot. She had to clamp a hand over her mouth to stifle a scream as a large indigo snake slithered over her sandaled feet. As it disappeared into the thicket, she knew that snakes would soon be the least of her problems. She was close to "Ding" Darling and its estuaries, a sanctuary for Florida alligators and the endangered American crocodile. If one of those prehistoric beasts decided she'd make a tasty snack she would, literally, be dead meat.

She gave herself a mental shake. She needed to concentrate on her human predator. Where the hell was Michael? Had he given up? Not likely. He'd been planning this for a year and had spent over a week staking out her car. Chances were that he wouldn't be discouraged after a short game of hide and seek.

Perhaps it was time to find a place to lay low and wait for help. She'd seen several spots that would have offered good camouflage and she probably should have taken cover in one of them but she hadn't been able to bring herself to hole up. Ancient memories had come back to haunt her. Too many nights she'd hidden in her room cowering, waiting for her father to come teach her a lesson. The similarity to her current situation was a motivating factor in pushing her forward. But, she reminded herself, she wasn't a helpless adolescent and logic told her that she was at risk of running into Michael if she continued moving about blindly. She needed to find a spot, swallow her fears and dig in. However, this was not the place. Her current position was far too exposed for her to stay put any longer.

She crept back into brush that thickened and grew taller the closer she got to the Sanctuary. In this particular environment being petite had its advantages. If she kept her head down she would be able to stand and still avoid being seen. It would make moving faster and would give her hands and knees some relief.

She felt like shouting in both pain and pleasure as she straightened both her legs. Then stooping like an old woman to ensure that her profile remained low, she began to move.

After only a few tentative steps, though, she heard the wail of sirens – a multitude of sirens. Hallelujah! The vast number of units suggested they were responding to her current situation. A small laugh escaped. Situation. Jeezus. She must be losing it if she could categorize this mess as a "situation." It was a friggin' nightmare.

Knowing that help was near had her rethinking her options. She could simply stay out of sight and wait for that help to find her or carefully maneuver her way back toward the cottages where Colt and the troops would be gathering. No contest. Waiting wasn't her strong suit. She cautiously began making her way out of the thick foliage. When she heard something rustling in the brush behind her, she quickened her pace. It was probably just another inhabitant of the preserve but she wasn't taking any chances. Then, another noise and Cat bolted. She didn't get far.

41

C olt adjusted his headset. The radio would be useless
until the others arrived with the rest of the equipment but he was thankful Steve had neglected to leave his
headset behind. Colt would need to know what the authorities were doing once they arrived. He'd also be able to
communicate with the first responders on their status. He
prayed he wouldn't have to call for medics when they did
find Cat.

Just a few feet into the brush it became apparent to
Colt what Cat was attempting to do. She knew she didn't
have the legs to outrun Montgomery and she was smart
enough not to try. Instead, she was using the thick stands
of native vegetation as a maze in which to hide. It
appeared to be working. Montgomery had gone in one
direction while Cat had crawled in another.

Her trail was not clear but it was still easy enough to
follow if one took the time to look. Soft handprints were
distinguishable in the sandy soil along with the indenta-
tions left by her knees and feet as she scurried across the

ground. Even an untrained eye like Montgomery's should have been able to track her but there was no sign that he'd done so once they'd entered the brush. The rage that Gib had described must be blinding him to the obvious. Thank God for that much.

They followed Cat's convoluted route until it led them to a large, thick Palmetto. She'd stopped here. Why? It was obvious that she hadn't rested quietly. The disturbed sand told him that much. He parted the thick fronds of the plant and spotted a patch of red almost completely buried in the sand. Adam reached in and pulled a pair of shorts from the dirt.

"She's using her head," Adam tried to assure him.

Yes, it was a smart move to ditch the bright colored clothing but it tore him up to know she was making life and death decisions alone. Colt tucked the shorts inside his shirt then silently turned to pick up her trail again.

At one point, Montgomery had virtually stumbled over Cat's tracks but still hadn't followed them. In spite of the heat, a chill went through Colt when he'd seen the intersecting tracks. He was wondering how much longer would Cat be able to evade the bastard when his headset finally crackled to life.

"Captain. This is Steve. Do you read?" Steve asked.

"Roger that," he answered softly. With the emergency sirens blaring almost non-stop, Montgomery had to know that he was a hunted man. Still, Colt had no intention of giving away his location.

"Any luck?" Steve asked him.

"They don't appear to have met up. We're tracking her now. Give me an update on your end."

"Gib's on his way to the hospital. Don and Kevin are with him. He has a slight concussion but the good news is the bullet went clean through. He'll be okay." Steve knew that after Cat, Gib would top the list of Colt's concerns so he dispensed with that issue first. "The Rangers at "Ding" Darling have been notified. The park is closed but they're checking for stragglers, making sure the area is clear."

"Search teams?"

"It'll be dark shortly, Colt."

Steve didn't elaborate. It wasn't necessary. Colt knew with darkness approaching that the local authorities would not risk sending men into an area teaming with predators, both human and animal. Procedure would require them to wait until dawn before beginning an organized ground search. Colt didn't like it but he understood the decision. He'd have made the same one had they been his men.

"Are they're setting up a perimeter?" That would be standard operating procedure but it was a massive area to cordon off.

"Working on it now. Colt, just because the locals can't go in doesn't mean we plan on hanging back. The guys are gearing up…" All conversation ceased as a hair-raising scream ripped through the night air.

WHEN CAT REGAINED consciousness there was no question that she was in trouble. The bindings and gag, along with the fact that she was now slung over Michael's bare shoulder, did not bode well for her chances. On the other hand, she was still alive. When Michael had tackled her she hadn't believed that she'd remain that way for very long. He'd pinned her to the ground, quickly trapping her arms and legs. Unable to scratch, kick or bite she'd used her only remaining weapon - her voice. She let loose a cry that would have made a banshee proud, hoping it would pinpoint her location. The outburst had momentarily stunned Michael but he'd recovered quickly, silencing her with his fist.

Obviously, his plan hadn't been to kill her, at least not immediately, or she would have been dead instead of trussed up like a Thanksgiving turkey. Where was he taking her? Did he have another means of escape beside his car? A boat maybe? God, she hoped not. She remembered how easily they'd lost the sniper when he took off over the water.

From her inverted position, she couldn't distinguish where they were or what direction they were headed. From what she could see, the terrain was virtually the same as the one she'd traversed earlier. She couldn't hear any waves crashing onto the shoreline but, then again, there were no sandy beaches on this section of the island. Only mangroves. Still, the air felt heavier and alligators croaked nearby telling her that they were closer to the water than she'd been when Michael had caught up with her.

Surprisingly, her captor was jogging briskly through the brush. Neither her weight nor the dense growth seemed to slow him down. If it weren't for the arm clamped over her legs, she'd have thought he'd forgotten about her presence all together.

Michael suddenly came to a halt. Cat didn't have time to contemplate the reason before she was dumped unceremoniously onto the ground. He untied her hands but before the feeling could return he flipped her onto her stomach and tied her wrists behind her back. Once they were secured, he lashed them to her bound feet. Hog-tied. Her hopes of escape slipped further away.

Cat was convinced that Michael was no longer walking the mental precipice he'd been teetering upon. He'd fallen off that ledge. His voice was soft, cold and calculating as he described the torture he had planned for her. His wild, feral eyes darted from her to the trail then back to her again. With each threat of violence his eyes flashed brighter. An unholy grin spread across his face as he took one of her thumbs and pulled it until popped from its socket.

"Just a taste of what you have to look forward to," he said. "We'll get started after I take care of your friends. I want to be able to enjoy hearing you scream." Then he turned and slipped back into the brush.

Once the tears had started to fall, she couldn't stop them. She was tired, hurting and for the first time since she'd walked away from her childhood home, unsure if she would survive the night. She didn't want to die out here alone.

'You're not alone anymore.' Colt's words echoed in her head, covering her like a warm blanket. He was out there somewhere. She knew it. Felt it. She just needed to hang on until he arrived.

She blinked, clearing away the tears. Bawling wasn't helping a damn thing. She needed to focus her energy elsewhere. Contorting her body, she studied her bindings. She recognized them as strips of cloth from Michael's shirt, which explained his bare torso. The knots resembled a colorful pit of snakes winding in and around with no obvious beginning or end. But they weren't snakes. They were cloth and cloth could be torn. She began to struggle against the bindings, attempting to break the Gordian knot. She accomplished little but a shift in her position. Looking around for something that might help her, she spotted a mature Saw Palmetto a few feet in front of her. The native plant had a particularly nasty feature that she'd become all too familiar with during the afternoon. The edges at the base of each frond were covered with sharp, serrated teeth. The larger the plant, the bigger and sharper the teeth. She had the cuts and scratches to prove it.

Determined, Cat began to flop and squirm until she had wiggled her way under the low growing palm. While the distance had been short, she arrived at her destination feeling like she'd run a marathon. Every muscle in her body ached. Her thumb hurt like hell and the percussion section of the Naples Philharmonic was playing an unending chorus in her head but these complaints paled in comparison to her need for water. The heat and exertion had left her on the verge of dehydration. In addition, the tight-fitting gag had sucked every ounce of moisture from her mouth. To compound her misery, a dried, saucer-shaped leaf shed by a nearby Sea Grape lay only inches from her face. It was filled with rainwater from last night's storm. The liquid taunted her.

She was close enough now to reach a low hanging frond of the Palmetto. Craning her neck, she pressed the side of her head into the sharp teeth. The gag, along with strands of her hair, caught. After several small tugs to insure it would hold, she slowly lowered her head until she slipped free of the material. She didn't dwell on her success. Instead she disregarded the sand, dirt and probably a host of invisible creepy, crawly things and slurped up the water from the leaf. It tasted like nectar.

When her tiny water supply was exhausted, she turned her attention back to her bindings. She managed to position herself so the makeshift ropes butted up against a row of teeth and began to rock against them, dragging the material back and forth against the spiked edge. After every dozen or so swipes, she'd strained against the bindings, testing their strength.

Fighting exhaustion and cramping muscles she continued her struggle toward freedom. There were times she thought she'd heard Michael returning but he never materialized. Had he'd gotten lost in the dark and unfamiliar territory? Maybe he'd fallen prey to the swamp. Wasn't she due for a break? Then just as quickly as those hopes began to soar they crashed to the ground as a hand clamped over her mouth.

42

"Shhhh, Kitten, it's me," Colt spoke softly into her ear. Instantly her fear vanished, giving way to relief. Colt dropped his hand from her mouth and quickly began to work on her bindings. As his knife sliced through the ties, he caught sight of the loop of fabric caught on a nearby plant. Montgomery had obviously wanted to keep her silenced after her bone chilling scream. Colt's blood boiled at the abuse she'd been forced to endure but mixed with the anger was a sense of amazement. No matter what Montgomery had done to her, he hadn't been able to break this woman. She'd fought him every step of the way and was still fighting when Colt found her.

Free of their bindings, Cat's arms and legs dropped to the ground like ten-pound weights. Pain arced through her, protesting the sudden repositioning of her limbs. She dug her teeth into her bottom lip to keep from crying out.

As he eased her onto her back, Colt continued the struggle to maintain his composure. Despite the almost nonexistent light he could see her bruised and battered face. He'd already noted the dislocated thumb as he'd removed her bindings. Her right eye was swollen shut. Blood caked on the cheek beneath it. He saw no obvious signs of broken bones, though, and, considering the effort she'd been putting into her escape, he was reasonably confident that none of her injuries were life-threatening. Still, the urge to rush her to the paramedics who were standing by at the cabins was almost overwhelming.

"Can you hang on a bit longer?" he asked brushing the hair from her face. "Adam and I need to clear the way."

A small nod was her response. Pulling her shorts from inside his shirt he tucked them into her flexing fingers. "You did good, Cat," he said softly as he laid a kiss on her cheek.

COLT TAPPED Adam on the shoulder as he emerged from the brush. It was time to put an end to this. They'd followed Montgomery's trail from the point where he'd overtaken Cat. She'd successfully managed to pinpoint her location with her scream. Colt had recognized it for the verbal flare that it was but that knowledge hadn't stopped his heart from lodging in his throat when he'd heard it. After they'd reached the site, the tracking had been relatively easy but painstakingly slow. They were being careful not to spook the unstable Montgomery - not with Cat as his hostage. Hanging back, waiting for the chance to safely rescue Cat was the hardest thing Colt had ever done.

As they'd come closer to the wetlands, it added to Colt's concerns. Darkness and water were as much their enemies as the lunatic they were pursuing. If Montgomery slipped by either of them, he could easily lose them in the marsh. What few telltale signs a tracker could use in that environment would be obliterated by the darkness. Of course, that was assuming he could avoid the predators that hunted in those waters. Poisonous snakes, alligators and crocodiles roamed freely throughout "Ding" Darling but they preferred the swampy areas of the refuge.

Before Montgomery had left Cat alone, Colt had considered having the Sheriff's office send up the chopper that had remained on standby at South Seas Resort. Once spotted, a good pilot would be able to herd the pair back toward dryer land but they'd tabled that idea. Montgomery was already unstable and the distinctive whop-whop of chopper blades could make him even more unpredictable. He hadn't wanted to risk that, not while Montgomery had Cat and with the clear trail he was leaving, there was no need to take that risk yet. In his twisted mind, he probably thought he was the one doing the hunting. Adam spotted Montgomery first. He signaled Colt then slipped around to flank their prey. Colt waited, giving his friend time to move into position. The buzzing of insects and the rustle of nearby leaves reminded him that humans weren't the only ones stalking prey tonight. The Sanctuary was a hunting ground for creatures of all shapes and sizes although rarely of the two-legged variety.

Colt silently parted the branches of the shrub in front of him. He could smell the sweat and fear that permeated the air. Apparently Montgomery had enough sense remaining to be scared and with good reason. Colt wanted him dead. The desire to put a bullet in the man's brain was so strong he was having difficulty fighting it. In all his years with the Army, with all the kills he could claim, he had never relished taking a life. This bastard, however, deserved to die. He had raped and abused God knew how many women and come close to killing his friend and partner. Above all, he'd hunted and hurt Cat. If Montgomery escaped or slipped through the justice system again, the carnage would continue. He was a sick, twisted son-of-bitch who needed killing.

Logic had Colt raising his Glock. A single shot to the head would bring this nightmare to an end. A single shot, he told himself, which would be justified. A single shot that would turn him into a cold-blooded killer.

"Drop your weapon," Colt shouted. Montgomery immediately turned and fired but Colt was already moving.

Montgomery fired again. He was either a lousy shot or wild with panic which didn't mean he couldn't get lucky. Colt placed a round into the dirt near Montgomery's feet. It was followed by another well placed bullet from Adam. Montgomery was out flanked, out-numbered and out-gunned but the man was obviously unable to fathom that. He turned and started shooting in Adam's direction.

Colt was done playing. He took aim and fired at Montgomery's shoulder. Adam followed with a shot to the thigh. The two hits should have incapacitated him but madness held its own kind of adrenaline. Montgomery had managed to scurry away into the brush. Colt joined Adam and the two cautiously advanced on the dense foliage where they'd seen Montgomery disappear. A gun lay on the ground but their target was nowhere in sight. Damn. He should have taken the bastard out when he had the chance.

Their quarry was bleeding heavily and would be easy to track. Montgomery probably wouldn't get far but as much as he wanted to finish it, Colt would let the Sheriff and DNR deal with the clean-up. In his current condition and with no weapon, he'd be lucky to make it to sunrise. It was time to get Cat the help she needed.

A tight knot formed in Colt's gut when he returned to find Cat lying motionless in the same spot where he'd left her. He said a quick prayer that she was asleep and not unconscious. He supposed she'd have welcomed either escape. Unconsciousness, though, could mean her injuries were more serious than he'd first thought. He railed at himself for wasting precious time going after Montgomery. "Let me have your pen light," Colt said, extending his hand toward Adam. Raising her eyelid, he flicked the tiny beam across Cat's pupil. Immediately, she batted his hand away. The fist in his stomach loosened.

"Stop it," she croaked. Cat wanted to kill whoever had awakened her. The minute Colt had left her she'd struggled into her shorts then blissfully had let exhaustion claim her. Regardless of her surroundings, she was safe. Colt had found her.

"Yes, ma'am," he said, smiling in relief. He lifted her off the ground, briefly passing her to Adam while he cleared the confines of the prickly plant. Once Cat was back in his arms, they quickly made their way toward the strobing lights on the horizon.

Within minutes they met up with the other members of his team who'd been headed in their direction. No one offered to relieve Colt of his burden. Instead, they spread out – some clearing a path, the others protected the rear. As they neared the buildings and safety, a scream echoed throughout the Sanctuary. The sheer agony of the cry told Colt no one would be finding Montgomery in the morning – at least not all of him. The hunter had become the prey.

43

C at woke with a start, her breathing short and her heart racing. She forced herself to focus on her surroundings and quickly got both under control. She wasn't trapped in the swamp. She was in the hospital. Colt was in the chair next to her bed, dozing. He looked rumpled, unshaven and exhausted.

Her last clear recollection was begging for water as she was strapped onto a gurney. Her mouth had felt as dry as the Sahara but the by-the-book EMTs had ignored her pleas. Instead they started an IV to force fluids into her system. Her gaze dropped to the hand where they'd inserted the needle. Having anything anchored under her skin registered high on her personal creep-factor scale so she quickly averted her eyes when she saw the IV remained implanted beneath her skin.

The fluids they were pumping into her system weren't doing much for her parched mouth. She hungrily eyed the pitcher of water on the bed table currently parked near her feet. She made two unsuccessful attempts to reach it before she dropped back against the pillows, cursing her stiff, aching muscles.

Colt was suddenly looming over her. "Are you okay?" he asked anxiously, interrupting her steady stream of expletives. He hadn't intended to fall asleep but the events of the night had obviously caught up with him. The doctors and nurses had told him to go home, assuring him that Cat was not seriously injured. Like there was any way he'd be leaving her.

"I'm fine," she snapped, pissed that she hadn't been able to accomplish a task as simple as reaching for a glass of water. She took a deep breath and opened her eyes to see Colt's worried face staring back at her.

"I think I should be asking you that question. You look like hell."

The woman was a poster child for domestic violence and she thought *he* looked bad? It started as a chuckle but quickly developed into a full-fledged belly laugh. Each time Colt thought he had his humor under control a glance at the woman glaring back at him through one good eye would set him off again.

Steve and Adam watched the two from the doorway, grinning. The doctors had assured them all that with a little rest and fluids Cat would recover quickly. But Colt had remained withdrawn since emerging from the brush with Cat in his arms. His sullen mood had some of the team members worried he might return to the solemn place he'd occupied after his return from overseas. Apparently there'd been no reason for their concern.

"What's so funny?" Steve asked.

Colt wiped his eyes with the back of his hand and smiled as he explained. "She thinks *I* look bad."

Steve and Adam directed their attention to the woman

in the hospital bed. One eye, dark and swollen, a half a dozen stitches inched across the cheek beneath it. Insect bites and bruises covered almost every inch of her exposed flesh and she wore a brace on her left hand. She obviously didn't appreciate their assessment because she turned her scowl to the two men, which had them joining Colt in his laughter.

WHEN THE PHYSICIAN'S assistant made rounds that evening he informed Cat that she could be released the next morning. She didn't want to spend the night but no amount of arguing had changed his mind. He did give her permission to shower, though. Cat was celebrating that concession until Colt refused to give her any privacy while she washed off the remaining dirt and sand. She decided to forgive him, however, when he offered to shampoo her hair.

After a nurse's aide cleared away the dinner tray, Cat tried again to get Colt to go home for the evening but the stubborn man refused to leave. Instead, he pulled up the second visitor's chair, propped his feet on it and picked up a newspaper someone had left. Cat turned on the television to catch the news.

She had just begun to drift off to sleep when the door to her room opened. Light spilled in from the hallway, followed by Gib pushing an IV pole and wearing his signature grin. She'd been told that he was recovering in a room at the other end of the corridor but getting down there to see him had been another battle she'd lost to Colt.

He didn't try to stop her though, when she slipped from the bed to throw herself at Gib. Colt did, however, station himself at her side, holding the back of her hospital gown closed and ready to catch her if her unsteady legs gave way. Eventually, he promised himself, he'd get over worrying about her every move – at least he hoped he would.

Cat and Gib hugged each other as tightly as their injuries would permit. As much as she hated tears, Cat let them fall. Neither said a word. None were necessary. They'd both come perilously close to dying at the hands of a madman. The result was a bond Cat knew would always remain between them.

"There's no permanent damage," Gib assured her when she broke away to study him. "The doctor says I'll be good as new in a few weeks."

"I'm not sure I can wait that long."

"For what?" Colt asked.

"To kick his ass," she answered, her eyes boring into Gib. "What the hell were you thinking jumping a maniac pointing a gun at you? Do you have a death wish?"

"Me? You're the ninety-pound fairy who tackled that bulked up nutcase! Do you remember that or did the blow to your head affect your memory?"

Colt retreated to his chair to watch. This was the first time he'd had the opportunity to enjoy Cat's temper directed at someone other than himself. It was, as Rick had once remarked, quite entertaining. Colt also recognized the verbal sparring for what it was – a tool for Cat to deal with her fears. At the moment, her last big fear stood directly in front of her. She'd been terrified for Gib having left him injured, bleeding and unable to help. Now that it was obvious he'd pull through, she was cleansing herself of those emotions. First with tears. Now with temper.

It was Gib's reaction to her fit of anger that surprised Colt. He'd have expected him to turn on the charm in an attempt to sooth Cat. But, apparently, he needed to blow off a little steam, as well. The two threw barbs and accusations at each other until a floor nurse stuck her head in the room and ordered them to lower their voices. As soon as the door closed they looked at each other and burst into laughter.

Gib returned to his room a short while later and Cat had immediately fallen asleep. Colt settled back into his chair. His intent was to catch some sleep if he could ever take his eyes off this woman. His woman, he corrected, and then smiled. She'd beat him senseless if she read his possessive thoughts but she was his, as much as he belonged to her. They were a pair, a team, and partners, for life.

EPILOGUE

C at awoke in the king size bed at The Gardens Hotel. For their honeymoon, they'd returned to the place where they'd first made love. The French doors to the veranda stood wide open. From where she lay she could see Colt's feet crossed at the ankle, resting against the railing.

The fragrance of coffee, mixed with a touch of tropical blooms, drifted through the open doors. The early November weather had been perfect for yesterday's small ceremony on the Sanibel shoreline. Well, maybe not so small. By the time Colt's friends and family had arrived, they'd had quite a crowd. Still, they'd managed to keep things intimate. Gib photographed the wedding, of course, while Rick stood at Colt's side. Jason proudly gave the barefoot bride away. Ellie, sporting one of her bright and bold, feathered hats, was Cat's matron of honor. Colt's mother, who had arrived in town several days prior to the wedding, wept throughout the vows.

Both Cat and Gib had fully recovered from their injuries. Colt's rehabilitation, however, was taking a bit longer. It was painfully obvious to anyone paying attention that he was nervous whenever Cat ventured out unescorted. He was improving and, to his credit, he never tried to stop her. Oh, she still got the usual safety lecture before each trip but those were becoming shorter in duration. Good thing, too, because she was out and about more often as her plans for the native plant and design center began to gel. By this time next year she'd have Sanctuary Gardens in full swing and, provided the zoning was approved, it would be on the property currently owned by their neighbors, the Copeland's. The couple was moving back to Atlanta to be closer to their daughter and grandkids. They'd been able to work out a very nice deal with them to lease the property. The current gardens would be ideal for showing off mature specimens of the plants she planned to sell.

"Are you going to daydream all day or are we going downstairs to breakfast?" Colt stood as he had just a few months ago, leaning casually against the doorframe, his chest and feet bare. Her heart still fluttered.

"Give me a minute," she said, stretching like her namesake. As she did, the sheet slid slowly down to her waist. Colt didn't take his eyes off of her. Who needed breakfast when you had this feast before you?

AFTERWORD

AUTHOR'S NOTE

This story is a book of fiction. While many of the places and estab-lishments actually do exist (and thank God for that!) just as many are solely products of my imagination. In those cases, any similarities to real people or places are purely coincidental.

C. F. Francis

ALSO BY C. F. FRANCIS

Looking for more? Enjoy a small taste of "Lovers Key", the next installment in *The James Gang* series.

Just a few short minutes ago Josie Boussard had foolishly believed her torturous journey had finally come to an end. She'd stood at the door of *Island Images* and stared into the darkened photography studio. Her legs, already weak and unsteady, buckled as she read the *CLOSED* sign hanging above the names of the studio's owners: Gibson McKay and Colton James— Steve's former Special Forces Commander.

Daylight was hours away. Tears stung as they'd channeled down the open wounds on her face. Colton James, was the key to finding Steve. Without Steve, she had no one else she could turn to. Nowhere else to run.

The sound of tires on asphalt invaded her world of self-pity, bringing her back to a place of urgency and fear. She needed to get out of sight. After she'd wiped the tears from her eyes, she'd spotted the patch of utter darkness across the driveway and had painfully made her way toward it. A garden. *Perfect.*

It took every last ounce of Josie's reserves to navigate her battered body over the fence that surrounded the property. She crawled the last few feet to the massive potting bench she'd spotted once inside the small jungle. She shoved aside the bags of potting soil that rested on the lower shelf of the bench, then slid her long frame onto the rough wooden platform behind the wall she'd just created. Pulling her knees upward in the tight space, Josie clasped them to her chest, shivering against the unusually cool Florida night. Her eyes drifted shut as she said a prayer that no one would find her before morning.

Made in the USA
Columbia, SC
22 November 2021